damiano
DELUCA

USA TODAY BESTSELLING AUTHOR
PARKER S. HUNTINGTON

Asher Black
Niccolaio Andretti
Ranieri Andretti
Bastiano Romano
Renata Vitali
Damiano De Luca
Marco Camerino
Rafaello Rossi
Lucy Black

AUTHOR'S NOTE

Hey, readers!

Firstly, if you haven't read *Renata Vitali*, it's the prequel novella to *Damiano De Luca*. You don't need to read it to read *Damiano De Luca*, but I recommend it because it's the story of how these two met.

A part of me wants to skip the author's note and send y'all on your way to the prologue, because that's what it was like writing this book for me. It was passing my normal stops and diving into territory I was unfamiliar with.

Truth. Deception. Two sides of one coin. Two opposites intwined so thoroughly, you can't appreciate one without acknowledging the other.

I've written about a ton of heavy themes before, themes that all mean a lot to me—courage, forgiveness, resentment, and duty. But nothing intimidates me more than speaking of truth and deception, because these two cuts deeper.

So, I found myself wondering what lessons I needed to learn, what lessons I wanted to teach others... And here it is:

Thinking you know someone and learning later you couldn't have been more wrong, that you've been deceived, is gut wrenching. It annihilates relationships in ways nothing else can. Friendships, love, companionship—none of these survive without trust. In the face of deception, deception always wins.

You can't ask people not to deceive you, but you can choose not to stick with them when they do. You can choose not to deceive others, to be pure of heart and intentions. And above all, do not deceive yourself.

WITH SO, SO, SO MUCH LOVE,

Greenlight - Jonas Brothers
Do You Think of Me? - REMMI
Crowded Places - Rynn
You Found Me - The Fray
Goodnight Moon - Go Radio
It Ends Tonight - The All-American Rejects
Stay - Mayday Parade
Miserable At Best - Mayday Parade
We Don't Have to Dance - Andy Black
I Miss You - blink-182
Dear Maria, Count Me In - All Time Low
Jet Black Heart - 5 Seconds of Summer
All over You - The Spill Canvas
Dancing On My Own - Calum Scott
Fuck Apologies - JoJo ft. Wiz Khalifa
Highway Don't Care - Tim McGraw
ft. Taylor Swift & Keith Urban
Mr. Brightside - The Killers

"If ever I am gifted the opportunity to betray you, I'll take it.
If life hands me the chance to destroy you, I will.
Today. Tomorrow. Ten years from now.
I will always seek revenge.
And you will never stop looking over your shoulder."

Ten years ago, I crushed Damiano De Luca's heart,
vowing false promises I never delivered.

The revenge? Didn't happen.
The destruction? As if I could.
Betrayal? Not. A. Chance.

We were 18 when I left, taking my secrets with me.
Now at 28, there's no trace of the jaded mafia prince
with the protective streak.

He's crueler. Colder. More calculated than ever.
And he's glaring at me from a funeral pew,
looking at me and my wedding ring
like we should be the ones buried six feet under.

The war is back on, but I'm not that teenaged girl anymore.
This time, there will be blood.
And it won't be mine.

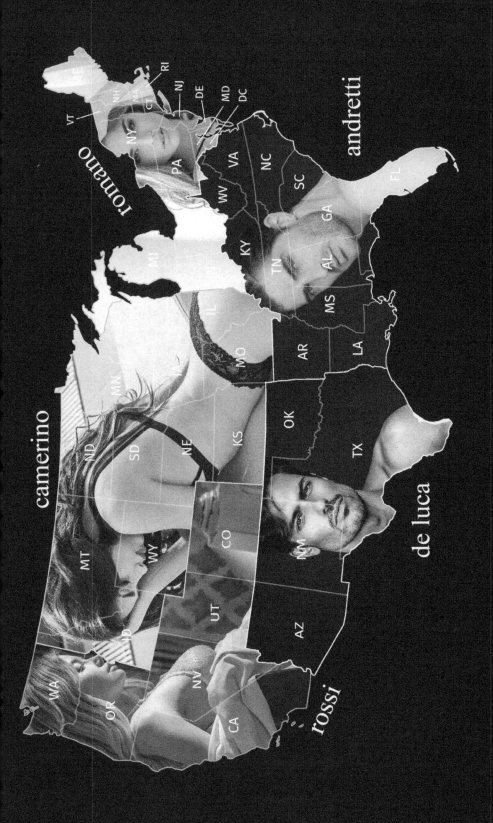

For Chloe.
Always for Chloe.

Who gives a fuck about your first love? Give a big round of applause for your second love, because they taught you love still exists after you thought it never could again.

— THAT ONE PINTEREST PIN

de·cep·tion
də'sepSH(ə)n/
(Noun)
The action or practice of deceiving someone by concealing or misrepresenting the truth.

Deception is an act of twisting the truth. Betrayal. Distrust. Suspicion. All bred by deception and blossomed in relation-ships. Sometimes, when you spend your life deceiving others, the line between fact and fiction is blurred, and you begin to deceive yourself.

That's the worst type of deception. Self-deception. If you're trying hard to convince yourself something is true or untrue, take a step back and re-evaluate. Be true to yourself. Above all, be true to your heart. Know what your heart wants and chase it relentlessly.

> ❝ The greatest deception men suffer is from their own opinions.
>
> — *LEONARDO DA VINCI*

Damiano De Luca

*T*o live is the rarest thing in the world. Most people exist. That is all.

Nana used to say this. She'd pass it off like it was her quote, as if Oscar Wilde wasn't a prolific writer any decently read human being would recognize. The words, however, were true. I felt them each time I yearned for something more, though I'd never tell Nana that.

Nana also used to say, you get what you're brave enough to ask for. Except this particular line was bullshit. You get what you're an asshole enough to take. I knew that the second I met Renata Vitali, and her amber eyes widened and her lips parted like she was already mine.

Only Ren didn't know it yet.

And back then, how she felt about me hadn't mattered.

Not until it was too late.

Renata Vitali

We could never have loved each other. We were too different. Too haunted. Too jaded. Too volatile. Too combatant.

We fought, and an earthquake rumbled the earth across the world. We touched, and lightning struck the same place twice. We kissed, and a tornado tore through towns nowhere near Tornado Alley. Being together meant destruction, and I may have been a Vitali, but no matter how much I tried, I wasn't bred for cold-hearted carnage like the rest of my family.

And Damiano De Luca *was* carnage, the secret De Luca son, wrapped in designer clothes and a faint, too-cool-for-me sneer, whereas I was the mafia princess, out of my league but too stubborn to admit it. Thing was, I'd never done anything to antagonize him. Not immediately, at least.

So, I never understood why he'd hated me from the second I moved into his home, exiled to De Luca territory by my own father. I may have been mafia royalty, but Damiano De Luca was the distant prince. Him, the conqueror; me, the conquered. He ruled the land I walked on, and it was his laws that governed my life.

It took me years to learn what I should have known from the start.

Twisted princes didn't love.

And when they became kings, they destroyed.

> There's a degree of deception in silence.

> — *DON LEMON*

Renata Vitali

Sixteen Years Old

Sometimes, you know when catastrophe is about to strike you. A screech of tires. Oxygen masks shooting at you from above your airplane seat. The numbness spreading across your face before a stroke.

There were no warning signs for me.

My heart was calm when Angelo De Luca turned the corner of

the East Wing hallway, seconds after showing me what would be my room for however long Papà's punishment for me lasted.

My heart was calm when, not a minute later, I darted to the room next to mine, and my fingers twisted the door handle without a moment's hesitation.

My heart was calm as I eased my way into the bedroom. The one that belonged to the secret De Luca son. *Damiano*, his dad had called him, not an ounce of affection in his voice.

I should have known better.

In this world, there was only one reason to hide a child if you were a mafia boss for one of the Five Syndicates. The thought of learning firsthand what was wrong with Angelo De Luca's secret son should have scared me.

But in the rare moments I'd seen my father, he had taught me that fear was weakness, and weakness was death. It wasn't a quaint lesson, nor was it a father's honorable attempt at keeping his daughter safe.

It was a warning.

Against him.

He was the threat in my life. Always would be. I'd been here less than an hour, but every second I spent in Devils Ridge, Texas reminded me of that.

Don't be weak.

You're a Vitali.

Vitalis don't feel fear.

Christ, a whole continent away, and Papà's voice still plagued my mind. Usually, he inspired anger. Today, determination darted from my head to my toes as I began my search for a cell phone or landline in Damiano De Luca's room.

Like my room next door, this room felt un-lived in. Unlike my room, someone had been living in this one for longer than all of one point two seconds.

Telltale signs of neglect painted the room. Crisp, clean sheets —untouched for who knew how long. Aged air—stale with a fading hint of aftershave. A sole eighteenth-century dresser, coated with a fine layer of dust.

I should have considered what that meant. That even the maids hadn't entered this room in some time. I didn't. Maman deserved to know that I'd seen Papà pounding into his secretary before he sent me to Texas to live with the De Lucas—without a phone and beleaguered by explicit instructions never to be in contact with one, lest I be given an opportunity to tattle to Maman.

I wasn't the type to listen, but people were like scampering rats when it came to my family. Or maybe they were cult followers—frail and obeisant, followers begging for a command, all too happy to hide the electronics from me. This meant searching for a damn phone in foreign territory proved nearly impossible.

It startled me how much control Papà had over people, even an ocean away. As the head of the Vitali family, Papà was *il condottiero*. The leader. In layman's terms, if the syndicate territories across the world were states and their bosses were governors, the Vitali family would be the federal government. And Papà? He'd be president.

Still, he may have made the rules for the mafia underworld, but I made my own rules. Those included doing all I could to defy his. Like finding a phone. I scoured the room, optically tracing every inch.

My heart was calm as failure met my eyes. There was a neat stack of laundry on the desk, a journal that peeked out from beneath the pillow-top mattress, and a box with north of twenty grand worth of Gurkha Black Dragon cigars tucked away in a built-in humidor beside the Alaskan king-size bed. But no phone.

Murmurs sounded from the hallway, and still, my heart was calm as I searched the room for a hiding place. Locked closet. Bathroom across the hall. Curtains tied so tightly together, even my thin waist couldn't hide behind them. Four-poster bed with a bottom blocked off by 18th century wood.

Silly, naive Renata Vitali.

Would I ever learn to plan for the worst?

Yet, my heart was calm when the handle to the bedroom door twisted, and I realized there was nowhere to hide.

My heart was calm as I perched myself in the center of the bed, looking as ready for my first encounter with Damiano De Luca as I could in old designer sweats stitched for rebellion and a samurai bun that weathered the eight-hour private flight from Italy to Texas.

My heart was calm as I accepted the inevitability of discovery with grace.

My heart was calm.

My heart was calm.

My heart was calm.

Until I saw him for the first time, and it wasn't.

2

> ❝ Only one deception is possible in the infinite sense
> —self-deception.

— *SOREN KIERKEGAARD*

Renata Vitali

Sixteen Years Old

You're a fighter, Renata.

Maman had drilled that into my head at a young age, and I'd always agreed. Never felt like there was another option. After all, why be weak when I could fight?

How arrogant of me to think I would always have the luxury of choice.

Angelo's secret son—and I just *knew* it was him—had swung the door open, his eyes landing on mine in an instant. If he was surprised, he didn't show it.

But I sure did.

In a so-cliché-it-decimated-my-ego moment, my eyes widened, and my lips parted. Choice had been ripped away from me. There was no fighting my reaction, because I wasn't equipped to handle this. To handle *him*.

Suddenly, I understood what Monet had felt when he'd destroyed his own art because it wasn't perfect enough. I'd laughed it off in Art History class, but staring at Angelo's son, I wasn't laughing anymore. Every boy I'd ever lusted over proved inadequate preparation for this moment. He was the indescribable, the *je ne sais quoi* people sought but didn't dare imagine.

Angelo mentioned we'd be attending the same high school, but looking at him, I could hardly believe we were close in age. He towered in the door frame, his body already well above six feet. His muscles were lean but sinewy, and calling him a high school boy would be like calling my dad's yacht a boat. Damiano De Luca didn't look like a high school boy. Heck, he didn't even look like any man I'd ever seen.

While the boys at my former Connecticut boarding school wore spiked hair slathered with layers of gel, his head boasted a simple gentleman's cut, hair buzzed short at the sides and left longer at the top. Prominent cheekbones and a strong jaw lined his face, along with a hint of stubble, which made him appear older than he was.

And his eyes... Something about them shook me. Screamed at me to pay attention. I was sure those haunted, panther-black eyes played a good game of poker to everyone else, but to me, they were splashing limbs, begging for a life raft. And I wanted to throw one to him. Wanted to reach out and save him from whatever pained him, but they hardened a second later and cut me out.

He took me in, and I swore, he saw past my façade. Saw past the frumpy attire I had curated for my meeting with his father. Saw past the shitty, dark blonde dye job I'd touched up on the flight; the un-plucked brows; the bitten finger nails and chipped, mismatched polish; and the baggy tee and sweats, which hid my curves.

I'd done this for the past five years, altering my appearance because I saw more worth in slithering under the radar than drawing attention. He was the first to give me this look, one that dared me to question him as he saw past my lies.

At eleven, I'd asked my mother why she never bothered with the spa treatments and pretty dresses the other moms would fuss over. I knew she was pretty. Papà always made sure I knew he would never marry a French commoner had it not been for her beauty.

But as the years passed, the layers of her beauty slipped away like water leaking past a broken dam until only the fractured foundation remained. Maman moved to the Hamptons in New York while Papà remained in Italy, and I wondered why she never tried harder.

When I asked, she laughed, poked my side, and said in her pretty French accent, "I'm going to poke you again. Dodge it." Minutes passed, and she tried again, but I was ready and easily dodged it. "With warning, your ears are perked, and your eyes are ready. But silent threats do not warn you, *ma petite guerrière*. They attack, lethal and unapologetic."

I wanted to be lethal and unapologetic.

An hour later, a screech tore past my lips when she pinched my hips out of nowhere. The next day, I traded my pretty dresses for loose band tees and baggy jeans that hung on me like an over-sized condom.

But now, sitting before this stranger, I saw no worth in my

mother's wisdom. My trusty barrier crumbled, and I scrambled to build new ones as his lips curled into a sneer and he eyed where my body pressed against his bed.

"If you want to sleep with me, you'll have to try harder, Princess."

Princess.

I hated that word. It reminded me of the role I played in the mafia world, one which included enduring torment from a tyrant father. Petty jealousy came from all sides, and I fielded it like a press secretary at the White House.

I'd been prepared for my mafia princess status to cause friction in De Luca territory, but I hadn't been prepared for the goosebumps Angelo De Luca's son elicited when he called me such a ridiculous name in his sparse Texas accent.

It was on the tip of my tongue to say I didn't want him.

Lie.

But being sprawled on his bed wasn't a sexual invitation, and I had an endgame to think of. I stood on my feet and met him just short of the doorway. "Just seeing what I'm dealing with here."

His eyes ran down my body and returned to mine. Maman always referred to them as a rapturous shade of amber, but I was sure that, like mine, his opinion was less favorable. He cocked a brow, and I realized that I was staring, my hand suspended in the air by my side like an idiot.

Had I been about to touch him? I slid my foot back as subtly as I could, taking whatever distance the movement allowed.

His lips twitched, and I felt the most ridiculous urge to touch them. "Have your fill yet? I may have to charge admission, and I guarantee you can't afford the price."

Pull yourself together, Ren.

I tilted my head up to meet his eyes. I was tall for sixteen, but he was so much taller. "The most I'd part with for you is the gum beneath my shoe."

Amusement danced behind his eyes before they slid, once again, down my body. "I have no doubt you're the type with plenty of gum beneath your shoe."

What was that supposed to mean?

I reminded myself that I had a goal. "Well, this has been riveting, but I'm jet lagged. Bye."

I stepped forward before he could answer and bumped into his shoulder on the way out, using the movement to distract him as I slipped my fingers into the pocket of his hoodie. My pointer and thumb fingers swiped his smartphone, and I hid it in the sleeve of my cardigan as I barreled past.

He was right. I was a princess. But sometimes, the princess saved herself. Except, I'd stolen his phone, and just like earlier, I hadn't planned for the worst that would come.

And making an enemy of Damiano De Luca was the biggest mistake I'd ever made.

3

> A deception that elevates us is dearer than a host of low truths.
>
> — MARINA TSVETAEVA

Damiano De Luca

The Present

Liars were a dime a dozen. Good liars, rarer. But the best liars were the ones who lied as much to themselves as they did to others. The woman beside me was a liar. I usually read people well, but with her, I wasn't sure which category she fit in.

Ariana De Luca fidgeted in her seat, a movement that would have gone unnoticed to the untrained eye. I let the silence simmer a moment longer as I reveled in her discomfort. The wooden pillar dug into our thighs, but I knew it wasn't the source of her irritation.

"Am I bothering you?"

We were at a funeral, after all, so I kept my voice low and my eyes forward, where Giovanni Romano was giving what was probably a moving eulogy for his deceased twin, Vincent. I wouldn't know. It was hard to pay attention when the woman that very same Giovanni had been asking around about sat beside me.

"No." Her voice wasn't clipped, but it didn't welcome conversation either.

I suppressed my smirk, quelling the part of me that loved stirring up shit. Really, Ariana De Luca was the shit-stirrer by entering Romano territory with my last name. Did she think either family wouldn't notice?

Silence spilled between us, no doubt heightening her discomfort. I studied her as she sat beside me. Looking at her was like looking at a picture of a younger Nana. Un-fucking-canny. Same Italian features. Dark hair. High cheekbones. Upturned nose.

Little Tessie Romano made her way to the seat between us, scrambling over a few laps along the way. If Dad were here, he would have dripped disdain. As far as I was concerned, everyone here could thank me for his absence—though bloodstains littered my path to the De Luca throne.

I allowed Tessie a small smile. "*Ciao, piccola. Come ti senti?*" When Ariana stiffened, it occurred to me that she didn't speak Italian. Because riling women up was a specialty I took pride in, I continued in the language, "Your uncle was a good man. He will be missed."

Tessie turned to me. "*Grazie, Damiano.*" Her somber eyes

squinted in a sudden smile, and she waved at a brunette as she walked past.

Fuck. Me.

Nope.

This wasn't happening.

Ripples of shock trickled into my bloodstream. The brunette turned, but I already knew who she was. Remembered the words she had speared me with before she'd left me. She'd promised revenge, and I'd been patiently waiting.

Renata Vitali was still the siren she'd always been—only different. Gone was the out-of-a-bottle blonde, replaced by a torrent of chestnut waves, which she had confessed was her natural color all those years ago. Full lips, the same come-fuck-me shade that laid squarely between ruby-slippers red and raspberry pink. Seductive eyes—part honey, part copper, framed by lashes thicker than Warren Buffet's bank account. In the sea of heavily made-up women here, it struck me that she was still comfortable enough to wear her face bare.

Since she'd left, she traded her rich-girl sweats for a fitted black dress with a slit, barely-there pencil skirt. It was intoxicating. It was toxic. It was lethal. Even in ratty jeans and a hoodie, she attracted attention. Never on purpose. But *this*... this held purpose.

I had waited years to see her again, and now that I had, I didn't know if I wanted her to stay or leave.

"Tessie, I've missed you." Her smile flattened as she met my eyes. "D."

D for Damsel.

She'd given me the nickname ages ago, and I was thankful she still abbreviated it in public. Small mercies.

Ariana started, which was a fair reaction. I was the new head of the De Luca family. Not many dared to use a tone with me, but Ren wasn't just anyone. If anything, she had more power than everyone in this room—me included. It suited her. Damn, did it suit her.

I debated calling her "Knight," but it was too intimate a first greeting for nearly ten years spent apart, so I settled for the nickname she loved to hate. "Good to see you, Princess."

To be fair, she *was* a princess.

A mafia princess.

Ren's eyes narrowed, tracking my every breath as I said goodbye to Tessie and followed her out the side of the church. It wasn't lost on me that I was always following Ren, even when I didn't realize it.

She reeked of strength. Wore it like a little black dress, hugging every delicious inch of her skin. Back when syndicates worldwide had engaged in costly, deadly wars, the Vitali family had been elected to run peace talks. Then, they became the mafia world's government. The most powerful family in the underworld. Renata wore that power well.

It was weird seeing this side of her in public when she'd done everything she could to hide her strength back then. Most guys weren't into girls who were smarter, more formidable, and just plain *better* than them. I was almost thankful for those douches.

That mentality had kept Ren single my junior and senior years of high school. Now, I guessed not. I eyed her ring finger, where a rock the size of the emerging hole in my gut rested. She followed my gaze to her finger, then lifted her chin and cocked a brow.

I met her stare. "Unapologetic and defiant as always, I see."

"Because I'm wearing a ring, and you didn't put it there?" She crossed her arms, and that damned ring teased me as it glinted in the light. "Save the chauvinistic bullshit for a damsel that would swoon."

Her pun wasn't lost on me. Neither was her attitude. I wouldn't win this argument with Ren, so I didn't bother trying. I reached for the door, one-hundred percent sure it was rude of the

De Luca head to miss the funeral. Probably a thousand times worse for the Vitali representative—still couldn't believe it was *her*—to miss it.

The door was locked. I pulled on it harder. Still locked. I'd never wanted to be a tight-wearing superhero and walk through the door's metal more than I did now.

"Fuck."

My eyes shifted to Ren and narrowed at how calm she was. It always unnerved me how cool and collected she never ceased to be. Like that time I'd caught her snooping in my room. Or when she'd pickpocketed my phone moments later.

I crossed my arms. "Did you plan this?"

"Don't flatter yourself, Da—" She cut herself off, but I knew what she'd been about to say.

When we were good, she was Knight, and I was Day.

When we were bad, she was Princess, and I was Damsel.

Needless to say, she was usually Princess, and I was usually Damsel.

I started to walk away, making my way to the front of the church. She made me feel unhinged, like the body my soul occupied wasn't mine. We'd been away from each other for about ten years, but somehow, we'd instantly reverted to how we'd been.

"Damsel!"

Nope.

Don't even think about it.

Keep walking, Damian.

I turned around. "What are you even doing here?!"

I'd thought she was gone. Escaped from the mafia world, like only a Vitali or someone like Asher Black could get away with. She sure as hell did a good job of staying off my expanding radar.

Fuck. My chest heaved up and down, each breath more cumbersome than the next. I needed to leave before I did something that piled on the mountain of broken glass between us.

Placid as ever, her attention wandered to a cat that sprang

across the alley before returning to me. "Representing the Vitali family."

"The same family that sent you off to boarding school at eight years old?"

She crossed her arms. "My mom moved nearby."

I ignored her. "The same family that sent you to De Luca territory and left you there for fourteen months?"

Yeah, I knew sending people off to live in De Luca territory was considered punishment in the syndicates' circles. After all, I knew what we'd once been. The De Luca name was a stain on the Five Syndicates. From my dad's unhinged behavior to the notorious story of my great-great-grandfather killing my great-grandfather, we were the laughing stock, like the extra character writers threw into horror flicks for the sole purpose of killing off later.

I was trying to give the family a better reputation, but I couldn't build a reputation on what I had yet to do. One bad deed was enough to ruin a million good ones. Unfortunately, the roads in De Luca territory were paved by bad deeds. Bricks made of poor decisions, mortared together by blood. I wasn't sure I was capable of enough good to offset the bad.

Just one of many reasons why I was personally in New York City to attend Vincent Romano's funeral. That, and I actually respected the man, which was more than I could say about most people.

Ren straightened her shoulders and lifted her chin. "Papà had his reasons." Her thumb twirled that offensive rock around her finger like a nervous tick that served the sole purpose of transferring her anxiety to me. Except I knew firsthand that she had no ticks, and if she had any anxieties, she held them closer to her chest than heat to a flame. Renata was a Vitali, after all, and she'd trained every flaw out of her body by kindergarten.

"Did they involve my father and his hands?!" I sucked in a breath and swore. I knew what had happened in the bathroom hadn't been illicit, but she didn't know I knew. "That was uncalled for. I apologize."

And still, she remained unfazed. If I didn't know her better, I'd think I stood in front of a sociopath.

"If you can't control your emotions, there are treatments for that, which don't involve tormenting me with your juvenile behavior. I was going to suggest a truce for this weekend, but I now see there's little point in that." She stepped around me like I was an overeager dog she could sidestep. "If you'll excuse me, I have a funeral to attend and a name to represent." Her heels *click-clacked* with every step she took toward the front doors.

Just like that night she'd left me, she was unapologetic.

Just like that night, she didn't look back.

Just like that night, she smeared my heart across the pavement with each step.

And just like that night, I still wanted her.

> **"** All deception in the course of life is indeed nothing else but a lie reduced to practice, and falsehood passing from words into things.

— ROBERT SOUTHEY

Renata Vitali

"**M**iss Vitali, I haven't seen you in a while." Frankie Romano approached me after the closed-casket viewing ended, clasped my shoulder with an over-sized palm, and kissed me on the cheek. Dark gray colored his hair at his temples, and he looked every bit the refined mafia leader he was. "What have you been doing with your time, Renata?"

Frankie led the Romano syndicate, which ruled northeast America. He was stern but fair and only resorted to violence when other options had been exhausted. I respected him for that and for leading the strongest of the five Italian-American crime syndicates without heavy bloodshed.

Dragging my eyes away from Damian, who stood beside one of his soldiers, I flashed a polite smile at Frankie and took a step back from him. "I graduated from college early through an accelerated program, and I've been an elementary school teacher for a while now."

"An elementary school teacher..." I doubted much dumbfounded Frankie Romano, but I guessed the mafia princess becoming a teacher did.

"Yes." My lips quirked upward, though I tried to smother the smile. Gosh, life outside the mafia had chipped away at my hard edges. Except when it came to Damian. Around him, I could fortify my walls quicker than a fired bullet slipped past its chamber.

"A Vitali schoolteacher." He shook his head, but it was lighthearted teasing. We had an odd relationship. We weren't close, and we didn't see each other often, but when we did, it wasn't strained. Kind of like his brother, Vince, he adopted the father-daughter vibe with me better than Papà did. "I suppose crazier things have happened." Frankie's eyes drifted to Damian, and I read the subtext.

I'd been prepared for Damian's rise. Yes, his existence had surprised me when we first met. Yes, Devils Ridge did a good job of hiding Damian's identity under Angelo De Luca's orders. But living in Devils Ridge gave me perspective, and I knew without a doubt that Damian would take over his father's throne. It was never a matter of how but when.

On the other hand, the other syndicates had no warning. Not

only had they not known he'd take over the De Luca syndicate, they hadn't even known he existed. Damian had to unease them.

"It's not crazy," I offered Frankie. "If you know Damian, you wouldn't think it's crazy."

I told him this because I might have been avoiding Damian, but he still deserved respect from other syndicate bosses. And Frankie deserved a warning, too. He let me live in Connecticut— Romano territory—without asking what I did there or invading my privacy. Granted, my last name probably helped convince him.

"Do you know something I don't, sweetheart?" the pet name slithered out of his mouth, oozing with condescension.

I took no offense to it. Some would get irritated by his tone, and throwing people off balance had a tendency to make them talk. A subtle but effective method. It just wouldn't work on me, no matter how much time out of the mafia had softened me. I didn't respond to verbal provocation.

I nodded and deadpanned, "Yes."

My eyes crawled the length of Frankie, cataloging his body language. I wondered if he helped me maintain my privacy in Connecticut out of the goodness of his heart or to gain favor with my family. I never knew if someone was helping me because they liked me or because they wanted me to think they liked me.

The Vitali family governed the Italian crime syndicates across the world after wars had caused massive loss of lives, drawn attention to the syndicates, and wiped out a few families. The underworld needed a neutral party to keep everyone above the line, and my ancestors had the connections and wealth to be elected. We gathered an army, more money than anyone could possibly spend, and networked in all branches of governments in all countries syndicates existed. So, it was very possible Frankie treated me well to gain my family's favor. It was also very possible he didn't give a flying fuck. He was a Romano, after all, and they were second only to the Vitali.

He pulled a cigar from his pocket and offered me one. "But you won't say..."

I shook my head. "A cigar contains as much tobacco as an entire pack of cigarettes."

Frankie shrugged. "Suit yourself." He rolled the edges of the cigar over his lighter flame, warmed the cigar, and removed the band.

I studied his movements and elaborated, "No one knew Damian existed. The only way that happens is if Angelo gave orders within his syndicate to keep Damian a secret." Sequestering Damian in Devils Ridge helped, too. Until he dethroned Angelo, Damian rarely stepped foot outside of Devils Ridge.

Frankie took a drag and puffed the smoke away from both our faces.

It still smelled, but I ignored it and continued, "No one bothered to keep tabs on the De Lucas, because Angelo didn't hold a candle to the other syndicates and the De Luca syndicate is mostly straight-laced oil money. That negligence is on everyone." I met Frankie's weathered eyes past the smoke. "But have you ever wondered why Angelo gave the order to keep Damian a secret?"

He drew the cigar away from his lips and stared out at the crowd that had gathered in the church's side lot. "He didn't want us to know he had a potential successor."

"Yes, but it's one thing to have someone who can succeed you through lineage. It's another thing entirely to have someone who others would *want* to succeed."

"So, everyone in the De Luca syndicate wanted Damian to take over, which means Angelo's either an asshole or Damian is that good... and we both know Angelo's an asshole. He's not right in the head either."

Frankie underestimated Damian. Back in Devils Ridge, I'd always suspected Damian saw value in being an unknown entity.

"Have you considered the possibility it's both those reasons?"

"Truthfully, I haven't really talked to the boy."

"*The boy* is nearing thirty, and he revitalized a failing syndicate in less time than it takes to become a dog trainer." My tone slipped past my lips sharper than intended. I was being defensive when I was no longer supposed to care about Damian.

After his coup, Damian dredged his syndicate up from the trenches. No syndicate compared to the Romano syndicate, but the De Luca family now rivaled the Camerino, Andretti, and Rossi syndicates.

"You sound impressed. Maybe even a little indignant." Frankie paused, his cigar hovering at the edge of his lips as he raised a brow. "Or perhaps like you care, Little Ren."

Well, fuck.

I redirected, hoping he didn't see through me, "Frankie, I like you. I chose your syndicate to lay roots in, and you've given me privacy. So, I'm offering you advice here as someone who has lived in Devils Ridge. As someone who has lived with Damiano De Luca for over a year. He's not someone you should take lightly."

"Noted, sweetheart." He gave me a sweet smile, and given the morose setting, he looked almost at peace. "Just so you know, Renata, you're not fooling me. Your eyes have been darting to him every other second. You don't just sound like you care. You look like you care, too."

His eyes scanned my face. Ten years ago, I never would have given anything away, but the civilian lifestyle didn't give me much practice in concealing emotions. I needed to get my shit together if I wanted to survive this weekend.

Frankie shifted his gaze to Damian, who stared at me unapologetically from the opposite end of the lot. "The others don't take well to him being here."

I turned my body away, so I couldn't see Damian in my line of sight anymore because Frankie was right. I *had* been staring. "By others, do you mean you?"

"No, I couldn't care less if he's here or not." He stressed, "There are more important things in life to worry over than petty prejudices."

I faltered. He'd just lost his brother, and I hadn't been watching my words. "I'm sorry, Frankie."

His loss hung between us like a swaying noose, a reminder that if we ever decided to move on, it would always be there to rob us of our breaths. Vincent Romano's death had ended the Andretti-Romano war, bringing the syndicates closer than they'd ever been. He sacrificed himself not just for his family but for peace between all of the syndicates. For what? A world I could barely stand? One which forced me to build walls higher than the Great Wall's?

"Don't worry about it, kiddo." Frankie straightened up his bespoke three-piece suit, looking like a black-haired cross between George Clooney and Robert Redford circa *Indecent Proposal*. A group of women nearby clung to his every move. "For what it's worth, I'm happy you're here. You're always welcome in the city." He stared past my shoulder before returning his gaze to mine with a smug look pasted on his distinguished features. "As much as I'd like to watch this unfold, I have to head to the cemetery first."

"Watch what unfold?" I started to ask, but he was already walking away.

Not a second later, a shadow darkened my path. I forced myself not to turn around as Damian's lips found my ear as he spoke, "Talking to yourself?"

I pictured the barbed-wire fence outside the state prison I usually passed on the drive back to Connecticut. Criss-crossed steel. Spiked metal. Sharp edges. Twenty feet high. I needed to build walls like that within me. Fast.

Pivoting to face Damian, I backed up a little, so his scent wouldn't make me lightheaded anymore. "Most people can take a hint when someone doesn't want to talk to them."

His eyes dipped to my arms when I crossed them, and he looked almost satisfied by the defensive gesture. "You're leaning into me, Princess."

I drove my heels into the ground, forcing myself not to adjust my body at his words, because he was right. I *was* leaning into him, and I hadn't even realized it. But I wasn't about to admit he was right.

They say one lie is enough to cast doubt on every truth, yet no amount of lies could ever absolve me of the worst truth of all —Damiano De Luca meant something to me. My brittle heart would never heal. I was condemned to him forever.

We stood so close as he bent forward and continued to murmur in my ear, "The way I see it, I see past your bullshit, your body is speaking an entirely different language than you think it is, and the only person who can't take a hint is you. So, I'll spell it out for you, Princess." He gestured at my body, which was *still* leaning towards him. "This isn't the body language of someone who left me. This is the body language of someone who has never stopped wanting me. I'll figure out why you left ten years ago, and I'll figure out why you're here now."

I couldn't believe Damian's audacity. Who spoke like this to someone after a decade apart? Though I saw traces of the boy I'd once loved in him, he had also changed. Confident, powerful, and unpredictable. The kind of guy my mom would have warned me away from as a kid if it weren't for the fact that he was exactly the type of man tailor-made for a mafia princess.

I swallowed, forcing down the way his words and presence sped up my heartbeat. I'd forgotten this feeling. Since leaving Devils Ridge, I'd stayed away from the fuck-you-with-his-eyes, take-what-he-wants-with-both-hands, padlocked-chest-full-of-secrets type of guys. I was the goldfish who took her first dip in the ocean, decided it was too big to handle, and begged for a cozy little fish bowl she could swim safely in. I was the anti-Nemo.

So, I shook my head, denial running deeper in my veins than

drugs in an addict's. And I couldn't deny I'd always been addicted to Damian, though my words said otherwise, "You don't know what you're talking about."

He leaned back against a random car, not a care in the world as to who it belonged to, despite standing in a lot full of dangerous mafiosos. "There's nothing cute about this denial act." I opened my mouth to protest, but he cut me off with his hard voice, "Don't bother denying your denial. It's an insult at this point, and I may give no fucks, but my soldiers don't take insults lightly."

Leaning against his car had put some much-needed distance between us, but I could feel the ghost of his breath across my face as he reprimanded me. I shoved down this stupid lust and mocked, "Touchy, touchy, sweetheart."

"I've worked hard for everything I've earned, Princess. If I don't defend my kingdom, I deserve to be dethroned."

"You speak as if I give a damn."

"We both know you do." His eyes dipped to my wedding ring, and he backed off the car, reached his pointer finger out, and stroked it.

I pulled my hand back, suppressing the tingles of lust that stretched the length of my spine and spun my mind a thousand different ways. "I'm not here to talk to you."

"Ah, the crux of the matter. Why you left. Why you're here. Feel free to explain either."

"It's been ten years, Damsel. Shouldn't you be over this?"

"You can lessen what we had all you want, Princess, but it's never going to change the fact that you loved me so much you used to say my name in your sleep."

"You're lying."

He ran his eyes down my body, pausing a moment on my chest, which swelled with each breath drawn. "If you remember, the air vent on the wall separating our rooms stood above both our beds. I could hear everything, and you spoke my name like it belonged on your lips."

He was right. I'd dreamed of him. Still did sometimes. I'd always been this unaffected girl. So aloof. So collected. But Damian nicked my armor, and a few years after I'd left Devils Ridge, I finally put the armor down.

So, here I was, with dangerous attraction simmering in the air and no protection against it. The spark between us had always been my problem. I could never truly push him away, so when I left, I knew the only way to succeed was to stay away.

But I was no longer away, and my demons weren't the type that could be confronted.

The least I could do was try to find my way out.

I stepped back and picked at a strand of lint on my sleeve, doing my damnedest to look unaffected. When I finally returned my gaze to him, he didn't look convinced. I spat out, "You can rewrite our history all you want, Damsel, but it won't change our future."

Taunting laughter rippled out of him, and he looked like temptation in his bespoke guanaco-woven suit and derisive sneer. "You don't get it, do you? You being here changes everything." He winked at me—freaking winked at me—and left, his soldiers trailing after him like well-trained lapdogs.

My mom had always taught me that life was a never-ending game of chess. And this game? It felt like he'd just claimed another piece.

> **❝** Appear weak when you are strong and strong when you are weak.

— SUN TZU

Renata Vitali

Ten Years Old

One spring evening, when the rain had sunk the wheels of our town car a foot deep into mud and I'd run out of books to read in the house, I found Maman in her library, staring over a chessboard.

I liked all sorts of things other ten-year-old kids didn't—

books, debate, and speed math, for instance. Chess had never been one of them. Papà liked to play it in the cigar room when other mafiosos visited. A men's game, he called it. I wondered what he would say if he knew Maman liked to play, too.

"Come." She gestured to the spot across from her. "Sit."

This chessboard was her throne, and it overlooked her empire. A floor-to-ceiling glass wall separated us from the beach. I always appreciated the wealth Papà took for granted. This view, most of all.

I loved this room. Loved everything about it, including the way my mom looked so out of place with her distressed style, which Papà complained made her look like a commoner. In Maman's defense, there was nothing common about her.

I slid into the seat and hid a grin at Maman's white Sonic Youth band tee. I wore the same one in gray. "Who are you playing with?"

"Everyone."

That made no sense to me, but I pretended it did. "Doesn't that get tiring?"

"Not if you know how to do it well." A smile curved her lips, and despite the fact that she was the only woman in the Hamptons who sported band tees, loose jeans, and Chapstick (and only on the best of days), Maman was the prettiest woman in the world when she smiled. "Do you see this? The dark pawn is at e5, and the light pawn is at e4." She moved the white knight. "And now the knight is at c3." Here eyes met my mine, too serious for a cozy rainy day. "Do you know what this is?"

The infamous Vienna game.

Papà had shown this to me a few years ago when he caught me staring at one of the many chessboards he kept in the house. "The King's Gambit is an aggressive attack. The opening of petulant kings trying to prove their worth." Indignation coated his voice, and even at seven, I heard it. "The Vienna game is a delayed King's Gambit. Slower play with the same result."

Years later, I still remembered his words. "Papà said the Vienna game is the opening of kings who do not understand that patience is wasted time."

Amusement swam in Maman's eyes. "Your papà can be a fool at times, pretty girl."

My jaw dropped. "Maman!"

I'd never heard anyone speak of Papà like this. He was the head of the Vitali, for goodness sake!

"Oh, hush, my love." She winked at me. "You won't tell." Her thin fingers, weighed down by an enormous diamond ring, moved a piece on the board. "Your father can learn a thing or two from the Vienna game." Maman met my eyes. "White plays quietly, and the dark king?" That unassuming smile filled her face. "The dark king never sees her coming."

It was a lesson I should never have forgotten.

6

> " Self-deception is sometimes as necessary a tool as a crowbar.

— MOSA HART

Renata Vitali

Seventeen Years Old

The workers in the De Luca household liked to gossip in Spanish, which was close enough to my native Italian that I had an idea of what they said. Señor Damian, as the maids called him, came home more often than usual lately, and they blamed me.

I loathed the sense I saw in their logic.

If ever there was a cold war between two strangers, this was it. I'd stolen Damiano De Luca's phone. That didn't exactly set a remarkable first impression. He hadn't confronted me about it, but I knew he knew.

After sending Maman an email and erasing my digital tracks, I slipped the phone on the floor by his bedroom door. Maybe he would think he had dropped it.

A girl could hope.

That had been three days ago. Days passed, and tense silence thickened each time I heard him walk by my door. Thing was, I knew the heavy footsteps held intent. Syndicate royalty didn't make noise as they walked. Training took care of that.

But each firm step Damiano De Luca took was deliberate. Like a move made on a chessboard, thought ten steps ahead. In fact, life in the De Luca household felt exactly like a chess match, in which I held no control over the board.

Maman always had the Vienna match laid on the chessboard in her library. Every now and then, she'd move a piece. Sometimes, a week apart; sometimes, a year apart. The dark king never sees his demise coming, she'd tell me each time I noticed a moved piece.

But I'd spent enough time looking at that chessboard to see my demise coming. Heard the breaths of impending doom each time I left the confines of my room. Felt the ironclad fingers of vengeance wrap around my neck whenever I dared to sneak food from the kitchen. Smelled the metallic blood of ruin trickle down my body whenever I dodged across the hall to use the bathroom.

I sensed it now as I grabbed a change of clothes and darted to the bathroom I shared with Damian. Like the other houses in Devils Ridge, Texas, the De Luca household was antiquated. Built in the 18th century, the house had been renovated only twice—once during the Victorian era, so it matched the aesthetics of the other Victorian-style homes in town, and once again a few years ago when the contractors had decided that introducing anything more than the minimal number of modern amenities would jeopardize the historic integrity of the home.

Historic integrity, my ass.

The East Wing bathroom had three rooms—a toilet room, a vanity room, and a bathing room. The door to the bathroom led to the bathing room, where a small bathing pool laid in the center, like I was on the set of Game of Thrones.

It occurred to me what a waste of water filling and draining this pool was, but I wasn't going to bathe in Damian's soiled water. I slid my silk robe off my shoulders and hung it on the hook beside the door, along with my change of clothes.

One of the maids had warmed the pool and filled it with bubbles earlier, and I dipped a toe into the water, exploring the temperature. My waist barely kissed the water before the door swung open.

I moved quickly, covering my breasts with the bubbles as I plunged fully into the pool. My eyes met Angelo De Luca's as he stepped past the threshold, busting every myth about evil being incapable of entering a room uninvited. Or was that vampires?

"Miss Vitali." He took a step closer, and I forced myself not to move away from my spot against the closest pool edge to the door. How someone so slimy and decrepit could spawn someone who looked like Damiano De Luca was beyond me. "My sources tell me you turn seventeen years old today." The gap between us lessened. "Another year closer."

Another year closer to what?

Goosebumps traveled across my skin, and I forced myself not to eye the open door. It was late. The last of the East Wing staff had retreated to their quarters after drawing my bath. I trusted Angelo De Luca like I trusted a jock to do his own homework. I was alone with this sinister excuse of a man, and though calm had nestled itself inside my body from a young age, it burrowed deeper, hiding somewhere between apprehension and concern.

Still, I didn't allow my anxiety to manifest. I ignored him, reached for the shampoo, and formed a lather in my hair. A gust of wind flew in from the open door, chilling the exposed skin on my neck. I wanted to dip lower into the water, but being vulnerable in front of a man who enjoyed feasting on prey wasn't an option. Instead, I continued washing my hair.

His jaw ticked as I ignored him. "You are a guest in my household, Miss Vitali. You will not disrespect me."

"You're right." I tapped my foot beneath the water, hoping to expend the energy of my anxiety and replace it with amusement. "A person's a person, no matter how small."

Pretty sure that wasn't what Dr. Seuss had meant when he wrote that.

Oh, well.

Hard eyes burned my skin as some of the bubbles covering my breasts fizzled and died. "Careful, little girl." He crouched and reached out. I forced myself to act aloof as he cupped the side of my face and shut his teeth with an audible *snap!* "I bite."

During my boarding school's unit on Irish literature, I'd come across a Laurence Sterne quote: "Respect for ourselves guides our morals; respect for others guides our manners." Clearly, Angelo De Luca had neither, but it dawned on me that if I stayed here long, perhaps that would be my fate, too. I begged any higher power to not let me succumb to the De Luca madness.

Angelo's palm wandered down my cheek, past my collarbone, and toward my left breast. Goosebumps met his touch, and he cackled near my ear. "I scare you, don't I?"

He did, in the same way I feared poisonous spiders and walking home alone late at night. Logically. Clinically. And entirely detached. These things could hurt me if I let them, but I wouldn't let them.

"While we're exchanging fears, yours is my family." I stepped into his touch, enjoying the way his eyes flared in surprise. "I may fear you, Angelo, but I'll still face you. The fears we don't confront grow into limits, and I have no limits. But you?" I taunted him with my laughter. For a split second, I felt less like Harry Potter and more like Draco Malfoy. "You're bound by them each time you move."

"I could kill you right now, and we'd see just how scared I am of your family." Angelo's grip on my flesh became brutal, and his hand rested beneath the water, just short of reaching the top of my breast. Figured that'd be the time Damiano De Luca chose to enter the bathroom we shared.

His eyes took us in, narrowing on his dad's hand beneath the water for a split second before a sneer twisted his lips. "I put up with you fucking the help, Angelo," he spoke as if he owned the household, "but I will not put up with you further threatening the De Luca name by fucking the Vitali child."

The Vitali child.

Good grief. I'd asked the housekeepers for Damian's age. As of today, we were the same age, yet that was what I was to him. A child. Somehow, those words were all I could focus on. It wasn't lost on me that he may very well have just saved me from his father, but something I would come to learn about Damiano De Luca was, his presence crippled my logic. It didn't just cripple it. It nuked it, then buried it six feet under until I wasn't sure my logic had ever existed.

Angelo stood from his crouch, and I'd never seen so much hate a father held for his son as I saw in Angelo's eyes. "Finally home, son?"

Damian leaned a shoulder against the doorframe, amusement radiating off of him in waves, but I saw past the show he put on for his father. He was taunting him, just like I had taunted Angelo earlier. A defense tactic that shouldn't have built a connection between us—especially given the way he spoke of me as a child instead of an equal—but it did. "Obviously, if you're looking at me and we're in this house..."

Angelo met his son in three long strides until they stood

mere inches apart. "One day, I will learn what it is that you do when you are gone, and I will destroy you."

A smarter man would have tempered his anger and hid his weaknesses. Instead, Angelo had laid his cards bare for me. The friction between him and his son and the ensuing power struggle between them weren't for outsider eyes and ears, but here I was, an unwilling voyeur with a front row seat. Who could blame me for pocketing the information?

Damian remained unfazed. "How can you destroy me when all you're capable of is self-destruction?"

And that was when I knew he would win. That he would *always* win. Calm, cool, and collected, Damiano De Luca was everything his father should have been as the head of one of the five American syndicates.

Damian's eyes shifted to me, reminding his father of the audience. Angelo pulled his shoulders back, standing taller than anyone in the room thought he was, and left.

My eyes met Damian's, and I wore the calmest expression I could manage. "Those who plot the destruction of others often perish in the attempt." I dipped my hair back into the water, rinsing the shampoo from my scalp. The tops of my breasts peeked out of the water at the movement, and I was painfully aware of my audience of one.

"Quoting Thomas Moore doesn't make you smart." His gaze swallowed mine as I lifted my head from the water, shock at his knowledge of the Irish poet driving my actions. "It makes you unoriginal."

"Coming from the boy plotting to dethrone his father, I'm not so sure I trust your judgment on originality. Read too many Marvel comics?" I grabbed the soap bar and ran it across my skin. "Is it the Loki and Odin relationship or the Blade and Lucas Cross relationship that inspires your every move?" My words may have lashed, but as I dipped the bar of soap under the water and rubbed at my body, I couldn't shake the feeling that I'd never been this physically vulnerable in front of another human.

But Damian wasn't his dad, and he didn't seem the slightest bit interested in my body. "You should have stayed out of things that are none of your business, Princess."

Excuse me?!

Being in Devils Ridge hadn't been a choice and being in this home had been even less of one. His father was the one who barged into the bathroom, and now Damian had the gall to accuse *me* of imposing? So much for kindred spirits.

If I were the type to lash out, I would have. Instead, I remained composed as I rinsed the rest of the soap from my shoulders, ascended the steps out of the pool, and stood in front of him. "If your intent is to provoke me, it's not working."

Water dripped from my naked flesh, but his eyes never wavered from mine. "I have no intent when it comes to you. You are a pest. A flea. Nothing more than a common house fly. Something that is beneath me to swat at. The door will remain open, and you'll eventually fly away. But until then, stay away from me and stay out of my business." Condescension was an ugly look on anyone but him. He stepped closer. "I wouldn't want to accidentally hurt you, Princess."

The air chilled my wet skin as it brushed against me. Or maybe it was his words that chilled me. That lasted for about a second before his father's voice boomed in the background as he yelled at one of the poor staff members in the opposite wing of the house.

Myriad emotions ran through Damian's eyes before he filtered them out. It didn't matter, though. The damage had been done. I'd seen the emotions, and rather than latching onto the moment of vulnerability like a vulture clutching onto a dead carcass, I saw a kindred spirit I wanted to help.

A damsel that needed saving.

I lifted my chin and measured my words. "I'm no princess."

He laughed at me. "What else would you be?"

I thought of Maman's chessboard and the never-ending Vienna game. I wasn't the king, but I certainly wasn't the pawn either. "I'd be the knight."

"Fine, Knight."

"Fine, Day."

His eyes narrowed at the nickname. I didn't wait for him to call me out on it as I reached for my robe, slipped it over my shoulders, and walked past him as collected as I could with a thin silk robe sticking to my wet skin.

Truth was, Day wasn't short for Damiano.

It was a play on Damsel.

He didn't know it yet, but that was exactly how I saw him.

It should have been a bad thing, but it wasn't.

The world might not have seen him as one, but to me, Damiano De Luca was the damsel— trapped in this gilded tower, lashing out at his dad for an escape—and I was the stupid knight in shining armor who wanted to save him.

> He who tries to protect himself from deception is often cheated, even when most on his guard.

— PLAUTUS

Renata Vitali

The Present

"Have you seen him?"

"Maman!" My eyes darted around the cemetery for prying eyes, and I pressed my phone tighter against my ear. "This is hardly an appropriate time for this."

"It's always an appropriate time for a mother to ask her

daughter whether or not she's seen the boy she likes." The laughter in her voice squeezed my heart.

I knew she was hurting over Vincent Romano's death. I should give her this. I should play along. Then again, she had played her part in teaching me to build barriers around myself during my childhood. She could reap what she had sowed.

"In no world will Damian and I coexist peacefully. It's just never going to happen."

I regretted spilling to Maman after I had fled Texas. Fled Damian. At the time, I didn't even have it in me to be angry at her for abandoning me in Devils Ridge. Never mind my unanswered hidden texts and emails to her, heartbreak took over. For the longest time, I couldn't see past the pain.

Nearly ten years ago, Maman suggested I distance myself from Damian and recuperate, and I agreed. After all, why would I want to be near the boy I'd just run away from, tail tucked between my legs, knowing it was the wrong thing to do to someone who didn't deserve disappointment from yet another person in his life?

Now, Maman wanted me to reacquaint myself with him, and neither I nor my ego understood it.

"You left for Texas, and when you came back, I didn't recognize you. Your walls had been built higher than I'd ever seen them, and I thought you needed time. It's been nearly ten years, Renata. Ten whole years, baby girl." Her shaky inhale startled me, sucked the air out of the space, and made it impossible to breathe. "You need to learn to trust, my darling girl, or you will die alone. Neither of us want that, right?"

I begged to differ. My barriers protected me. Back then, the ugly clothes and unkempt appearance had caused many to underestimate me. The one time I had shed my walls had been for Damian, and look how that had turned out.

I'd since lost the frumpy clothes, but the walls around me never wavered. I rebuilt them, and then I built walls around those walls just because I liked to look at them. It was safer that way.

"I trust you, Maman. You are all I need. All I'll ever need." I also needed this conversation to end. "Maman, I'd love to talk more about this"—I approached the crowd, hoping she could hear their murmurs, think I was busy, and abandon the open-yourself-up spiel—"but everyone is at the cemetery already, and the burial is about to begin. It would be exceptionally rude to remain on the phone."

"Ren—"

"—Bye! Love you, Maman."

I hung up on her, feeling zero percent guilty and one-hundred percent sick of the emotions clogging my throat. I pushed them down, one by one.

Anger.

Frustration.

Betrayal.

Mistrust.

Love.

Lust.

Loneliness.

Sorrow.

Misery.

Fear.

Swallow. Swallow. Swallow. Swallow.

If emotions were sustenance, I would never have to eat again.

Don't be weak.

You're a Vitali.

Vitalis don't feel fear.

I repeated the mantra Papà had forced on me since birth until my feelings slipped away, leaving an emotionless façade. I only ever had to try to remain aloof around Damian. Usually, emotional distance came naturally to me. With Damian nearby? Not so much.

My heels wobbled as they sunk into the plush grass as I walked past the rows of tombstones surrounding me. New York could be unpredictable in the summer, but the weather this year sweltered more than usual. Today, however, was nice enough. I didn't know if that made me happy or sad. Vincent probably would've thought it was hilarious to be buried under the ground on the one nice summer day this year when he wasn't around to even appreciate it. I, on the other hand, didn't have Vincent's humor.

I stood near the front, far enough away to be respectful of the Romano family and close enough to adhere to the Vitali's place at the top of the hierarchy. The crowd for the burial ceremony outnumbered the closed casket viewing earlier. Vincent Romano clearly earned the respect of many, though that didn't surprise me.

My eyes remained forward as Lucy Black sidled next to me, her husband Asher—the Romano's former fixer—a couple rows ahead of us. I didn't know her. She didn't know me. Why was she next to me?

"Hey, I'm Lucy." Her eyes shifted to me. "Are you a Romano? I've never seen you around."

Oh.

She didn't know who I was.

My brows furrowed until I realized she only asked because I stood in a row ordinarily reserved for the Romano family. "Vitali. Renata Vitali." The instinct to flee settled deep in my legs. I had to force them to stay rooted to the ground.

"Oh." She paused a beat, and we stood in silence as the crowd grew in size. Pretty soon, we'd exceed the maximum capacity of the private cemetery. "I like your hair."

Were married people always this congenial? Couldn't she be happy next to her husband?

"Thank you."

She paused a beat. "He keeps staring at you." She bit her bottom lip, like she was stopping herself from saying more.

I dug my nails into the sides of my thighs. My eyes begged me to turn and meet his gaze. Instead, I grit out, "Who?" I didn't need to ask to know Damian stared at me from a few rows behind us, but not asking revealed more than I wanted to a stranger.

"Damiano De Luca."

His name sounded wrong coming from her lips, like it wasn't meant for her to say. It didn't escape my notice that I didn't hold any claim over him. Then again, it was me he stared at. Thousands of people gathered here today to mourn Vincent Romano's life, and he'd been staring at me since I clocked him earlier.

The attraction we once had still persisted because all of me stood on alert, too close to breathless for comfort. I was used to attention. I never wanted it, yet I had attracted it all my life. But even though I'd spent fourteen months blossoming under Damian's attention, I'd never gotten used to it.

I forced myself to speak. "You've met him?"

"Asher introduced us earlier." She kept her eyes averted from Vincent's casket up front, and it occurred to me that she might have started this conversation to distract herself. "He's kind of intimidating. Actually, not just kind of. He's *really* intimating."

I couldn't imagine having the privilege of speaking so freely.

I felt Damian's eyes as I shifted. "I'm sure there are women who think the same of your husband."

"True. But my husband isn't staring at me like *that* right now, and we're newlyweds."

Why was it so hard to breathe?

I forced myself not to adjust the collar of my dress. "Perhaps the De Lucas are still as ill-mannered as they used to be. We're at a funeral after all, and it's rude to stare."

"I shouldn't have brought it up." Lucy giggled a little, which startled me given the setting. "Sorry, I'm a tad bit tipsy. Okay, I'm really tipsy, and I'm trying so hard not to talk a lot right now, but I really want to talk a lot. I don't know why I had to drink so much today."

Right.

Syndicate funerals involved an unreasonable amount of drinking. Shots with the immediate family before the viewing. Shots during the viewing. Shots before the burial. Shots after the burial. Shots at dinner. Shots at the remembrance party. Shots to close the funeral day. Lucy had no meat on her. She didn't stand a chance.

"Eat a big meal before Vincent's life remembrance party tonight." I glanced at her, studied her glazed eyes, and ignored the way Damian's attention made my skin itch. "And stop by Duane Read for charcoal or carbon capsules."

Her eyes lit up. "To absorb the alcohol?"

Was he still staring at me? Why was he still staring at me?

"Yes."

Look away, Damsel.

"I can't imagine charcoal binding to alcohol well,"—my briefing had mentioned it, but with Damian so close, I'd forgotten that Lucy majored in some field of biology—"but I'd like to test it. Maybe on myself. Like a guinea pig. I've always had the spirit of a guinea pig. They're soft and furry. I had one once."

Her words slurred together a bit as she rambled on and on. "Well, a foster brother of mine had one. I think he ran away or something, because my foster dad—he was a total asshole, and I hated him so much, thank goodness I left—told me the guinea pig would never come back, short of an act of God, which was something he would never inspire."

She stopped to hiccup. "But even if he could inspire an act of God, I don't think it would be to resurrect a guinea pig. Or was it a hamster?"— Good lord, did she blurt out everything that came into her mind?—"I actually don't know what the difference is. Either way, it was really cute. It had these tiny little whiskers, and it'd just eat anything I'd throw its way. That wasn't much, by the way, because we had no food or money or anything really."

She turned to face me. "What was I talking about? Oh, right. God. No, acts of God. I think the act of God he'd inspire is, like, unlimited beer or something. Not resurrecting a guinea pig. Why are we talking about guinea pigs?"

Good grief, I needed her to sober up and stop talking like Captain Jack Sparrow needed rehab and a colonic.

I turned to Lucy and nailed her with a fake smile. "We were talking about charcoal or carbon capsules. They've never failed me." Not that I drank often. I changed the subject before she could give me a verbal essay on charcoal versus carbon. "Vincent was one of the best men I've ever known. I can't imagine any other mafia figure garnering this crowd. Not even my own father."

This had to be the worst redirect. I didn't want to talk about my father, and I wanted to talk about Vincent even less. I pushed away the spasm of pain at the thought of Vincent's death, trying my best to build some emotional distance.

And emotional distance included overcoming the torment of living in a world where Vincent Romano no longer existed. To be honest, that world scared me. He and Maman were the purest parts of my life in the mafia world.

Don't be weak.

You're a Vitali.

Vitalis don't feel fear.

I could almost feel the phantom sting of my dad's palm striking my face. A feeling which had always accompanied those words.

For the first time today, I focused on the feeling of Damian's gaze on my back. It was better than the pain of losing Vincent. When I was younger, Maman used to take me into the city, and the two of us would have dinner with Vincent nearly every time. It hadn't taken me long to become suspicious of why these dinners remained so secretive. Unmarked town cars with tinted windows. Car swaps. Obscure dinner locations. Private dining rooms.

If I had to bet on something, it'd be that Maman and Vincent had been in love. They may not have shared a physical affair, but it had been, without a doubt, an emotional one. That should have upset me. After all, Papà's infidelities pissed me off.

But Maman was different. She was the parent who loved and protected me, and every piece of me needed to do the same for her. That was why, when Maman had asked me to represent the Vitali name at Vincent's funeral, I agreed. She couldn't come without raising suspicion, and Vincent had been my second father in every way short of marrying my mom. I was sure he would have, too, had my father not been a Vitali.

"Who's your father?"

Wow, she really had no clue.

I ignored her question. My eyes shifted to Lucy, and I hoped she could see the sorrow in them. It was the truest thing I had to offer. "I'm sorry for your loss."

She shook her head, her movements fervent and resolute for someone inebriated. "Don't be. He lived and died on his own terms. It's more than most of us can hope for."

Her words cut me unexpectedly. Nothing about my life could be described as "on my own terms." If that were the case, I would be standing beside Damian, not rows apart, my skin burning at the way his eyes stayed glued to my body. Itch. Scratch. Burn. I wanted to do all three the longer he looked at me.

How could he stand the sight of me after the way I had left him?

I could see this snowballing in the near future, and I unleashed an impulsive plan to stop it. I lifted my arm and pretended to scratch at an itch on my elbow, making sure the sun glimmered off the giant diamond on my wedding ring finger. It shone in a way that I knew reached two rows back.

From the corner of my eyes, I saw Damian glance away.

My heart tightened.

Unhappiness coursed through my veins.

And for the life of me, I couldn't explain why I'd done what I'd just done.

Nothing about this felt like living on my own terms.

> 66 Don't tell me of deception; a lie is a lie, whether it be a lie to the eye or a lie to the ear.

— SAMUEL JOHNSON

Damiano De Luca

"Impetuous" had never been the word to describe me. I had dethroned my father with careful planning and only a dash of outside help. It had taken years and more patience than most possessed, but I'd done it, and I'd done it well.

So, my reaction to Ren's presence bewildered me. I spent the church ceremony boring holes into the back of her head with my eyes when I should have focused on the mystery of Ariana De Luca.

The burial at the cemetery had been spent studying everything that had changed since Ren left. The developed curves. The provocative disposition. The all-knowing upward tilt of her lips. That goddamned ring on her finger.

By the time the Romanos laid Vincent to rest, bad decisions pushed themselves to the forefront of my mind. I stood at the peak of the hill, Ariana walking away to my right and Ren slipping into her car on my left.

The right decision—the obvious decision—would be to turn right. To pursue Ariana and elicit answers. To put the De Luca organization before my unyielding heart.

I didn't make the right decision.

Swerving left, I took five long steps to Ren's town car and slid into the back seat beside her. The divider rolled downward, and a gun pointed at my face. I ignored it, steadying my eyes on the siren that, somewhere along the line, had replaced the girl with the sweats and messy bun.

She kept her eyes on the row of headstones out the window. "Yes?"

"Call off your lapdog, Princess."

Her driver cocked the gun.

Ren's lips curved up. "Is this role reversal? Did you find a new kink? You're playing the Vitali, and I'm the subservient De Luca?"

Bitterness undermined her classical beauty and did nothing for me. Her insult brushed past me as I considered the agitation hidden beneath her façade. I'd done nothing wrong. All those years ago, *she'd* been the one to overreact. *She'd* been the one to threaten me. *She'd* been the one to leave.

She didn't deserve an ounce of my sympathy.

Yet, I was tempted to give it to her anyway.

I leaned forward, and her lapdog waved his gun. I turned my

head and pressed it against the silencer's muzzle. "If you're going to point a gun at me, use it." The front sight brushed against my forehead, and the smell of Cheetos dust wafted from his finger situated on the trigger.

He retreated a millimeter, and I dipped left into Ren's side, seizing the opportunity to unarm him. The gun went off, and the bullet pierced the window beside me before I snatched it from his grip.

His eyes grew as I released the magazine, and it plopped onto my lap. "Miss Vitali—"

Miss?

"You're fine, Samford." She met my eyes as he faced forward. "This will only take a few minutes." Her eyes shifted to the shattered window. "Seriously?"

"Untrained dogs are the worst, aren't they?" My gaze never wavered from Samford's through the rearview mirror, even as my peripheral caught Romano, Camerino, Andretti, and Rossi soldiers approaching the car with their guns drawn.

"I don't have time for this." Her words were ice, but she leaned into me without realizing it, and I knew she was still hot for me. At least that hadn't changed. It reminded me of before. Before we'd fallen in love, even. Back when we hated one another but still felt the lust that would never leave us alone.

"Somewhere better to be?" I faced her and struggled to process the frost in her eyes. "Why are you here, Princess?"

"Knight. Or Renata. Never princess."

I'd never figured out why that nickname bothered her so much. That, in turn, bothered me. Back then, I wanted to unravel the mysteries that were Renata Vitali. Nowadays, I'd settle for an apology because, fuck, I deserved one.

I bellowed a laugh. "Knights don't run away when things get tough."

"That's not what I did."

"Sure." Dissociative amnesia affected… what? Five percent of the population? Ren had always been the type to be in the minority. "You left, and it made no sense, and now you're mad at me. That's what happened."

The fuck am I doing?

Talking about our past stood at the back of the line on the list of things I should have asked her. At the very least, I could justify asking why she had come. It was a stretch, but that answer could *maybe* benefit the De Luca family name I'd risked everything to preserve.

"Damsel."

The sanctity of the just-for-us nickname died as she said it in the presence of her driver. It bothered me to admit that part of me died, too. But fuck, that nickname had spent more than a decade staying just between us. Now, here she was, giving it away freely like it was candy and she was a creeper driving a white van.

She shifted at the look I speared her with before she sighed. "It's been nearly a decade. Get over it."

Solid advice, if I was being honest.

The rift between us was a canyon. Deep clefts too rocky to scale. I wasn't even sure why I wanted to.

"When you're done dodging my questions, I'll allow you the opportunity to explain yourself."

She arched a brow. "The opportunity?"

I opened the door, avoiding the litter of window glass that scattered on the floor like sheep with no shepherd. "It's more than you deserve."

I stepped out of the car and turned to face the crowd of soldiers that had surrounded us. One of them arched a brow.

I considered what would irritate Ren most before I spoke. "Sorry, guys. She's on her period."

The door slammed shut behind me.

It echoed like it had that night she'd run away.

9

Renata Vitali

You have to be here, I reminded myself as I strolled into L'Oscurità, a Romano bar in an expensive part of the city.

Few things in life were worth stressing over. Damiano De Luca happened to be one of them. My poor heart hadn't dealt with the torment that was Damian in years and struggled to keep up. It scraped at my insides with each demanding beat as I perched myself on a barstool.

Normally, I was calm, collected, and cool—the three Cs my Vitali blood demanded of me. But in my little corner of the Romano bar, I wasn't sure who was winning—my heart or my head.

I had left this world. Begged Papà to set me free. Done everything I could to live a normal life with a normal teaching job in a normal suburban Connecticut town, close enough to Maman's place in the Hamptons that I could visit whenever she felt lonely.

I hated that I was here. I hated that, all these years later, I still felt something suspiciously close to love whenever I thought of Damian.

Upper-level mafia figures, attendees of Vincent's funeral this morning, replaced the typical bougie, annual-income-north-of-eight-figures clientele. Their presence darkened the room. That, or the overtime my heart had put in was messing with my head.

"I'll take a whiskey neat. Single malt Scotch." I slid my sweater down my arms, placed it on the courtesy hook beneath the bar top, and met Ariana De Luca's eyes. "Macallan if you have it, please."

"I have a 35-year-old in the back..."

"That'll do."

I skimmed the bar as she left to retrieve my drink. Asher Black, Niccolaio Andretti, and Bastiano Romano sat in a corner booth, and I made a mental note to send my condolences their way. The senior Romanos—Frankie, Eli, and Gio—sat at the opposite end of the bar, surrounded by a sea of suck-ups. I made another note to avoid them. Representatives for the Camerino and Rossi families showed up, too. All that was missing was a De Luca in the mix. Well, an out-of-the-closet De Luca.

My eyes sought Damian, and when they didn't find him, disappointment and relief filled me in equal measures. Ariana returned with the bottle of Macallan. Just in time, because Damian walked in.

Courtesy of the deep Vitali coffers, I slid six hundred-dollar bills Ariana's way, took my drink, grabbed my things, and made my way down the bar. Blending in came easily to me, and as I used a particularly large enforcer to shield me from Damian's line of sight, I knew I was in the clear but within hearing range.

I never cared enough about this world to be the eavesdropping type, but with Damian, it didn't even occur to me not to. It was like opening a bag of chips and finishing it in one sitting. It happened before I even realized what I'd done.

"Ms. De Luca." Damian used the voice he did when he pretended to act natural but was looking to stir up trouble. It always fooled everyone but me. "Penny for your thoughts?"

She ran a rag across the bar top and poured him a beer on tap, though he hadn't ordered and I knew he didn't drink often. "I like to think they're worth more than that."

Poor girl. I almost pitied her. Perks of being a Vitali included knowing things others didn't. For instance, while Damian remained blissfully unaware that he spoke with his half-sister, I knew when she'd been born, who she had been born to, and just how naughty Angelo De Luca had been all those years ago when Damian's mother still lived.

"A barter it is." Damian's voice dipped lower. "I've had one Hell of a month or two. Giovanni Romano has been asking about a girl poking around his territory. Imagine my surprise when my last name slipped past his lips."

"It's just a last name."

"Cut the crap, De Luca." I could picture the hard glint in his eyes. "You share my last name, yet I've never heard of you. Why is that?"

"Why would you give me a heads up about Giovanni?"

Skirting around Damian's questions never accomplished anything except diminishing his respect for you. "Answer the question, or I'll answer it for you, and you won't like my answer."

The enforcer that had been blocking me from Damian's view

shifted, and just like when we'd met all those years ago, our eyes connected, and we saw past each other's façades. Damian had always been a closed book, one that only I could open and read. But of everyone in this world, he was the only one who could say the same of me.

I shifted my eyes, but I knew he'd approach. Hell, Ariana De Luca knew it, too, because she took the opportunity to slip away to the other end of the bar.

"Princess."

"Damsel."

"Are you going to tell me what you're doing in New York City?"

I could feel his eyes on my face, but I didn't dare meet them. "Representing the Vitali name."

Really, my mom had sent me, but that didn't sound any cooler aloud than it did in my head.

"No." His arm brushed mine as he took the seat next to mine. "You're not."

I gripped the glass tighter between my palms. "Excuse me?"

What did he want me to say? That I was here to see him?

"I see past your lies." He nodded toward everyone else at L'Oscurità. "Don't treat me like I'm one of them." His breath brushed against my cheek as he leaned closer. "Treat me like I'm Day, and you're Knight."

Presumptuous.

That was what he was.

How else could I explain the way he talked to me after almost ten years apart? But his words rekindled the flame I held for him, the flame that had never once flickered in the nine or so years we'd spent apart. It was a piece of me I'd never been able to explain, and I'd given up trying long ago.

I finally turned to face him and met his eyes, silencing any hesitation that threatened to escape my body. "But you're not Day, and I'm not Knight. You're not Damsel, and I'm not

Princess. We're strangers who knew each other once upon a time, and that's all we'll ever be."

Other than forcing myself to keep my distance, there was no reason to be this harsh. His dad was no longer a threat, and I was no longer a child whose decisions could be influenced by others. Yet, here I was, wearing a big chip on my shoulder that, sometime over the past ten years, I'd named "Bitch."

If I were more honest, I would admit that fear played its hand here. I'd never open my heart again. Never.

He tilted so close to me, I knew others would think we were kissing. He smelled like he used to, and it took everything in me to not close my eyes and inhale. "You say I'm not the Day to your Knight, yet you lean into me like you're gravitating toward me. Like you start where I end."

"Stop this."

"I never understood why you hated that nickname. Princess. It was never an insult." He pried the glass from my grip and dumped the Macallan into his untouched beer.

My fingers tingled where his had brushed against them. "I was drinking that."

He ignored me, moving the beer glass over the bar counter onto the bartender's side before turning to face me. "I'll say this once, and you won't have a drop of liquor in your system when you're in bed tonight, your hands are itching to pleasure yourself to the memory of me, and you're looking for something but yourself to blame."

Jesus.

Those tourmaline-black eyes never wavered from mine. "Princess isn't and never has been an insult. I never saw you as someone who needed saving. It's one thing to be a princess sitting on a throne of glass, but it's a great deal more to be a princess that shatters glass ceilings while everyone looks the other way. People may overlook you, and maybe you've always wanted it that way, but I never did. I always saw you."

He stood, his eyes never once drifting to the nearby table, where a fight seemed inevitable. "But you know what? *You* left *me*, so next time you find yourself reaching out for help and grasping empty air, ask yourself why you pushed me away. Because I sure as Hell don't know."

I swallowed. His words hurt. Even worse, they were true. I'd forgotten how it felt to spend time with someone who could see past my barriers. He walked past them like they didn't exist, and he stirred mayhem within me. *We* were mayhem. My hands shook as he stepped past me and moved toward the table in the center of the bar.

Lucy sat there with two girls. A confrontational blonde stood in front of her, her arms crossed, a pissed off snarl a permanent facial feature.

"Wait!" I latched a hand onto Damian's forearm and immediately pulled it back. Damn the way my composure slipped around him.

What could I say to that? I had my reasons for leaving, but he didn't know them.

You could always tell him.

Could I?

That would open up more pain than I was interested in handling. Goodness, I had always prided myself in my strength, but I felt weak at the moment, embarrassed and haunted by my past.

So, instead of telling him what had happened, I dropped a bomb that should have been bubble wrapped, padded with foam, inked with a giant "FRAGILE" stamp, and delivered with more care. "She's your sister."

"What?" Incredulity spread across his face, and he leaned away from me.

I slid my sweater over my shoulders, so I had something to do with my hands that didn't involve comforting him. "Ariana De Luca is your sister."

His lips formed the beginnings of a snarl. "I don't know what stunt you thin—"

"Look at me, Day." I met his stare head on and tried to show him the truth within my words. "Your father had an affair with a stripper years ago. She worked for him at The Landing Strip but fled when she found out she was pregnant. I'm sure you can ask around to confirm. Her name was Aria Simpson." I added the last part in case he actually did ask around, but I knew he trusted me. I could see it in his eyes, and it wasn't lost on me how much yet how little things had changed.

"How do you know this?"

"I'm a—"

"—Vitali. Right." He shook his head, turned his body away from me, and walked away.

The most valuable part of knowledge was having it when others didn't. The knowledge I had given up made up far more than a morsel, and one day, when he had time to properly digest his new reality, he would look back and wonder why I had parted with this information.

I hoped, when that day came, he would draw the wrong conclusion.

10

> Deceiving others. That is what the world calls a romance.

— OSCAR WILDE

Renata Vitali

Seventeen Years Old

Two men look out through the same bars; one sees mud, and the other stars.

No matter how much I loved his poetry, Frederick Langridge and I probably wouldn't be friends. Langridge was all about looking up, finding the positivity in every situation. Lately,

I'd been looking down. Succumbing to pessimism that reached new heights each passing second.

Sitting in this room, day after day, felt like a life sentence. Looking out of the windows, all I saw was mud. Metaphorical mud—a syndicate boss would never boast anything less than perfect, manicured lawns—but still.

Mud.

Ugly, slimy, shit-colored mud.

For the past decade, school had been my refuge. Classes, my reprieve. Books, my daily vacation. Of course, Papà had made the decision for me to skip the remainder of the school year before I had arrived.

There'd only been two and a half weeks left, and the curriculum didn't exactly pose a challenge. Two great points of justification for someone who loved his daughter and wanted to give her a break; two even greater points of justification for someone who knew how much his daughter loved school and wanted to punish her.

But Papà didn't control everything, and defying rules came as easily to me as multi-variable Calculus. When the clock crept past two in the morning, I slid my padded socks on and cracked the door to the room open.

This had been my nightly routine since my second week here, when I'd figured enough time had passed since I'd gotten caught in Damian's room to sneak into the library. Now, months later, it was nearing the start of another school year, and I still hadn't been caught. I hadn't caught sight of Damian once, either.

After silence greeted my ears, I slipped past the door, gliding my feet in soft, gentle movements across the hardwood. A neoclassical oil painting loomed across the entrance to the library, Ludovico De Luca's stern face donning a foot-high frown. The painting never failed to give me shivers.

Ludovico De Luca had been the first De Luca descendant to step foot in America. He'd also been certifiable. I'd read in the

Vitali archives about how he killed his wife, son, and daughter-in-law. Some theorized he probably would have killed his grandson, too, if it hadn't meant the end of his legacy.

What I hadn't expected was the same damning historical account I'd read in the Vitali archives to be framed and hung in the library like a mounted taxidermy trophy. Like a memory to take pride in. People frequently dismissed the De Luca family as crazy for a reason.

I pushed open the double doors to the library, expecting emptiness like the best sanctuaries were.

Instead, I found Damian.

He rested on a maroon velvet divan, his legs propped up against two accent pillows fit for a King's crown. A first edition copy of Fyodor Dostoevsky's *The Brothers Karamazov* rested between his palms. The same copy I'd been reading and left lying on the side table last night.

How was I supposed to know anyone read in this house?

Dust covered half of the books in the library, Damian never stayed in the house longer than an hour, and Angelo De Luca guarded more rage than intellect in that skull of his. Nothing about this household screamed, "Literary!"

"There are goosebumps rising along the length of your arms." He didn't once look up from the book. Even if he had, several feet separated us.

Foreign jitters traveled up the length of my arms. They startled me, but I forced myself to tamper them. "I don't recall reading that line in the book." I took a seat on the divan across from his, resigned to his intrusion. It couldn't be worse than being cooped in the room.

He turned the page and managed to make the movement look masculine. "They're a physical manifestation of your attraction to me." His tone left little for debate. Like his words were fact, and daring to argue otherwise would be met with failure.

I thanked Maman for her lessons in composure. Without her,

my voice would be far less level. "So, my goosebumps, which don't exist,"—*lie*—"are a physical manifestation of my attraction to you, which also doesn't exist." *Double lie.* "I take it the rumors of insanity running rampant in De Luca territory are true."

At last, he met my eyes. "Those aren't rumors. They're facts."

But he didn't look crazy.

And despite how much I tried to convince myself otherwise, truth laced his words. No matter how out of the blue they were. I was attracted to him. And maybe there were goosebumps. Maybe.

If he could do random, I could, too. "Do you hate me?"

His eyes flicked back to his book. "Hate would require emotion, and I do not possess any of those where you are concerned."

"The hair on your forearms are raised." I ignored the lust that scratched at my stomach when his lips tilted slightly upward.

It felt like we were playing with each other. He may as well have pulled me close and whispered, "Play with me, Princess," in my ear. My heart beat that fast.

Instead, he tampered his half smile. "Is that so?"

"It's a manifestation of your attraction to me."

"Possibly," he allowed, and I couldn't handle what passed between us—a zing of realization as one kindred spirit recognized another. "It's certainly not natural."

Did he just admit that he's attracted to me?

I tapered my reaction. It took a beat, but I saw where he was going with this and cursed myself for not seeing it sooner. Could I blame the months apart from a classroom? "Do you really think neuroses can physically present themselves?"

Never in a million years did I think I would be here, sitting in the De Luca boss' library, discussing Freud's "Dostoevsky and Parricide" with Angelo's secret son. This wasn't a truce. This was literature, and somehow, at least tonight, it had bridged a gap between us.

He flipped a page. "It makes more sense than the alternative."

"Not to me." I tucked my feet under my thighs, leaned against the cushion, and allowed myself to get comfortable as I thought.

Freud penned an essay arguing that Dostoevsky's epilepsy began after his father died as a physical manifestation of his guilt over wishing for his father's death, but I'd never been convinced. I hated my father. Yet, I couldn't imagine wishing death upon him. At least, not without more provocation. Plus, I didn't believe emotions could develop into physical illnesses.

"Death should be a last resort." Hypocritical, coming from a Vitali, but that didn't make it any less true. "Not some trivial wish to be thrown about. And goosebumps, your example of emotions eliciting physical responses, aren't as severe as a condition like epilepsy."

He peered up from the novel and, for the first time since I had walked in, took in my teeny sleeping shorts and satin spaghetti strap shirt. His eyes darkened, and I watched his Adam's apple bob. "Would you have stayed if I accused you of developing a heart condition over your attraction to me?"

I eyed where the throw blanket pressed against his hips because he'd been right. I did have goosebumps. From the cold, of course.

"It wasn't an either-or situation. You weren't limited to goosebumps and cardiovascular disease."

But yes, I would have stayed, I admitted to myself, still unsure how I had gotten to the point where I sought being saved from my boredom by him. It also wasn't lost on me that he had implied he wanted me to stay.

"Perhaps." His hands untangled the blanket, flattened it as he held it open above the floor, and tossed it so it covered my body almost perfectly when it landed on me. "You overestimate my desire to converse with you."

"Which one of us was the first to speak?"

"If I recall, it was me... after I caught you sneaking around my room."

Okay, I walked right into that.

"You didn't catch me snooping. You caught my laying on your bed."

"Yet, you deny your attraction to me. Which is it, Knight? Are you attracted to me, or were you snooping?"

"What is it with you and absurd either-or scenarios?"

He set the book aside and swiveled, so his feet touched the floor and his forearms rested on his knees as he leaned forward and hit me with his unwavering stare. "Dodging my questions isn't going to earn you any respect from me, and seven days from now, when we start our senior year of high school, you'll be wanting that respect."

I met his actions, unfolding my legs and leaning forward, so mere inches separated our faces as we sat across from one another on divans crafted for royalty. "I have your respect."

"Is that so?"

"What do you call this?" I gestured between us. "Are you in the habit of discussing the psychology of literature with people you don't respect?"

At eleven years old, Maman had taken me into the city during what was supposed to have been a quiet weekend visit to her Hamptons home. She passed me a food stand hotdog, and we made the trek to Barney's. A bite in, I heard a whimper and caught the coiled tail of a stray dog. I glanced at my hot dog.

Maman cut her eyes to me. *Mon petit coeur saignant...*

I heard her warning loud and clear as she called me her little bleeding heart and yanked me into the safety of her waist. The hot dog slipped from my fingers, and the stray dog pounced at it, snapping at a pedestrian who walked past.

My head lowered as Maman placed a hand on each of my shoulders. "Renata, *ma petite fille*, you have a beautiful heart, but one day, your need to save cornered animals will get you bitten."

She lifted my chin until my eyes met hers. "Some scars do not fade."

It was one of the few lessons Maman had taught me that I had never taken to heart. Staring into Damian's eyes with less than a hand's width of separation between us, I reminded myself of the haunted look I had seen in his eyes—not once, but twice now.

It was too easy an inclination to want to fight him. But the desire to save Damian appealed in equal measure. Something in the way he held himself—too composed, too aloof, too unapproachable—had me convinced of his loneliness.

Lonely people started conversations with near strangers they seemed to hate, right?

Which had to be why I cut him off before he could say something that warranted a verbal lashing. "It's okay not to hate me. It's okay not to like me, too." I dipped my eyes to the blanket that had pooled at my lap before returning them to him. A little act of kindness, which had me second-guessing everything.

His eyes followed mine to the blanket. "Hate would require emotions, and I—"

"—don't possess any where I'm concerned. Yeah, I got it." The urge to roll my eyes burned at my irises, but that would have been counterintuitive to my point. "There's a difference between loneliness and solitude."

One was pain; the other, preference.

Perhaps that had been too deep, too much for two destructive intellects, searching desperately for outlets in a town that possessed none.

Why did it have to be *him* who lured me in with late night conversation that felt less like a tentative truce between enemies and more like a flirtatious argument between friends?

Why was it *him* who felt like the answer to my loneliness and I to his?

Maybe it was not choice but fate.

At least, that was what I told myself when I returned to the library the next night, and we read *Infinite Jest* together and argued over the psychological consequences of having absent parents.

I wondered what he told himself.

11

> " We are never so easily deceived as when we imagine
> we are deceiving others.
>
> — FRANCOIS DE LA ROCHEFOUCAULD

Renata Vitali

The Present

Damian observed his half-sister, a look I'd never seen in his eyes as she made her way to Lucy Black. Two women sitting at her table argued with the blonde. I saw the slap from the blonde before it came and studied Damian as he watched his sister stop it midway.

Pride.

That was the look on his face.

Jealousy.

That was the feeling it kindled inside me.

Stupid, right?

But as silence descended in the bar, and Ariana released the blonde's wrist, regret over the happiness Damian and I could have shared eclipsed the impassivity I had tried so hard to build during our time apart. It dawned on me that these weren't the feelings of someone who had initiated a breakup.

Silence remained in L'Oscurità as Ariana passed the blonde off to security, and Bastian reached Ariana. I noted their intimate body language, how in tune they were with one another's body. Either they were sleeping together, or they would be soon.

The volume rose to normal levels as security spoke with the blonde at the door, and Damian stared at Bastian and Ariana until the two parted. He wanted to talk to her. Bad idea. For both of their sakes and mine.

The bouncer kicked the blonde out, and Ariana skimmed her eyes across the bar before following. A minute later, Bastian followed her, and Damian followed him.

I eyed the tap beer Damian had mixed with my Macallan. "Oh, what the hell." Reaching over the bar, I downed a fifth of the gross concoction and followed the four of them, well aware of how ridiculous this situation was—me following Damian, who followed Bastian following Ari, who followed the blonde.

These men walked like panthers as they pursued Ariana and the blonde. I paused for a few seconds to slip off my heels and rounded the corner into the alleyway with lighter steps. The shadows hid me as I paused at the entrance. I could barely make out Damian or Bastian, but I knew both had guns drawn.

Moonlight lit the blonde as she swiveled and faced Ariana. "Stop following me!"

"Monica—"

"How do you know my name?!" Her features were unreadable from this distance, but horror seeped into her voice. "You're from the bar. You're one of them."

Ariana took a step closer, and the girl—Monica—yanked a gun from her waistband. Her hands shook as she pointed it at Ariana. I pulled mine out from my thigh holster as Bastian's dark shadow reached the edge of the light. His gun raised midway, Damian stood just far enough behind him to hold the advantage in a gunfight between the three of them.

The small gun wavered in Monica's hand. "Don't move."

Less than a foot separated Monica and Ariana. If I were Ariana, I would have latched onto the gun, twisted it down and away from me until Monica's finger broke in the trigger, and grabbed the gun. But the difference was, I had Vitali training since a young age, and she'd never been inducted into the De Luca fold to be trained.

Yet, that was exactly what Ariana did, her movements swift, clinical, and practiced. Monica screamed and clutched her broken finger to her chest.

"Calm down, Monica." Ariana held the gun to Monica's face, and just as Bastian broke past the shadows with his Smith & Wesson pointed at Monica, she added, "I'm with the FBI."

What the actual fuck.

Ariana spun the weapon she'd stolen toward Bastian. Damian strode into the light with his gun drawn on Bastian, and Ariana shifted her gun to him. I could walk away. I could turn around right now and pretend I hadn't seen this.

But I didn't, and though I couldn't bring myself to admit why, it was about as obvious as a stuffed bra. I approached with light steps, stepped over a pile of cans, and raised my gun to the back of Ariana's head, far enough away that she couldn't disarm me with any of her surprise FBI moves.

When she shifted, I *tutted*. "Don't bother." I figured Ariana was the only one the other two cared about, which was why she had my gun pointed at her head. "I'll shoot you, then your boyfriend."

Damian lowered his weapon, and the trust that took didn't escape my attention. "Ren..."

Monica took the opportunity to run, and Bastian started after her.

Ariana shook her head. "Don't. She has an ankle bracelet. What she knows, I can... I can figure out a way to explain to my boss."

I cocked my gun, though I didn't plan on using it. "Your boss. And who would that be?"

Damian took a step forward. "Renata—"

"Didn't you hear her? She's in the FBI." I may have distanced myself from this world, but it didn't change my blood. I was a Vitali. The utmost governing authority in the mafia world. I rarely exercised my power, but I wouldn't hesitate to do so now if it threatened Damian. "This can be a Vitali matter if I make it one. Choose your words wisely."

Bastian dropped his gun to his side. I stared at him until he secured it in his holster.

"What do you want?" He cocked his head, then shook it. "What's the Vitali position here?"

If Papà were in my position, he would place a bullet in Ariana's temple and be done with it.

I wasn't my dad.

I lowered my gun. "We'll be watching from afar, so long as you can deal with this internally."

The Romano family could shoot Ariana, lock her up in one of the private prisons they owned, or recruit her. Whatever it took to preserve their secrecy. But I suspected Bastian would deal with this himself—without involving his family.

"What's the catch?"

Honestly? I didn't really care, but I knew my family would. I also knew that Damian could get caught in the crossfire if it wasn't handled right, but I needed to trust my gut and let Bastian handle this. "There will be consequences should you mishandle this."

Bastian nodded and left with Ariana, leaving me alone with Damian.

I almost wish they hadn't left.

12

> Hateful to me as the gates of Hades is that man who hides one thing in his heart and speaks another.
>
> — HOMER

Damiano De Luca

I took a step toward Ren, my eyes narrowed and throat bobbing. "You were here for me. To have my back."

I would never get used to having someone who I could count on to always look out for me. We could be best friends or worst enemies, and I knew Ren would have my back. It should have been nice instead of bittersweet, but we'd never had a cookie cutter life.

Ren holstered her handgun and shook her head, and I wasn't sure if her denial pissed me off or excited me. "How do you figure?"

"You held the gun to Ariana, threatened to shoot her, then threatened to shoot Bastian. But not me."

My anger at her for leaving me ten years ago eased, and fuck, I wanted her all over again. Call it daddy issues, but I had a soft spot for people with pure hearts like hers. This was the girl I fell in love with. The one who came in guns blazing, eyes calculated, always defending me, even when I didn't need it. How could I not want her? Find me a man who could resist her, and I'd find you a beachfront property in Oklahoma.

She shrugged, such a pretty little liar. "And?"

She wanted to avert her eyes. I could see the urge in the strained edges of her glare. But I had always had the ability to bulldoze past her barriers, and she had another thing coming for her if she thought I wasn't prepared to do so now.

Ren lifted her chin. "You weren't a threat."

"But I am, Princess." One more step and I'd have her backed up against the wall. "I'm the biggest threat you've ever met."

"How so?"

"Because you care enough to save me."

"You didn't need saving."

"No." I took that last step, moving her against the bricks. She could have left, but she didn't even try, so I raised my hands to either side of her face until my palms touched the abrasive surface and caged her in. "But you did it anyway."

"I'm the knight in shining armor, remember?" She could hide behind her bravado all she wanted. It didn't fool me. Hell, her eyes dipped to my lips. Needy. Hungry. Impatient. I could rest easy knowing her desire for me would never waver.

I shook my head. "Don't do that."

Earlier today, I had been prepared to hate her. But she was here, and I saw the same girl I fell in love with. The fearless girl who had always had my back. I didn't hate her. In fact, I couldn't help but want her.

She leaned into me, and I suspected she didn't even realize what she'd done. "What?"

"Don't make this a joke. It isn't one."

"You're supposed to be mad at me." Her brows furrowed, and those full lips parted.

I wanted to bite it.

But I glanced down at her hand, and that damned ring taunted me. "I am."

"I'm supposed to go to bed with my 'hands itching to pleasure myself to the memory of you.' Remember?"

"You will."

I leaned in and inhaled her vanilla scent. She still used the same shampoo. It made no sense, but it felt like victory, and I took the opportunity to memorize her scent all over again.

She tilted her chin up and met my eyes. "So, why are you so close I can feel your breath against my lips?"

Good question.

Two could play the evasion game.

"Are you going to tell me why you're here?"

"In New York or this alley?"

"Both."

"To represent—"

"Princess."

She infuriated me, yet I still needed her. If it were lust, I could have walked away. It wasn't. It was nearly a decade of repressed pain, a flash of history, and the future we never had because she'd run away. I couldn't say no, because the second I saw her again, I knew I still cared.

Her calm façade began to crumble. "I'm here to represent the Vi—"

"*Knight*. Cut the bullshit."

She closed her eyes, but I knew she couldn't fight the memories, because I couldn't either. They surrounded us, trapping us until we suffocated in our past. "Stop asking me these questions."

"Just answer this one: why did you save me tonight?"

Say it, Ren. I can't, so say it for me.

"I didn't save you." Her eyes flickered open, and I was met by amber. The sight was nearly enough to catch my hope as it sank to my stomach. "I have no doubt you could handle yourself. It's them I worried for."

She was doing it again. Trying to make this less of a big deal than it was. But her words echoed like a distant memory I shouldn't have forgotten.

I cocked a brow. "Really."

"They're weak... but that's not who you are. Is it, Damsel?"

Jesus.

She'd gone there.

She'd gone to the words of our past.

They were as good as proof that some part of her still wanted me, and I could work with that.

But I wanted to walk away. I wanted to fly to the opposite end of the earth and live somewhere that hadn't been touched by Ren and our memories. I also wanted to scale the rocks. To climb the canyon between us, despite its jagged, suicidal ridges, and reach the other side. The side where I could lean forward and capture her lips between mine, and she'd thaw under my touch like she had all those years ago.

I wanted to kiss her, and be with her, and love her.

And I swore, by the end of this trip, Renata Vitali would be mine again.

13

> ❝ Nothing is more common on earth than to deceive and be deceived.
>
> — JOHANN G. SEUME

Damiano De Luca

Seventeen Years Old

"I think it's unrealistic. Impossible, even."

Who knew, between the two of us, Princess would be the pessimist and I, the idealist?

I eyed the article of great-great-grandfather Ludovico on the wall, careful to keep my eyes off of Ren. I was well aware that I enjoyed our nightly literary debates way too much. "You don't think people have the innate goodness in them to rally for a common goal?"

The magazine felt heavy in my hand. Not because it was an issue of Playboy, nor because it was a limited edition 1984 run, but because it was the only thing keeping me from striding across the library's timber floors and kissing Princess. Vitali blood or not, I wanted her. Craved her in ways I'd never allow myself to pursue. She was, after all, a Vitali. And I was, after all, a lowly De Luca prince.

"Think about it like this. Decent people don't commit hard-core crimes, nor do they always follow the rules. They sneak into the carpool lane or speed when they shouldn't, but they're not out there murdering people. They don't go out of their way to donate all their non-basic essentials, but every once in a while, they'll volunteer at the local animal shelter. They're just... normal. Balanced. Trying to live their lives as best as they can, but sometimes their best isn't *the* best." She sat on the divan across from me and set her copy of *The Toynbee Convector* down.

Her eyes darted to my *Playboy*, which held the original copy of the short story we were discussing. "Say there's a normal distribution of goodness in the world, and the average person, at 50%, is a decent person. That would mean there are 34% of less-than-decent people, 13.5% of bad people, and 2.5% of awful people. That's billions of people that aren't even decent. You think *they* could muster up all that gushy goodness to create a utopia based on the crazy rantings of a self-proclaimed time traveler?"

"Fucking hell." I shook my head, ignoring how hot her arguing made me. I wanted to pry that paperback from her hands and replace it with my body. "Did you really just ruin Ray Bradbury for me?"

"Maybe you should learn to debate better."

"Maybe *you* should learn to—"

My dad's voice rang in the hallway as he yelled at one of the maids. Ren's disappointed eyes met mine before we both scanned the room. She scrambled upward and slipped behind the nearest floor-to-ceiling drape, hiding like we were doing something wrong by spending time with each other. Maybe we were, but it didn't feel wrong until someone invaded our bubble.

"Ah, there you are, my prodigious son."

I turned to Angelo as he swung the double doors open, and they struck the doorstoppers. "Obviously." I paused a beat, a carefree smirk I didn't feel curving my lips. "I didn't think you knew what 'prodigious' meant, but hey, I didn't think you could find the library either."

"Shut your fucking mouth or your biggest life accomplishment will be cleaning toilets at The Landing Strip."

My dad owned The Landing Strip, the one and only strip club in Devils Ridge, but he didn't know I frequented the place. Not for enjoyment, but to network. To show the De Luca soldiers and *caporegimes* how they could be treated if they supported me.

And I *had* cleaned the toilets there. I helped the staff, got my fucking hands dirty, made jokes with them on their breaks, asked them about their sons and daughters, and showed them just how much more I cared for them than my father did. Just one of my many steps to dethroning Angelo.

I dipped a hand into my pocket and leaned a hip on one of the divans. "What do you want?"

"You see the Vitali girl lately?" He sneered and whistled at the same time, which was kind of impressive if you thought about it. "She's growing."

I leaned further against the cushion and forced myself to remain impassive. "You're sick."

Angelo took a seat on the divan closest to where Ren hid. "There's an opening at The Landing Strip."

"And?"

"And it's time we made that Vitali girl earn her keep." Behind my dad, the drape shifted. Ren must have been pissed, or creeped out, or both.

"Earn her keep? You've been cooped up in this town too long, old man." I eyed Ren's copy of *The Toynbee Collector* beside him. "That idiom no longer refers to room and board."

"What?"

"Never mind." I ran a hand down my face and contemplated the millions of things that could be running through Ren's mind right now. "Seriously, what do you want?"

"The Vitali girl working at The Landing Strip."

I couldn't be related to Angelo.

Just fucking couldn't be.

He was the sperm that should have been swallowed.

And I was his offspring.

What did that make me?

The muscles in my neck tightened. "She's a minor, and she's a Vitali. Either of those reasons alone should be enough to dissuade a rational person fit for the position of De Luca mafia boss."

He ignored my dig—just barely, I suspected. "The Vitali need to know their place."

"What do you think happens when a minnow picks a fight with sharks?"

My dad stood up, his fists clenched at his sides. "Watch your mouth, son."

I had been.

For eighteen fucking years, I had been.

But I felt my plan coming to fruition, and I needed him to lose control for it to work. I needed him to take a swing at me and make contact. Somewhere visible, where the physical proof couldn't be missed. A black eye, perhaps.

"Oh, Angelo. You don't get it, do you?" I shook my head and tsked. "You're the minnow. The Vitali are the sharks. And they will eat you alive." I rose from the divan until we stood eye-to-eye, arms width apart. "Feel free to facilitate your own death, but leave the De Luca name out of your mess."

"You will not disrespect me like this."

"I already have." I'd always taken his abuse without a word, and maybe he'd gotten used to it because his eyes expanded before forming angry slits. Still, he needed more provocation. I let loose a deep, disrespectful chuckle. "Or what, Dad? You gonna kill me like Great-great-grandfather Ludo killed his son? I dare you to fucking try."

Hatred brimmed in me, such a contrast from my time spent with Ren, and with her mere feet away, I wanted to stand up for myself. I didn't want her to see me like this. Didn't want the patience I needed to take over the syndicate to coerce me into taking the emotional abuse my dad had been spewing my way since childhood. Didn't want to wait for this damned plan to work before I destroyed him.

But I needed him to punch me. I needed there to be physical proof of him losing control for the soldiers and *capos* to see. An inkling of doubt lurked in my conscience. Ren didn't need to hear this.

Too late.

Dad swung at me, his form all brute and no finesse. I feigned a dodge to maintain appearances of a fight but let his fist connect with my face. It connected hard enough to leave a bruise. He adjusted his suit while I fell to the floor. As he towered over me, a sharp laugh struck the air before he walked away.

I leaned my head back onto the floor, thinking about the million times he had dished a similar punishment to me. Usually with a belt on my back. This time around, the marks would be visible. This was what I wanted, wasn't it?

Self-pity clogged my throat, making the breaths I forced myself to take sluggish. A few seconds after the door clicked shut, Ren emerged from behind the drape and stared at me. She moved a step closer, and a lock of hair loosened from her bun and covered her right eye. Didn't matter. I had the color memorized.

She looked particularly angelic in that moment, though. The light blonde hair. Pale skin. Eyes an inhuman shade of amber. But I preferred her naughty side. The one that argued with me— all strength, backbone, and sass. I wondered which side she'd give me now.

I waited for her to say something. The more time passed, the more I convinced myself she'd rub what had happened in my face. Self-pity didn't flatter me, but I did nothing to stop it from building.

I could have curled my lips up into a smirk. Made a witty remark. Told her how hot she looked from this angle. But that would make a mockery of our friendship—and we were friends, even if she didn't know it yet. Hell, sometimes it was even hard to admit our friendship to myself.

She opened her mouth, and I braced myself for her words. "Pick yourself up, Damsel." My eyes hardened at the nickname, the context striking me harder than I would ever let on. I opened my mouth to retaliate, but she beat me to it. "Angelo De Luca is weak, and when you dwell on the punishment he dishes, so are you." She brushed the hair out of her eyes, giving me half a second to absorb her words. "But that's not who you are. Is it, *Day?*"

One day, when I didn't have my head so far up my ass, I would look back at this moment and realize it was precisely the moment I fell for Knight.

14

> " You can fool some of the people all the time, and all of the people some of the time, but you cannot fool all of the people all of the time.

— ABRAHAM LINCOLN

Renata Vitali

Seventeen Years Old

G irl power. Noun. Power exercised by girls, specifically in the context of supporting oneself and fellow women. Origin: coined by American punk band Bikini

Antonym: Laura Willis.

Laura had supporting herself down to a T. I would give her that. But when it came to empowering other women, she fell as flat as a slashed tire. It had taken me five seconds at Devils Ridge High to realize exactly the type of obstacle she would pose for me, and months later, I could confirm the accuracy of my initial assessment.

Which was probably why pickpocketing her phone wasn't the best idea I had ever had, but other than my nightly forays with Damian in his home library, boredom had become a sibling of mine. Plus, I needed a phone to contact Maman.

Devils Ridge, like other small towns, possessed more gossip than a lifetime subscription of *Us Weekly* magazines. Only, nearly everyone in this town had mafia ties, turning it into an incestuous community of shared dirty little secrets.

One of which was the ban that had been placed on phones for me.

My teachers kept me away from tablets, phones, and laptops. No one would lend me anything, Angelo had cleared the household of stray electronics, and I'd never ask Damian for a phone because I didn't want to break the tentative truce he and I shared by reminding him of how we'd met in the first place.

I wasn't normally a thief, though I happened to be good at it. The thin metal felt powerful in my hands as I leaned into my locker and typed out the password I'd seen Laura entering during AP English Lit the week before. It opened without trouble, and I pulled up her browser app and checked my emails.

None from Maman.

My head and hands buried in my locker, I drafted an email to my mom.

From: Renata Vitali
To: Margot Vitali
Subject: Earth to Maman?!

Hey Maman,

I tried to reach you months ago on a phone. It wasn't mine, and I no longer have access to it. I haven't heard from you, and I'm worried about you. Are you okay? I'm sure Papà told you where I am and gave you orders not to contact me, but just know I'll be looking out for word from you just in case.

I'm staying with Angelo De Luca—he has a son!—at their mansion. Papà gave the order to remove communication privileges from me. Papà wants to silence me, Maman, because I saw him doing something he wouldn't want you to know. Honestly, I would rather tell you what happened in person. I know you cannot defy Papà and move me back to Connecticut, but maybe you can visit. I can tell you in person.

I miss you Maman. You're probably worried about me, but don't be. I'm fine. I'll stay fine, too. I just needed to tell you that I'm safe, and I need to talk to you. I'll find a way to get access to the internet again soon.

Love You,
Ta petite guerrière

A hand gripped my scalp and yanked my hair back before I could press send. The phone clattered to the floor as my face left the locker. Laura's eyes met mine. Crazed. So crazed I knew she'd forgotten her place below me in the mafia hierarchy. The hierarchy that was probably the only reason these kids had left me alone all these months.

Damian emerged through the crowd, his eyes leaping from Laura to me. We'd been doing the secrecy thing, and this marked the first time he'd been near me at school. There was nothing to out. We weren't in a relationship, but there would be implications to the complicated relationship we did have.

Still, I wondered what he'd say or do, so I waited for his reaction instead of sending an elbow backward into Laura's gut and taking care of this in my least preferred method of dealing with people—physical fights.

"Stop." Damian's voice bounced off the narrow hallway walls.

I liked where this was going.

He took a step forward, looking particularly menacing with the shiner Angelo had given him a couple days ago. "She's a Vitali." He shook his head when Laura's hand tightened on my hair—she had a thing for him, and his defense of me had to be eating away at her ego. "Stop, Willis."

My scalp burned, but it was worth it to see Damian defend me. I knew how he behaved at school by heart. He didn't defend anyone. He kept to his corner and let the kids come to him, like a king, indulging his loyal subjects. This... this was everything.

Laura turned up her chin, but it wobbled, and her hands shook on my scalp before she lowered her head in submission. "Because you're protecting her?"

"No." Damian's eyes flicked to me, and they speared me for all of point one seconds before he dismissed me with his gaze. "Because she's nothing."

And that was my cue to leave.

I swallowed my emotions, pushed my heel down onto Laura's foot, swung an elbow backward into her stomach, and twisted away when she released my hair with a surprised yelp. Violence didn't satisfy me, but I needed to get out of the hallway, and it was the quickest way. Plus, the De Lucas had invaded Devils Ridge. The staff would do nothing, and either way, in the eyes of the international syndicate court, my Vitali name justified any action I chose to take. I could kill Laura, and there would be no repercussions.

I didn't bother addressing either of them as I closed my locker door, swung my book bag over my shoulder, and made my way to the library for the rest of the lunch period. About ten minutes before the bell was set to ring, Damian pulled out the chair across from the table I sat at, a worn copy of *Nightmare Abbey* open before me. I'd just gotten to the part where Marionetta torments Scythrop. Fitting if you asked me.

"I never took you as an anti-romance type of girl."

I turned the page. "Was it my lack of faith in humanity that persuaded you otherwise?"

Our banter marked familiar territory, which he didn't deserve. He'd hurt my feelings, which meant I cared, and I *couldn't* care. His opinions shouldn't have mattered to me. They were only words, and he was a pitstop, not the finish line. He hated me; I hated him. That was the familiar territory that should have superseded this weird friendship that had burgeoned between us.

"You're mad at me."

Did it matter? This arrangement would be over when I turned eighteen in a few weeks and could flee without legal reper-cussions.

"Anger would require emotions, and I don't have any of those where you are concerned." I cocked a brow and met his eyes.

They were so talented at guarding things. At school, he played off his dad's onslaught of abuse well. But I saw the real him. The rage simmered on a loop, and I knew I would never figure out how to extinguish the flame. A part of me wanted to watch him self-destruct, just so I could be the one to pick up the pieces.

Some knight I was.

"Okay, I deserved that, but in my defense—"

"Those words are usually the predecessor to some lackluster excuse—almost always offensive, and one hundred percent likely to piss me off. You're better off stopping now."

He closed his eyes and ran a hand over his face. "I was an asshole out there, but it's better that way."

"Excuse me?"

"It'll get worse if they know we're friends. Plus, you can handle a few schoolyard bullies. I have no doubt about that, though I do doubt they can handle you."

My lips twitched, and I knew we were both thinking about the elbow I had swung at Laura. Violence was never funny, but I couldn't help myself. Damian's excuse could have been as simple as a De Luca protecting one of his own. I could understand that and part ways without spending more than a few sleepless nights dwelling over it.

But here he was, in front of me, and *that* I didn't understand.

"Why are you here, Damsel?"

"You have until the bell rings." He slid something across the table to me.

I glanced down at it.

A phone.

The library had been empty when I entered, but I still checked before clutching onto the contraband device. My mouth opened and hung there, unsure of what to say in this situation. Did I thank him for the phone or toss it back at him, offended at the idea that he could buy my forgiveness?

I didn't want to do either, so instead, I unlocked the phone, pulled up my email account, and sent the email I had drafted earlier before logging out and deleting the history. We had five minutes left until the bell rung, and I didn't know where this left us.

It wasn't like I thought we'd figure things out in five minutes, but not trying didn't feel like an option. I'd meant it when I likened us to kindred souls, chasing away loneliness in each other. I didn't want to lose that.

I only had a few weeks to go before I was old enough to leave

Devils Ridge on my own. Damian shouldn't have mattered, but he did.

"Princess?"

Oh. I'd been staring. I slid the phone to him.

He stood and pocketed the phone. "See you tonight."

"Tonight?"

"Yeah. Tonight." He slid the chair back under the table. "This doesn't count as our library date."

Date, he'd called it.

Shut up, stupid pitter-pattering heart.

> **"** We are never deceived; we deceive ourselves.
>
> — JOHANN WOLFGANG VON GOETHE

Renata Vitali

The Present

Two things can be said of humans: we will all die, and we are all big, fat fucking liars. By age four, nine out of ten of us have grasped the concept of lying. By the time we become adults, six in ten of us can't go ten minutes without lying. Those sixty percent? They lie an average of three times per ten-minute conversation.

I know what you're thinking.

I don't lie.

… At least not that much.

That's what the liars in the UMass study thought, too. Point is, everybody lies. A lot.

Even me.

Especially me.

I lie to myself every day.

Each time I'm close to the truth, I slip backward into deception, where it's safe. Where my heart is safe from the one thing that could save it. But as I saw the indecision on Damian's face, that hint of vulnerability he only managed to show around me, the truth pushed through for a glorious second, and I grasped onto it.

Confession: there had been a time when I had loved Damiano De Luca. Seeing him again showed me how little I had healed.

Maybe that explained why I still wanted to save him. Why I wanted to ease his pain and make him feel better. Learning he had a sister had hurt him, and I wanted to take that pain and obliterate it. That should have been a warning for me to run away.

Instead, I straightened my back and lightened my tone. "Come on." I pressed both palms onto his chest and pushed, easing the tension between us with space.

He took a step back, the moon's reflection glinting off his eyes. "Come where?"

Good question.

The alley's brick wall dug into my back, but I didn't dare step forward into his body. "I have no idea."

Interest shone in his eyes, but he looked me over. His eyes cataloged my body language before he settled for running a hand over his face. "I should get back to my hotel. It's getting late. Do you have a car to take you back to wherever you're staying?"

"Worried about me?"

His eyes flicked over my body, and my pulse thrummed as he studied me. Just when I thought he would answer, he took another step back and started to walk away. I hated watching him walk away, but I couldn't say anything about it, because once upon a time, I'd done the same thing.

I opened my mouth.

Don't do it, Ren.

You don't need a ride.

You don't need Damsel.

He'll be fine alone.

You'll be fine alone.

"Wait."

Holy hell, what did I just do? I stared at his back as he paused his retreat. He stopped in an instant, like he'd been waiting for me to make the first move, but that was a silly thought. I had wronged him. How could he want me after that?

He turned to face me. "Well?"

Stop this right now, Ren.

I took a step toward him. "Will you give me a ride?"

Why did you just do that?

He didn't answer for a moment. Tense silence filled the gap between us like water in a sinking ship. "Fine."

I followed behind him as he led me back to L'Oscurità, sending a text to my bodyguard to head to my place before me. Damian's driver pulled in front of the bar, stepped out of the car, and opened the door for us.

I slid in first. "476 5th Avenue."

It was a five-minute drive, give or take. If I could last that without caving, it would be a miracle.

Damian entered after me, and his hip brushed against mine. "What hotel is that?"

I didn't answer and stared out the window, wondering what the hell I was doing. That look in Damian's eyes had since fled, but I knew tonight shook him. With a secret sister in the FBI, how could he not be shaken? But it wasn't my responsibility to help him. We were nothing to each other.

He relayed the address to the driver, and I felt him turn to face me as the electronic soundproofing barrier between the passenger cabin and driver lifted. "Word about my sis—Word about *Ariana* cannot get out."

It felt so good to hear his voice again. I could feel it on my skin and in the air. He was everywhere. In my past. In my head. And worse, beneath my skin. I steeled myself against him, embarrassed by my weakness.

"Obviously." The words bit out of me. My self-preservation instincts built walls of sarcasm around me. I had prepared myself for seeing Damian again. Clearly, not well enough.

"I meant within the mafia community."

"That's obvious, too."

"Will you be reporting back to the Vitali?"

I had no choice. Everything that happened while I represented the Vitali name needed to be reported. But there were no rules dictating who I had to report to. I could report to my mom. She ran the Vitali archives, because Papà saw her as nothing more than a glorified trophy wife and secretary. He wouldn't press her or me on what happened at the funeral processions because, while he probably should have been here representing the Vitali name, he couldn't step foot in New York.

My dad was afraid of the embarrassment that would come if Maman ever chose to leave him. So, they had an unspoken agreement. Maman got New York and the surrounding states, and Papà got Italy and everywhere else. But since Maman had a secret relationship with Vince, I didn't trust her to not be overly emotional at his funeral and draw suspicion. Which was why I agreed to come out of the woodwork and represent the Vitali.

Maman's relationship with Vince was also leverage I could hold over her to keep Ariana's position in the FBI a secret, not that I thought she would say anything if I asked her not to. We always did our best to look out for each other.

I turned to face Damian and took in his tense, closed-off body language. "I have to report to someone. Failing to do so will escalate the situation and draw attention to Ariana, you, and possibly Bastian. I can report to my mother, since she sent me here, and let her choose to do what she will with the information. That's the best I can do."

It was more than anyone else would have done. In reality, this was a solid course of action. Probably the only course of action that wouldn't involve bloodshed, and I was sticking my neck out for Ariana, a total stranger, because I knew Damian cared. But I downplayed my actions and hoped he wouldn't look into my motives.

It worked, because his lips turned down at the corners. "And what do you think she'll choose to do?"

"I have no idea, Damsel." I poured myself a glass of champagne from the mini fridge. "Maybe nothing. Maybe something."

He took the bottle from me and drank straight from the rim. "I need a straight answer, Knight."

My pulse thrummed when he shifted and our thighs touched. "My mom keeps the records. Other than that, she keeps her head out of the family business." I emptied the champagne glass in one gulp, so I had something to do other than focusing on our proximity. "So, she'll probably record what we've learned into the archives, and if no one decides to look, no one else will find out."

"And what are the chances that no one will decide to look?" His words bit, but he didn't seem anything but comfortable beside me.

"I don't know, Damsel."

"Are you purposely being difficult?"

Arguing. This was territory I could work with.

I cut him with a glare. "I've been out of the mafia world for nearly a decade, Damsel. Excuse me if I have no interest in maintaining ties with the Vitali."

"They're your family."

"I'm my own family." I went to chug my glass, and it would have been badass, had it not been empty.

He handed me the bottle, and I placed my lips right over the spot he had drunk from. I tasted him. Goosebumps rose up my forearms, and I loathed the lack of control I held over my own body. The innate calmness I'd had before meeting Damian all those years ago remained a distant memory.

"What are the chances no one will decide to look?"

"I already said I don't know. Has this past decade made you senile?"

"Knight..." That growled warning sent sparks throughout my body, straight to my core.

I forced myself to focus on my irritation, allowing myself a rare moment to shed my calm façade and lash out. "Look, I'm a fucking elementary school teacher! Okay? I don't know anything about the Vitali anymore. I can guess if that's what you want."

I leaned back in the seat and stared at the ceiling. "I have to tell my mom. It'll be above board that way and give us both protection. My mom's not only a good person, but she's also trustworthy. If I ask her to be discreet, she'll be discreet. So long as nothing eventful happens this weekend, no one will ask to the see the records. Hell, no one cares about a funeral. It's why I'm here and not my dad or my mom."

That, and Maman's emotional affair.

He didn't say anything for a few minutes. "An elementary school teacher?"

A smile pushed at my lips. "Shut up."

He laughed, and it was so unexpected and carefree. Nothing held back. I had no idea how I expected myself to stand a chance against him. My resolve weakened as the car came to a halt in front of the library.

Damian slid out first and gave me a hand. "The New York Public Library? It's not even open."

I ignored his hand, knowing he'd feel the sweat on my palms if I took it. "I know people." In reality, the head librarian was a friend of mine I'd met at a conference. I stepped toward the entrance and turned back to face him. "Are you coming in?"

"Why?"

Because I want to make sure you're okay.

"We need to go over the details."

Lie. We could hash them out in a minute and part ways. I needed to make up my mind. I either wanted Damian or I didn't. It wasn't fair to either of us to drag our interactions out.

Damian hesitated for a moment before he turned to his car. Defeat coursed through my body. He said something to his driver, who took off a few seconds later. I drove my heels into the ground to fight my anticipation.

He made his way to me and cocked a brow. "Well?"

I chose not to wonder why he entertained me. Instead, I turned, walked up the steps of the limestone structure, and smiled at the night guard when he opened the door for me and Damian. "It's upstairs."

This was a bad idea. I knew this, but I didn't stop. Trying to stop this would be like trying to stop lightning from striking the ground. I was only human, and any effort to do so would only get me hurt.

We passed the main reading room, which looked like the dining hall in Harry Potter, and I led him up the stairs, past dozens of rooms full of books, and into my little nook. In the early- to mid-1900s, secret apartments emerged across New York libraries for live-in caretakers. This one had become my sanctuary when I stayed in the city, but I didn't stop to think about the implications of sharing it with Damian.

He leaned against one of the stacks that surrounded my full-sized bed as I stripped down to my underwear and tossed an oversized shirt over my torso. It fell down to the top of my thighs, and I considered throwing on sweats, but there was no point. It wasn't anything he hadn't already seen from me.

When I turned to face him, his eyes weren't on my body like I had thought they would be. They remained transfixed on the diamond resting on my ring finger until I slid under my covers, hiding the rock beneath the duvet.

The ensuing silence made me uneasy.

"When I wake up, I'll meet with Bastian and relay a course of action." Damian's eyes scanned the shelf next to the bed, and he dragged a finger across the worn book spines. He flipped through the stack of books I had put aside for myself. A small smile tipped the corners of his lips when he saw Dostoevsky, the first book we'd read together.

I cleared my throat until he stopped his snooping. "He's gonna wonder what your interest is. Will you tell him she's your sister?"

"No. I'll use the situation to leverage a favor or two from him."

"Smoke and mirrors. It's ballsy."

"It'll work." A beat passed, and Damian took a step back. "Why am I really here, Knight?" He stared at me with naked desire and something else I didn't dare consider.

I debated lying, and I should have, but there were already too many lies between us. Keeping track of them tired me. "I didn't like that look in your eyes earlier. Like your world had flipped, and you had no control."

"Knight." He shook his head, but it wasn't disappointment in his eyes. "Always trying to save me." He didn't sound mad about it. Just matter of fact.

I would have preferred anger. At least then, it wouldn't feel like he knew me too well.

I didn't answer. I didn't trust myself to. People heard the word "saving" and associated it with victims. But no sane person could see Damian as a victim—myself included. He just had this pain buried deep inside of him, and I wanted to be the person who took it away. Call me selfish, but it was just as much for me as it was for him.

I shouldn't have come to New York. This wasn't fair for either of us. I couldn't be near him without wanting to be with him, and he... too many people in his life had let him down. Perhaps me most of all.

Damian's eyes latched onto the paperback beside my pillow.

I considered hiding it before grabbing the book and tossing it to the foot of the bed. I nodded my head at it. "Go ahead."

I didn't breathe as he took a step closer.

He took a seat on the mattress. *"The Toynbee Convector."* He cleared his throat, and it took him a moment to continue speaking. "Which story are you reading in the collection?"

My toes curled as his hip brushed against my leg. "Not the one you're thinking." My eyes drifted shut. "I'm halfway through 'One Night in Your Life.'"

Another lie.

Stop it with the lies, Renata.

You're better than this.

He deserves better, too.

Yesterday, I had finished "The Toynbee Convector," the short story the collection had been named after. But it was a story from our past, one we had shared in the De Luca library in Devils Ridge. Mentioning it would bring up memories I had forced myself to forget. I couldn't go there, even though we both knew his presence here already blurred lines.

"I know what you're doing."

My heartbeat picked up. "Nothing."

Gosh, when had I become such a liar?

I turned until I faced the wall, away from him. I could still feel his body heat against my legs. "I'm doing nothing."

"Sure." He kicked off his shoes; removed his suit jacket;

unbuttoned his tailored button down, so it hung open; and settled beside me.

I stilled as he lifted the covers, and the length of his body brushed against my back. "What are you doing?"

"Nothing," he mocked, like we were eighteen and in love again.

Why were we doing this to ourselves?

This wasn't one of our library dates, where we joked around and fell in love with each other. We were tense. Angry. Full of painful history. Playful mocking was nothing but a lie.

But noise filled the air as he opened the book and flipped a few pages. "I'm doing nothing."

And then, he read the first line of "The Toynbee Convector." I knew him well enough to know this was his way of thanking me. His way of evening the score without addressing the emotions that came with seeing me again. It shouldn't have meant anything.

But just like all those years ago, I gave a piece of my heart to him. I wondered who was hurting who here.

The engagement ring felt as heavy on my finger as the lies I'd been telling myself for the past ten years.

16

> We like to be deceived.

— BLAISE PASCAL

Damiano De Luca

Must-stained pages stifled my breathing as I roused from a deep sleep. I lifted the book off my face and stilled when Knight's arm tightened around my waist. We'd never done this. Never spent the night beside one another on a bed. I felt like a virginal teenage boy again, and I wasn't sure if I welcomed the sentiment or abhorred it.

Lifting her arm off me, I slipped out of the bed, hoping her time away from the mafia had dulled her senses enough to keep her sleeping. By the time I slipped my suit jacket on, her breathing remained level, and I could have taken the moment to sneak away.

Instead, I stared.

Her differences stood out to me. The cinch of her waist. The volume of her hips. Her natural dark hair color popped against the pink of her lips. She was the same girl, but so, so different. I wanted to memorize her all over again. I also wanted to get as far away from her as I could.

She'd taken me here to get my mind off things.

I had read a story of our past to her to thank her.

Neither of our actions changed the fact that beneath that duvet laid a rock the size of a nickel.

Fuck.

I still wanted her. Seeing her again reminded me of everything I'd missed about her. I turned and left before I pushed her before she was ready.

My driver showed up with a pair of clean clothes, and I changed into the jeans and white tee as we pulled up to the Wilton University campus, the meeting point Bastian had texted me a few minutes ago.

Another town car pulled up beside me, and I slid into the back beside Bastian.

His face remained blank as he took a sip of a smoothie the same shade as Kermit the Frog, shit you'd never see a grown man doing in small-town Texas. "You hear from Renata Vitali?"

I pasted indifference on my face while swallowing the bitter taste of hearing Ren's name from another man's lips. "Yes."

We sat in silence.

He shifted in his seat. "… And?"

"And she agreed to discretion, so long as the matter is sufficiently handled on your end."

"What does discretion entail?"

"It means the encounter will be slipped into the Vitali

archives, and so long as no attention is drawn to this weekend, there should be no reason for anyone to investigate."

Translation: don't fuck up and draw attention to us.

"What does she want in return?"

"I've taken care of that."

"In exchange for what?"

In truth, I still reeled from the revelation of having a sister and the overwhelming urge to protect her. But in case Bastian didn't know this, I planned on keeping it a secret and misdirecting him.

I considered my options. The Romano family represented the strongest syndicate family. They had more pull than every territory in America.

My head hit the headrest as I relaxed into the leather. "One day, probably soon, you'll take over the Romano family. When you have the power, you'll use it to bring the De Luca family back into the syndicates' inner circle."

Perhaps I was an asshole for taking advantage of the situation. That didn't bother me. Though it was worth mentioning that I really did want my sister safe, and I'd welcome a future where we could get to know one another... but I also wanted a future for the De Luca name I'd fought so hard to save. I had an opportunity here to get both, and I planned on taking it.

"And if I don't take over the Romano family?"

"You will." I turned to face him. "Your uncle is dead, and your dad and remaining uncles are approaching retirement ages. You're next in the bloodline. Or have you forgotten that?"

His face stayed blank, but his jaw shifted a tick, and I knew I had him riled up. My specialty. "Your discretion and the Vitali discretion in exchange for a seat at the table?"

"Yes."

"Fine." He pulled out a pen and thick contract paper with the Romano letterhead and seal at the top. "If word gets out, this agreement will be nullified, and retribution will be sought."

"Understood." I watched as his pen moved across the page. "Have you heard of The Benefactor?"

I'd be lying if I said I had reached the De Luca throne on my own. I left a trail of blood, sweat, and tears. And the most important factor was also the one I never fully understood. Someone helped me from the start. An anonymous colluder. One who didn't ask for anything in return.

I always suspected he or she was connected to the Romano territory. Hell, I'd once gotten a package from The Benefactor that I had traced to Romano territory. I'd traced everything since. It all came back to Romano territory.

"Why?" Bastian's pen stilled, and he didn't look up from the paper. "Are you amending the agreement?"

"No."

He continued writing. "Then, we have nothing to discuss, De Luca."

"Your family wanted me here." I kicked a foot up on the mini fridge. "You may as well treat me like a guest."

His thinly veiled irritation amused me. "I can assure you we couldn't give two shits whether you're here or not."

"Oh, we have plenty to discuss, Romano. I received a handwritten invitation to Vincent's funeral, sent from your territory. Vincent is your *capo*." I nodded to the paper he held. "The letterhead and seal on the invitation was from your family." He finally looked up at me, and I pressed on. "Last I checked, the Hamptons is your territory. This involves you, and if it doesn't, your territory has more leaks than a used condom. Which is it, Romano? Are you involved or are you a used condom?"

"American politicians and foreign dignitaries vacation in the Hamptons. The Romano family stays out of the Hamptons as a courtesy for the work the politicians and dignitaries on our payroll do. In fact, the only mafioso in the Hamptons is..." His eye twitched, and he paused and looked down at the contract before handing it to me.

I waited for him to say something. When he didn't, I considered pressing my luck but decided to keep the small win. Instead, I skimmed the contract, took the pen from him, and twisted the cap off the opposite end. A small blade sat at the end of the pen. Pressing it to my thumb until crimson smeared across the surface, I stamped my thumbprint onto the contract.

Syndicate agreements were always signed in blood.

> " The people of the world having once been deceived, suspect deceit in truth itself.

— HITOPADESA

Renata Vitali

Most mafiosos anticipated the roundtable discussions after the passing of a high-ranking syndicate member. They represented a shift, an opportunity to gain leverage or lose it. It was my job as the Vitali representative to assure that no war broke out as four syndicates attempted to take advantage of the bereaved syndicate in their period of grief.

I suspected this wouldn't be difficult given the reverence Vincent Romano had garnered, but I wondered how the syndicate representatives would take my presence. Traditionally, the Vitali head—Papà—would lead these meetings. Since he couldn't step foot in New York without breaking his agreement with Maman and she couldn't come without risking the secrecy of her relationship with Vince, the five syndicates were stuck with me.

Lucky all of us.

The passing of a *caporegime, consiglieri,* underboss, or boss was a three-day event. A day of funeral processions. A day of negotiations. A day of celebration. Usually, the syndicate whose member died constituted the only somber party on the day of negotiations. Today, every single face possessed a grave expression.

It was the ultimate show of respect to Vincent Romano.

Only his death could elicit grief in every syndicate.

As the Vitali representative, I sat at the head of the oval table. As leaders of the bereaved syndicate, Gio, Frankie, Eli, and Bastian Romano sat at the opposite end of the table, taking up the most space.

The other four syndicates were allowed one representative each. Marco Camerino on behalf of the Camerino family. Rafaello Rossi on behalf of the Rossi family. Ranieri Andretti on behalf of the Andretti family. And Damiano De Luca on behalf of the De Luca family.

I tried to ignore Damian as I opened the giant book in front of me and began to read. "We are gathered here today to respect the passing of a valued syndicate member." Electric power coursed through me as I commanded the room, but all I could feel were Damian's eyes on me.

I swallowed before continuing. "The roundtable proceedings exist to remind us that the passing of Vincent Romano is not an opportunity for malfeasance, revenge, nor avaricious behavior. In a moment, I will open up the discussion for peace talks, starting with the De Luca family and ending with the Romano family. Are we in agreement?"

After a round of "ayes" across the table, I nodded to Damian and asked, "What would the De Luca family like to request?" A snort came from the transcriber, and I cut her with a vicious look. "You may be excused."

Damian's eyes burned holes in the side of my face, and I couldn't meet his stare. I didn't want to see his reaction to what I'd done for him. I didn't think I could handle it.

"But—"

"Bring in your replacement on your way out."

Transcribing for a historic roundtable negotiation was a privilege she clearly didn't deserve. She may not have believed that a De Luca deserved a seat at the table, but I knew Damian better than anyone else, and no one deserved it more. No one.

As she left, my eyes traveled across the room, the warning clear in them. I had just spoken up for a De Luca when, as the Vitali representative, I was supposed to be the neutral party. I didn't say anything that favored Damian's syndicate, but the act of removing the transcriber was close enough for lines to be drawn.

I couldn't explain it. Hell, I couldn't control it. It wasn't just my desire to make up for the past. It was more than that. Damian deserved respect, and I wanted to be the one to help him gain it. Never mind the fact that he had left me this morning and I hadn't heard from him since.

The replacement transcriber entered the conference room with her head down. She sat at the desk in the corner of the room. Once she scooted her chair in and rested her fingers on the keyboard, I nodded my head to Damian. I finally turned to face him.

He gave me that look. The same look he had given me when I had witnessed his dad punching him, and I'd told him to pick himself up. That he was stronger than his self-pity. (I would always believe that.)

Damian cleared his throat. "The De Luca family declines to put forth an agenda in respect for Vincent Romano's passing."

His words hung in the air.

Unprecedented.

The *clacking* from the transcriber halted. Frankie swore, and Bastian stared at Damian with renewed interest. I could feel the surprise and respect Damian had earned with his words, but I couldn't emotionally process what he had said.

Damian had passed on an opportunity for leverage. One I knew he desperately needed. He was the only one I'd ever told about Maman and Vincent, and when my eyes met his, I knew he had done this for me. Even when friction existed between us, we looked out for one another. I swore, I'd never been more attracted to Damian than I was in this moment.

My body tensed as the aches of losing Damian ten years ago and losing Vincent recently traveled through me. Beside me, Damian reached for my hand under the table. I wanted distance from him. Hell, the hypocrite in me wanted to hate him for leaving without a goodbye this morning—even though he hadn't meant to fall asleep at my place in the first place.

But I could never hate him.

Not when I knew who he was.

As his thumb stroked my hand in a soothing motion, another wall of mine shattered. I flipped my hand upside down and inter-locked my fingers with his. He squeezed my hand, and a decade of lost time pulsed between our palms.

What were we doing?

Why couldn't we help ourselves?

I turned away from Damian, keeping my expression measured. Our hands remained under the table, where no one could see them. I suppose old habits die hard, and just like it was my instinct to stick up for him when I could, it was Damian's instinct to hold my hand when he saw me in pain.

The rational part of me knew I needed to let go.

The larger part of me, the one that still loved Damian, refused to.

The room had gone silent, and no one knew how to react. Some tried, but they couldn't hide their respect for Damian. Pride and melancholy warred within me as people other than me recognized the type of man Damian was. One of honor, respect, and worth.

I gathered my voice and broke the silence. "The Rossi family may begin."

The *clack* of typing sounded from the transcriber again as Rafaello began to speak. "The Rossi family declines to put forth an agenda in respect for Vincent Romano's passing."

I clenched my free fist beneath the table to tamper my emotions. The Rossi family had followed Damian's lead and passed on an opportunity for leverage. Vincent—the same Vincent who had watched Disney flicks with me and taught me that it was okay to cry—had managed peace, even in his death.

I nodded to Marco Camerino, who cleared his throat. "The Camerino family declines to put forth an agenda in respect for Vincent Romano's passing."

Damian squeezed my hand beneath the table, and I knew he understood how much this meant to me. I kept my face neutral as I nodded to Ranieri Andretti. Tension rose in the room, which I didn't bother dissolving.

He deserved it for killing Vincent, no matter the circumstances. It might have ended the Andretti-Romano war, but the expense had been far greater than any of us wanted to pay.

Sorrow built in Ranieri's eyes, and he gave a soft sigh. "The Andretti family declines to put forth an agenda in respect for Vincent Romano's passing."

I turned to Gio Romano, who didn't need my encouragement

to speak. "The Romano family declines to put forth an agenda in respect for Vincent Romano's passing."

And there it was.

For the first time in the history of the syndicates, no one leveraged for power. I dismissed the meeting, and an odd sense of peace gushed into me as leaders exchanged handshakes and the head of the Romano family clapped Damian on the shoulder and drew him into a hug.

The room emptied until only Damian and I remained.

I flipped through the book, so I had something to do with my hands and eyes. "Thank you."

"Ren," he murmured.

I refused to look at him, but my heart sped up, too quick for the emotions that clogged me.

"Ren."

"Mhm?" I kept my eyes on the book. Being a good liar had its perks, but today, my skills evaded me. I'd bet I looked plain stupid staring at a book while Damian watched beside me. I definitely felt stupid.

Damian reached out and slammed the book shut. "Look at me, Knight."

I dragged my eyes to his face. "I'm not good at this."

"Using your eyes?"

I rolled my eyes and stared straight ahead. I counted backward from ten to settle my heart, which beat too quickly thanks to him.

"Shit. This isn't going how it's supposed to go." He kneeled next to me, reached for my face, and gently tipped it toward him until I stared back at him. He held an earnest expression on his face. Open. Honest.

Basically, the opposite of mine.

Fuck, fuck, fuck.

I may have swooned a little.

"I just want to thank you, Knight." His hand still cupped my face, and his thumb brushed my cheek. "Accept my gratitude. There's nothing hard about it."

But there was, because accepting gratitude felt impossible beside the guilt I felt when it came to Damian. He had nothing to thank me for after I had run away from him and left him alone in that house with his dad. If anything, I should have apologized profusely to him. Another thing I could never bring myself to do.

I stared at Damian.

Silent.

His disappointed sigh struck me as he shook his head, then walked away.

The worst part was, I deserved his disappointment—and worse.

18

> Man is not what he thinks he is, he is what he hides.

> — ANDRÉ MALRAUX

Renata Vitali

Functioning alcoholics.

Every mafioso was a functioning alcoholic.

At least, they might as well have been with how many excuses they found to drink over the course of the funeral processions. After the peace meeting, the accords needed to be signed in front of an audience of upper-level Camerino, Andretti,

Rossi, De Luca, and Romano members, followed by a toast and a round of drinks at L'Oscurità.

I kept to myself after sprawling my signature across the accords album and taking the requisite shot. Another shot slid in front of me, and I took it, too. I liked having control. Growing up in a mafia environment encouraged me to find power anywhere I could, and that started with myself. So, the urge to get drunk and forget about Damian caught me off guard.

I couldn't be the first to leave, so I found a corner table booth and cradled a single malt between my palms—one-hundred percent aware of how I looked and unable to gather an ounce of care.

"They say you're a big, bad Vitali," a soldier slurred as he slid his way into the booth beside me, probably ten shots past drunk. His dad was a *capo*, maybe. "I have something big and bad to show you." He leaned into me, the scent of alcohol and jackass invading my personal bubble.

I raised my hand to push him off the bench, but a shadow approached the table, and he was unceremoniously yanked out of the booth and onto his ass.

The soldier looked up to Damian from the floor and scrambled to get up, stumbling along the way. When he finally settled on both legs, he stood level with Damian's shoulder. "I'm a fucking Camerino. Do you know who my dad is?!"

"No, but I know who I am."

"Who are you?"

The boredom in Damian's icy tone layered tension in the air as he looked down at the soldier and spoke, "I'm Damiano De Luca,"—the soldier's eyes widened, and I could practically see him sobering by the second—"and you'll show me respect."

The soldier's mouth opened, and he floundered for something to say before accepting the lifeline one of his friends threw him when they called his name from a few tables down. Neither me nor Damian watched as he stumbled away from us.

Our gazes never wavered from one another. The silence between us throbbed, expanded, and engorged until I finally broke it.

"Damian." I pulled a lock of hair away from my face and raised a brow. "This isn't a werewolf romance, you aren't my alpha, and you don't get to mark territory you don't own. I don't need you fighting my battles for me."

"That was hardly a battle, Princess."

"And it was hardly your business, Damsel."

He cut to the chase, "Eventually, this push and pull will get old, and you'll find yourself wondering why you bothered putting up a front in the first place. Give in, Renata. You have so many walls up all the damn time, always so scared. Take a leap for once in your life."

I raised my chin. "I take leaps."

He looked unimpressed as he stood in front of me in the corner booth, his body providing privacy from lurking eyes. "Name one."

My eyes narrowed, and I tilted to the side to fully face him, my legs dangling off the edge of the booth bench. "This." My hand reached out, and I gripped onto his belt buckle.

"Princess…" His voice started as a warning but trailed off as I slid my fingers down and stroked him through his pants. "What are you doing?"

Good question.

Was I trying to prove something to myself or him?

Either way, I didn't stop. He grew hard in my palm, and I wanted to feel him skin to skin, but I was all too aware of the crowd of people behind him. His hand stopped my movement, and he took a step back. I dropped my hand to my side and studied him.

He reached out and cupped my chin between his thumb and pointer finger. "This isn't you."

I pulled away from his touch. "So, first you want me to take a

145

leap, and then you tell me that it's not me when I do. Which is it, Damian, because even whiplash would struggle to keep up with you."

"Stroking my cock in public is hot, but it's not a leap. It's a distraction, and I see past it. I see past you."

I'd forgotten what it felt like to have Damian push my boundaries, to have him reach under my skin like only he could. In that moment, what I'd just walked into slapped me in the face. If I were being honest, I knew seeing Damian again would happen when Maman asked me to represent the Vitali. I could pretend that I did this for Maman, but the truth was, I chose to come. After leaving for ten years, I chose to see Damian again. I chose *this.*

Why in the world did I choose this?

Damian must not have liked what he saw on my face because he put more distance between us and said, "I'll see you at the dinner tonight, Princess, and I hope you'll surprise me."

And maybe I hoped I would, too.

19

> " Deception may give us what we want for the present, but it will always take it away in the end.
>
> — RACHEL HAWTHORNE

Renata Vitali

It felt wrong to celebrate after a death. I could handle the funeral on day one. I could understand the negotiations on day two. But celebrating Vincent's death on day three rubbed me the wrong way.

"You're celebrating his life, Renata."

I hated myself for making Maman talk about this. "It just doesn't feel right."

147

Lucy waved at me, and I waved back, thankful that I'd chosen this moment to call Maman. The last thing I wanted to do was socialize. Asher Black, her husband and the Romano family's former fixer, stood beside her, his arms wrapped fully around his wife from behind. Bastian, Ariana, Niccolaio Andretti, and a redhead stood with them. The six of them looked like the popular kids in a 90s flick—too untouchable to be approached.

I looked away.

Maman's stern voice reached my ears. "You're on the phone at a party intended for Vincent. *That* is what is not right."

My eyes skimmed the ballroom. Situated in a hotel owned by Asher, the ballroom's elegance matched the rest of the building. Crystal chandeliers. Pietra Firma marble flooring. Pearl accents. Still, I couldn't appreciate the refined beauty. My stomach churned with emotions, and I tried to blame it on this event.

Of course, Maman saw past me.

"Renata Vitali, you are lying to me, and I do not appreciate it." She let out a curse in French. "I try to understand you, but I cannot understand how you can love a boy and not try to be with him."

I didn't bother pointing out the parallels between my situation with Damian and her situation with Vincent. It would be cruel in light of Vince's death. Regardless, I'd never call my mom out. She was strong but also fragile in moments, and it was the latter which encouraged me to let her be.

I ignored the fact that even my mom was calling me out on my lies and twisted the wedding ring around my finger, my movements absentminded. When I realized what I was doing, I settled for adjusting the deep V of my red floor-length evening gown. "I don't love anyone besides you, Maman."

I cursed karma because Damian chose that moment to walk into the room. I couldn't look at his hands without remembering how they looked holding worn paperbacks over the hundreds of nights we'd spent reading together in his library. I couldn't look at his lips without remembering the substance in our conversations and the fact that I had only ever shed my walls for him. I couldn't look at his eyes without remembering how they stared into mine when I'd given him my virginity then left after he had told me he loved me. And I would never, ever retrieve the piece of me I'd given him in Devils Ridge.

"Renata?"

Damian's eyes skimmed the room and connected with mine in an instant.

"Yeah, I'm still here." Barely. "I just spaced out."

He took a step toward me.

"Are you okay up there?"

I tracked his path to me, Maman's words barely registering. I nodded, then remembered she couldn't see me. "I'll be fine." My phone slipped a little in my clammy palm. "I just wanted to give you an update. The roundtable went well."

Someone stopped to talk to Damian, and relief swept through me as his progress halted. But then the woman leaned too close to him and laughed at what he said. Her fingers rested on the lapels of his finely tailored suit, and I stilled.

You don't own him, Renata.

He's not yours.

Don't make the same mistake twice.

Protect yourself.

"Renata? Renata!"

"Sorry. Someone was talking to me."

Another lie for the books.

Maman cleared her throat. "What were the demands?"

I hesitated. "There were none."

The conversation between Damian and the woman ended, and Damian turned back to me. Our eyes locked, and I stuttered a shaky breath out.

Maman gasped. "What do you mean?"

He was nearly here.

"I mean"—I took a deep breath—"no one requested anything in exchange for the peace period. They just… agreed to it out of respect for Vincent." Silence filled the line. I couldn't imagine what went through her mind as I spoke. "Maman?"

A few more steps now.

"That's great." She cleared her throat, and my heart tightened for her and chastised me for focusing on Damian when my mom needed me. "I'll, uh… I'll log the transcription into the archives when you drop them off."

Damian stopped in front of me, and my eyes traveled from his shined shoes, to the way his tailored pants stretched across his thighs, to the perfect fit of his white button down, to his defined jawline, to his eyes, which stared at me with an arched brow.

He mouthed, "Stop checking me out."

My jaw dropped a bit. I made a point of rolling my eyes and swiveled, so he faced my back, breaking the spell.

What had Maman and I been talking about? Right. Logging the transcription.

I cleared my throat. "Will it bring attention to Ariana De Luca?"

"No." A ruffling played on Maman's end. "I'll make sure of it. And don't think I don't know that you're only interested in Ariana because of her brother."

I ignored the last half of her words. "Thank you." My eyes cut to Damian's as he walked around me to stand in my line of sight. "I have to go."

"Remember to drop those walls, Renata."

"*Bye*, Maman." I ended the call and slid my phone into my clutch.

Damian crossed his arms. "What'd she say?"

"Nothing."

In no scenario would I tell Damian that my mom all but begged me to drop the walls I had built around me. For him, no less.

"She's my sister, Knight. Don't I deserve to know what your mom said?"

Oh.

Right.

Of course, that was what he was talking about.

"She said there'd be no problems. Everything's good."

He nodded, taking my word just like that. His eyes skimmed the ballroom. "Does this remind you of prom?"

Prom, where I had shared my first kiss with him.

My eyes shifted to his lips.

His eyes narrowed, and he took a step closer. "Ren." His voice was deep and guttural and touched me in places he didn't belong.

I couldn't understand why he still tried to talk to me. I was nothing but walls and a shady past. His efforts to talk to me defied logic, and I was sick of not understanding his motivations.

"Why are you talking to me, Damsel?" I shook my head. "I didn't mean it like that. I just want to know why you're giving me your time. Our history isn't pretty."

"Why do you always focus on the bad stuff?"

"Look around, Damsel!" I nodded my head to the pictures of Vincent at the front of the ballroom. There were dozens more on easels throughout the room. "Bad stuff happens! People in this world don't gather together because good things happen. We're here because the bad things matter."

"You had my back in the showdown between me, Ariana, and Bastian. You had my back in the roundtable negotiations. You have always had my back."

If he kept going, his logic would break my shield, and I'd be vulnerable again, which could not happen. "I can't talk to you about this. I have to mingle."

He shook his head. "No, you don't. No one wants to talk to me, and you're out of the mafia game. No one expects you to make rounds of idle chit-chat. You showed your face. That's all they want."

"So, what are you suggesting?"

"Talk to me, Princess."

"Knight," I corrected automatically. "I'm not the princess. I'm the knight. And we are talking."

"No, *talk* to me. Spend the night with me."

"That's presumptuous."

"Not like that, and you know it. Spend the night talking to me."

I looked around the ballroom, full of people I didn't know or care about. Then, I looked at him. The only man I'd ever loved.

Damn him for chipping away at my walls.

"I can't."

"You can, but you won't."

"I don't know why you're pushing this!"

"Over the past three days, you stood up for me in front of a law enforcement agent and later in a room full of mafia bosses." He leaned forward, and I could feel his breath on my ear as he spoke into it. It fanned across my skin. "You're caring, brave, and badass. And by the end of this trip, you'll be mine."

I moved quickly when he backed up, startled by the way I'd leaned into his touch. I was seconds from leaving when I noticed he had my phone in his palm. He must have swiped it when he had leaned into me. Déjà vu hit me hard.

"Phone." I held out my palm. "My phone, please."

He typed something into my phone, and I racked my brain for anything damning he could find on it and came up empty. "You really should password protect this. You're a Vitali, for Christ's sake."

"I'm a schoolteacher, not a Vitali."

"As long as your last name is Vitali, you're a Vitali."

"I'm not having this conversation with you. Give me my phone back."

"Done." He slid my phone back into my palm. Our fingers touched, and he let his hand linger until I yanked mine back. A smirk lined his lips, and he gave me a mocking two-fingered salute. "See you tonight, Princess."

I opened my mouth to tell him he wouldn't, but he'd already walked away, and I didn't want to raise my voice and draw attention to us. Instead, I settled into my assigned seat at the head table in the ballroom.

Damian took the seat across from me as Lucy settled to my right and Bastiano Romano sat on my left. The way Damian stared at me had me sending discreet looks up and down the table to see if anyone else noticed. They were trained upper-level mafia members. Of course, most of them noticed.

Something had switched in Damian. That look in his eyes. The way they followed my every movement. He wanted me again.

But I had left this world, and he couldn't have me.

Renata Vitali

L ucy shifted her eyes from me to Damian, her smile not at all sly. I ignored her and focused on my dinner plate. When I chanced another glance at Damian, he finally stopped looking at me. Only, he was talking to the daughter of one of the Romano leaders, which might have been worse than looking at me.

I wished he had taken a seat further down the table, so I could have avoided the agony of wanting Damian to stop looking at me and any other woman. I spent the dinner concentrating on not looking at Damian, and he knew it because his leg brushed against my leg beneath the table every time I thought I'd been subtle in taking a peek out of my peripheral.

I was thankful when speakers started gathering on the makeshift stage. The lights dimmed, and the first speaker rose to the podium. He told a tale of the death of his sister. Vince had set his mom up at a hotel until she could care for herself, made and paid for the funeral arrangements, and listened to him as he talked about his sister for nearly eighteen hours straight.

Remorse speared my heart. When I'd distanced myself from the family, I'd also distanced myself from Maman. I hadn't seen Vince in eight years, and not a second went by where I didn't miss him. Listening to how great of a man Vincent was stabbed me. I missed out on eight years of memories, and it was my decision. One of many poor decisions I'd made in a lifetime of poor decisions.

I swallowed my emotions and pushed my chair back. Damian cocked a brow, but I ignored him as I made my way to the stage. The line of men and women allowed me to pass to the front of the stage, thanks to my last name. I was grateful, because I needed to speak before I couldn't bring myself to.

The memorial banquet was a celebration of the life of the deceased. The mic remained open, and anyone could share good memories they had of Vincent. I couldn't speak of the memories I had connected to my mom's relationship with Vincent, but I would give what I could.

Wild blinks shuttered my eyes as they adjusted to the spotlight. I cleared my throat and allowed myself a few minutes of vulnerability in Vince's name. "I was eight when I met Vincent

Romano. My English was awful at best, I hadn't dropped my Italian accent, and conjugations kicked my ass.

"I came home with an F on an English spelling test, so afraid to tell my parents." Gosh, I'd thought my problems were the end of the world back then. "I hid in the library, my chubby cheeks blotchy, tears streaming down my face, just a giant, blubbering mess.

"Vince came into the library and browsed the selection. I thought I was so sly, hiding quietly in my corner. Back pressed against the wall. Knees drawn to my chest. Of course, he had clocked me as soon as he came in, but it wasn't until he had a copy of F. Scott Fitzgerald's *The Great Gatsby* in his hand that he approached me.

"'Why are you crying?' he pressed me. I showed him my test, and still, he asked, 'So? Plenty of people fail all the time.'

"I glared at him, and with the attitude of an eight-year-old, I said, 'Not me! I'm a Vitali. I'm powerful!'" I let loose a soft laugh. "Obviously, nothing's changed."

When the room's laughter subsided, I continued, "Vince laughed. It wasn't mocking. It was patient. And then, he asked, 'Powerful?' When I nodded, he held up the Gatsby book and said, 'Do you know what this is?'

"I shrugged, my hand still clutching that damned test. 'A book?'"

I suppressed the sudden surge of sadness, which gripped my throat.

"Vince shook his head. 'Not just any book. The best book. Do you know who wrote it?' When I said no, he smiled at me and told me, 'F. Scott Fitzgerald. One of the greatest writers of all time. You want to know what else he is?'

"I shook my head again. Vince reached out, tapped the giant red 'F' on my test, and said, 'An awful speller. One of the world's greatest writers, and he was an awful speller. People aren't born perfect, Little Miss Renata. They don't live perfectly either. But the people who are perfectly happy are the ones who don't chase perfection, especially for power. Instead of learning to conquer others, they learn to be happy with themselves.'

"Being the brat that I was, I asked him why anyone would try to be better if they were already happy with themselves. And he told me, and I'll never forget this, 'If you want to be better, do it because it makes you happy. Not because you think it will make someone else happy or because you feel like you have to.'"

My eyes met Damian's, and my words battered me harder. I'd thought moving to Connecticut and living a quiet life was me doing things that made me happy. But if I were really happy, would I be second guessing my choice to leave Damian? Would I be trying so hard to rebuild the walls between us because I was scared of getting hurt again?

I faked a smile to the crowd. *"The Great Gatsby* is still one of my favorite books. Just like Vincent Romano will always be one of my favorite people."

Fake smiles and hollow greetings filled my path back to the table. Emotions packed themselves so tightly in my throat, breathing was a struggle. When I sat back on my seat, my phone buzzed. Even though it was rude, I turned the brightness down and read the message, needing the distraction.

Damian: I like it better when you smile for real.

He must have gotten my number when he had my phone earlier. He'd programmed his in, too. My head shot up, and I stared at him. He was talking to that girl again, but I knew some part of him was aware of my attention. How had this happened? He was supposed to hate me. I should have fought the urge to back him up in the alley and at the roundtable meeting.

Renata: You don't fool me.

Distracting me. And, admittedly, doing a good job of it. When my phone didn't vibrate again after ten minutes, I sent a follow-up text.

Renata: I know what you're doing.

A Romano soldier stood on the stage, and he spoke of a time when he'd been homeless, and Vincent had helped him get back on his feet. Vince gave him more work, set up a place for him to stay, and made sure he was fed.

I'd had the privilege of knowing one of the best people to ever walk this Earth, and I pushed him away, thinking I was justified because of the gray world he lived in. But if I really was so justified, remorse wouldn't be seizing my throat so tightly.

Just when I thought a tear would drop, my phone buzzed, and I gripped it tighter, like it was my lifeline.

Damian: Sending inappropriate texts in the middle of a memorial banquet?

Renata: Don't stop.

It was a moment of weakness, but I needed the distraction he gave me. And yes, I knew that was why he was doing this. He'd always been so in tune with my emotions, and it was our thing to always be there for each other, even when we shouldn't have.

Damian: You didn't say that to me last time I slid inside you. We should rectify that.

Renata: You were never this dirty back then.

Damian: I was also an eighteen-year-old trying to be a gentleman.

Renata: And now?

Damian: I'm no longer eighteen, and I'm no longer a gentleman.

Renata: Liar.

Damian: No one has ever accused me of being a gentleman before.

Renata: That's because they don't know you like I do...

I hesitated and deleted the last text before the illogical part of me decided to send it. It was too intimate, and while I welcomed the distraction, it couldn't go any deeper than silly texts.

Renata: Tell me something stupid.

He didn't answer for a while, and each second without a reply sent me deeper and deeper into grief over Vincent. I needed Damian to reply. *Damn it, Damsel, help a girl out.* I caved and studied him.

His phone rested on the table in front of him, and when he noticed me staring, he pressed something once on his phone. Not a second later, my phone buzzed. He must have had his message already typed out. His eyes stayed on me as I read his text.

Damian: You have a ring on your finger. That's pretty damn stupid.

My jaw dropped a little before I recovered. I typed something, deleted it, retyped, then deleted. His ankle touched my calf beneath the table, and my phone dropped from my startled hands onto the floor.

Lucy leaned over, picked the phone up, and handed it to me. If she'd noticed Damian's leg on mine while she was down there, she didn't mention it. Instead, she gave me a small smile and returned her attention to the stage, where mine should have been.

My phone buzzed again.

Damian: Tell me something stupid.

My heart lashed out from inside me. He slid his leg up higher, parting my dress at the high slit, and hooked his ankle around my knee. His conversation with the woman abandoned, his complete attention transfixed me.

I licked my lips. His eyes traced the path of my tongue. On the stage, an Andretti *caporegime* spoke of healing, moving forward, forgiveness, hope, and honesty. In front of me, Damian represented the possibility of achieving these things.

Take a leap, take a leap, take a leap, my heart begged.

Don't, don't, don't, my fear argued.

Make a damn choice, my brain demanded.

I typed, pausing every other word because I couldn't decide what was worse—sending the text or not.

Renata: I had a dream last night. You kissed me in it.

Damian: That's not stupid.

I didn't respond. This was a bad idea. Fifteen minutes and two more speakers passed. My phone buzzed. I forced myself not to check it, even when Damian talking with the Romano woman burned my eyes.

My phone buzzed again a few minutes later, and I caved.

Damian: In your dream, how did I taste?

Damian: You hate that I'm talking to her. What do you think that means, Princess?

It meant that I cared more than I should have. I needed to nip this in the bud, but I wouldn't because I needed the reprieve he offered more, if only for tonight. Tomorrow, I would wake up and leave for Connecticut. Tonight, maybe I could take what he offered.

Renata: I'm not sure how you tasted. It wasn't those lips you kissed.

His foot went slack and fell from my leg. He dropped his spoon in his soup bowl as he read his text. The new speaker spoke of Vincent as if he'd been a father figure. I stiffened. Damian's leg brushed against mine again, and I returned my attention to him. The phone buzzed.

Damian: Spend the night with me, Renata. No strings attached. Just one night. We can take it from there. I know you want to. I know you're afraid. Be fearless, Knight.

Renata: I know what you're doing.

Damian: I know. I'm distracting you, because you're hurting. And you'll accept my help, because that's what we do. I hurt. You help. You hurt. I help. Don't change us, Knight.

"Too late, Day," I whispered, and his eyes shot to mine from across the table.

21

“ Don't trust everything you see. Even salt looks like sugar.

— MARYUM AHSAM

Renata Vitali

Damian led me out the side to his car. By the time we made it to my nook in the library, I had questioned my decision to leave with him a million times. In the end, I knew I needed this. Damian chased away the pain. He did for me what drugs and alcohol did for others. Problem was, he was more dangerous than substances. If he wanted to, he could ruin me.

I sat on my bed, pulled my knees to my chest, and rested my chin on them. "Promise me something."

"Anything."

"Promise me that, when I wake up, you'll be gone."

His features darkened. "Ren..."

"Please."

He didn't answer for a moment. "Fine."

"Thank you."

He took a seat next to me and handed my oversized sleeping shirt to me. I shimmied into it as he turned away. My bare thigh touched the top of his hand as I wiggled out of my dress. He sucked in a breath, and I felt like I had when we were teens—always a heartbeat away from a kiss.

When I settled back against the headboard, he looked at me again. "Remember that song we slow danced to?"

I closed my eyes and pictured prom night. "A remake of Bryan Adam's 'Heaven.'"

"I heard it in my hotel elevator this morning." His hand reached out and gripped my thigh.

We sat beside one another, our backs leaning against the headboard and our legs lying flat on the bed.

I sighed at his touch. "Are we crazy for doing this?"

"Do you want to stop?"

"I think this is a bad idea."

"I think it isn't." He shifted, so his body hovered above mine, our faces separated by a short breath. "If you don't want to do this, tell me. But if you do, I'll chase away the pain. I promise, Knight."

I let out a shaky breath. "I don't feel like a knight right now." I felt like a pawn on Maman's chess board, incapable of bold moves. The weakest link.

How could Damian see my pain? *I* couldn't even pinpoint it. It was losing Vincent and the ghost of losing Damian all at once.

It was also confronting the idea that the past ten years of my life had been a mistake.

I'd pushed Vincent and Damian away. I could never get Vincent back, but now I had an opportunity to have Damian for the night. I'd be stupid not to take it.

I met his stare. "You'll be gone when I wake up?"

He didn't answer me.

"Damian…"

He pressed his forehead against mine. "Yes."

His answer hurt me as much as it helped me. Anticipation sprinted laps around my body. He climbed over me. I hooked my leg around his lower back, and he ground into my body until I wanted to tear our clothes off.

Our mouths met—anger, frustration, and lust meeting with each clash of our tongues. He sucked the tip of my tongue into his mouth. I stroked the roof of his mouth. Once. Twice. The third time, he lowered me from the headboard, pushed me onto my back, and climbed completely over me.

His hands dipped under my shirt. He slid them up, lifting the shirt with his movements until both palms cupped my breasts. I arched into him as he pinched my nipples. His lips left mine, and he buried his face in my neck and nipped at the skin, stroked it with his tongue, and sucked.

It felt so good, I could have cried. I'd missed his touch. Craved it in ways I hadn't realized. The tear slipped out before I could stop it. I didn't cry. That wasn't me. Never. But another tear greeted the last, and I was helpless to stop it. I had never had a real family. Didn't know what the word meant, let alone what it felt like.

I saw Maman part-time, and Papà might as well have been someone else's father for all I saw him. This world had somehow spit me out and made me different than everyone else. All the other syndicate families, at one point or another, had a family dynamic. Camaraderie. Loyalty. Honor.

Except Damian's. It explained why my soul reached for his. We were kindred spirits, and I'd lost him. After tonight, I'd lose him again. A final tear slipped out, and I swiped it away quickly before he could see it.

A moment later, he must have felt the tension in my body because he stopped and pulled back to look at me.

I didn't want him to leave but couldn't bring myself to ask him to stay. "You'll be gone when I wake up, right?"

He placed my head in the crook of his neck, and while I didn't shed the tears I wanted to shed, I let him hold me.

"Yeah," he said. "I'll be gone."

22

> "You may be deceived if you trust too much, but you will live in torment if you don't trust enough.

— FRANK GRANE

Damiano De Luca

R enata laid pressed against my side, snoring every now and then. She squeezed the arm wrapped around me, and I didn't dare move. The night hadn't gone as planned. I was supposed to slip inside her. I was supposed to remind her why we fit so well. I was supposed to make her beg, plead, scream out her orgasm, and beg me for another five.

I didn't even kiss her.

I had a long flight back to Texas and a full day of meetings. I should have closed my eyes and gotten some sleep. Instead, I spent the night with Ren as long as it would last, our limbs a twisted, chaotic knot I didn't want to untangle. Then, I begged the sun to retreat so I could have another hour. It didn't listen. If anything, it rose faster. Still, last night was the best night I'd had all decade, and I needed another one like it was a basic necessity.

This was real.

What Ren and I had was real.

I was many things, but I wasn't delusional.

This. Was. Fucking. Real.

And so long as she wanted me to, I would fight for us.

23

> Beware of the half-truth. You may have gotten hold of the wrong half.

> — UNKNOWN

Renata Vitali

I knew I had asked him to leave, but when I woke up to an empty bed, the pang in my chest reminded me of what a horrible idea being near Damian was. I had spent the past ten years convincing myself that I didn't care about him.

Now he was gone, and I didn't want him to be.

24

> « All war is deception.

— SUN TZU

Three Days Later

Damian: I said I'd be gone, but I lied. I'm not giving up on us. I made a mistake when you left ten years ago. I should have chased you better. I should have never stopped chasing. I'm not making that mistake again. I'll see you at the next summit in a month. We're not spending another ten years apart when we both want this. This is happening, Knight.

Error: Message failed to send. This number is invalid. Please resend using a valid 10-digit mobile number or a valid short code.

> **There is nothing more deceptive than an obvious fact.**
>
> — ARTHUR CONAN DOYLE

Renata Vitali

"Save some for the rest of us," Sally joked as I hoarded half of one of the pepperoni pizza boxes in the empty staff room. She was my best friend in Connecticut, which was sad considering we weren't really friends. Just colleagues who spent lunch period eating together on occasion.

My eyes lifted to hers, one hand on a plate full of pizza slices and the other shoveling a slice into my mouth. "Sorry," I spoke around a mouthful of food.

Her nails tapped the table she sat at, and in a conservative cardigan, silky blouse, and loose slacks, she looked more like a librarian than our actual librarian did. "If I didn't know any better, I'd say you were eating your way through a heartbreak. You look like me after Eric and I divorced." Her locker-blue eyes scanned my figure through oversized glasses as she tucked a blonde lock of hair back into her neat bun. "Just about nine years younger and forty pounds slimmer."

"No heartbreak here." I took a seat next to her and set down my plate on the cheap plastic tabletop. "I just haven't eaten pizza in forever."

Truthfully, I was stress eating. You know that feeling you get when you know something is wrong, but you do it anyway? After changing my number, I had that in droves, and it pushed me into the cushy arms of pepperoni, mozzarella cheese, and extra marinara. I paused. *Fuck, I forgot the parmesan.*

Like the mindreader she was, Sally handed me a few packets and smiled when I thanked her. "Are you going to tell me what is eating away at you?"

I tore a cheese packet open and sprinkled the processed parmesan onto a slice with the skill of a *Kitchen Nightmares* chef. "Nothing is eating away at anything except me with this pizza." To make my point, I chomped down on a bigger bite than I could handle.

My mind wandered to my phone, and I wondered if Damian had tried to text or call me since I left New York. Changing my number had been a spur of the moment ordeal, fueled by the fear and uncertainty I felt after waking up alone—even though, being the hypocrite I was, I'd asked him to leave before I woke up.

Sally handed me a napkin, which I dabbed against my face. Her mama bear instincts were strong despite our mere ten-year age gap, and she doted on me like she did one of her students. "Denial isn't just a river in Egypt."

"Denial isn't just a river in Egypt? Really, Sal?" I pointed a pizza slice at her as I retorted, "You know, if this conversation were an essay and you were one of your students, you'd fail yourself for either plagiarism or unoriginality."

"My students are seven and eight. They don't write essays." She took in my face, then paused, raised a manicured hand to her chest, and gasped. "Renata, you do *not* make your students write essays. They're in second grade!"

I set the pizza slice down and dabbed at the oil with a napkin because I knew the pet peeve would distract her. "It's a formulaic five paragraph structure on why family matters, not a research essay on the lack of bipartisanship in Washington. They'll manage."

"Do you have to do that?" Her eyes dipped to my fiery-orange, oil-soaked napkin, and she scrunched her nose before meeting my eyes again. "'They'll manage'? I swear, you were raised by tigers."

Close.

Vitalis.

"They'll write thank you notes to me from whatever Ivy League school they're accepted to in ten years." I shrugged and tossed the napkin at the trashcan by the door, nearly missing. "And yes, I have to do this. There's more oil than pizza on each slice."

She ignored me as I pressed a second napkin to the slice. Her unimpressed expression bounced off my shoulders. "I thought you were more fun than that. You're supposed to be the cool teacher. You had your students build miniature catapults last year, and they got to launch little ping pong balls at the PE teachers. I remember all that screaming and cheering—and all the shade my students threw my way for not adding catapults to my lesson plan."

"I'm not fun. It was an engineering, math, and physics lesson," I pointed out.

Sally opened her mouth, closed it, then opened it again. "I know what you're doing."

If you know what I'm doing, do tell, my brain begged. *I haven't known what I've been doing since I fled Devils Ridge. Passing time? Going through the motions? Making excuses not to apologize to Damian until too much time slipped by? Answer D, all of the above?*

My pizza no longer appealed to me, and I pasted the most innocent look I could conjure on my face. "Enlighten me."

"You're distracting me from my original question."

And I usually succeeded in drawing our conversations away from things too personal to discuss. I scanned my brain, wondering where I went wrong over the past five minutes.

"Is it a boy?" she pressed.

"When have you ever seen me with a boy?"

"I never see you outside of work."

Fair point.

I slid my plate away from me and crossed my arms. "It's not a guy."

"Then, why are you blushing?"

Oh, Jesus, Joseph, and Mary.

Blushing? Really? This was what I'd meant when I said time outside the mafia had softened me. I passed time by training, so I could still fight and shoot a gun, but I had the emotional forti-tude of a preteen popping her L.J. Shen cherry.

"Fine, it's a guy." I didn't elaborate, hoping the bell would ring before she could pick apart my sanity.

No such luck.

"Who? Do I know him? Does he live here?"

"No, no, and no."

She furrowed her carefully plucked brows. "'Who' isn't a yes or no question..."

"His name is Damian."

"Hot." When I didn't continue, she leaned forward and asked, "Well?"

"Well, nothing."

"I give great advice."

"Good to know."

"Seriously, I could have been a therapist or a life coach or a fluffer."

"I don't think that means what you think it means."

"Fluffer? Someone who fluffs someone else's ego. What else could it mean?"

"You know how movie sets film multiple takes of a single scene?"

"Yeah, sure."

"Porn sets do, too. To keep the men hard, they hire fluffers, whose job it is to suck—"

"Oh, my goodness! Renata! We're in a school."

My lips quirked up, and I finally relaxed. "You ask, I answer."

"If only that were really true..."

I ate in silence for a moment, pausing to study Sally. My teeth dug into my lower lip as I considered whether or not to take up her offer for advice. I mean, who else could I ask? Maman would just tell me to lower my walls, accompanied by a litany of other things I didn't want to hear.

Standing, I brought my plate to the sink and washed it before returning to my seat. "Have you ever been afraid to let your guard down?"

"Around a guy?"

I thought about it. "Yes, but also around everyone, I guess."

Who was I kidding? My walls had more guards than Fort Knox, and living trapped behind confines of my own making wasn't living. Happiness over the past ten years had been a lie I deceived myself into believing.

"I think most people have that fear of letting their guard down, especially if they've gone through something difficult in

177

the past. Take me and Eric, for instance. Dating feels nearly impossible after the divorce. Every time I convince myself to go on a date, I always feel like the relationship is destined to end, which is a horrible state of mind to enter a relationship in. Nothing can succeed if you don't give it a chance to."

"So, what do you do?"

"You take a leap, knowing you're strong enough to catch yourself if no one else is there to."

"I have a friend who used to date a guy ten years ago, and she recently met him again..."

"Your friend..." Sally started, clearly not believing this friend existed. "How did she feel when she saw him again?"

"Like the world flipped upside down, butterfly clips suddenly came back in style, people still communicated via AOL Instant Messenger, and floppy disks were the new biggest invention of our lifetime."

"So, her feelings never ebbed?"

"I guess not," I allowed, because who could get over Damiano De Luca? I was only human.

"Why didn't she try to make things work the first time?"

"She was scared."

"Of?"

"The boy's dad approached my friend and threatened to"—I considered how truthful I could be before settling for a minor substitution—"*disown* his son if she continued their relationship."

"So, she left."

"Yep."

"And she regretted it."

"Every day since."

"And the dad?"

"What about him?"

"Is he still a problem?"

"He stopped being a problem less than a year after she left."

"Then, why did she stay away?"

"She didn't explain to the boy why she left. Instead, she created a fake fight and fled, because she was afraid he'd stop her if she told him the truth."

"She could have explained that to him. Any reasonable person would understand."

I tugged at my dress, reluctant to admit the truth. "She was afraid."

"Of?"

"The problems in her relationship with the boy had never been just about the boy. In a perfect world, they'd be happily married by now. But the world isn't perfect, and she was raised by a woman who showed her how to never fight for love and a man who told her to never let her guard down. So, it wasn't just the boy I couldn't let my guard down for. It was *everyone*."

I didn't even catch my slip up, too caught up in the realization that I needed to fix my issues before Damian and I could ever have a chance.

"Can I offer you advice from someone who's seen you nearly every day for the past seven years?"

"Of course."

The sympathy in Sally's eyes struck me. "Sometimes, people don't build walls to keep others out. Sometimes, they do it to protect what's left inside." She reached across the table and took my hand, all pretenses of talking about a 'friend' discarded. "Remember—that brick you use to build your walls can be a brick you use to rebuild what's within them."

26

> A liar knows that he is a liar, but one who speaks
> mere portions of truth in order to deceive is a
> craftsman of destruction.

— CRISS JAMI

Renata Vitali

I smiled at Gaspard, Maman's majordomo, as he left me with a little bow and strode out of Maman's library. My eyes strayed to the books on the shelves, noting a few new limited editions sitting beside a box of Gurkha Black Dragon cigars, like the ones Damian used to have in his bedroom's humidor. Except I'd never seen him smoke. Come to think of it,

I'd never seen Maman smoke either. Expensive decoration. That was what they were.

Taking a seat in front of Maman's chessboard, I looked out of the floor-to-ceiling French windows and studied two birds perched on a tree.

"Thank you for coming, Renata." Maman kissed me on the cheek before taking a seat across from me. The way her smile consumed her face made her radiant, and I understood how Papà could be so worried and insecure that she'd leave him.

People loved Maman. Gravitated to her. She was kindhearted, empathetic, and someone I could tell all my secrets to. Hell, I'd even told her about Damian's existence before he rose to the De Luca throne. I spilled to her about falling in love with him and running away, and I trusted her to keep my secrets like I trusted Tijan to write a page-turner every time.

With her connections and magnetism, a divorce with Maman would embarrass Papà. Which was why she holed up in her fortress in the States, and Papà stayed the hell away to avoid poking the bear.

My eyes dipped to the chessboard, and I took in the pieces. "You've moved something."

"Good eye," she praised, that smile still glued to her face. "Knight to F7."

"This has got to be the slowest game of chess ever. You've been playing this exact game since I was a kid."

"It's a game of patience, yes."

"Not speed chess."

"Speed chess doesn't gratify."

"Tell that to the multi-million dollar World Rapid and Blitz prize winners each year."

Her bubbly laughter echoed in the room. "Remind me why I raised a smart ass."

I suppressed my smile with pursed lips. "You love me."

"That, I do." Her fingers traced her queen, and she continued after a beat, "I didn't bring you here to discuss speed chess, Renata."

"Why am I here? Not that I don't love seeing you..."

"We need to go over what's required of you before the next event."

"Event? Are you saying I'm going to the city again?"

"Yes, you had to have known that."

"I—" After a sharp inhale, I let out my exhaustion with a deep exhale. "What if I don't want to?"

I'd left the mafia for a reason. After fleeing Devils Ridge, Papà wanted me back in Italy to train as his second in command, but I needed out. I couldn't stomach being part of a system that birthed Angelo De Luca, and the lies, the deception, and the way people used one another sickened me.

So, I turned to the only thing left that I enjoyed—school. Mama helped me extricate myself from the Vitali, and I left for college, went on a fast track to becoming a teacher, and have been teaching second grade ever since. But being the Vitali representative at a function felt like too close a step to rejoining the mafia fold.

Maman repositioned the queen and clasped her hands together. "I pulled a lot of strings to get you out of the mafia, Renata, and I don't ask you for much. Your father won't come to America, even to represent the Vitali name, and I can't come because..." Her voice trailed off, but I knew what she'd been about to say.

She couldn't come because of her secret relationship with Vincent.

My eyes traced the fine lines on her forehead and the way her eyelids drooped a bit. Maman still grieved the loss of her love, and I was being an ungrateful daughter. A grudge-holding chicken, too, who couldn't see past her barriers but also resented the way Damian left the library nook.

"Please, do this for me, Renata."

I let loose the sigh that had been building the past few minutes. "Okay."

Maman covered the events and gave me a detailed binder of things I needed to say and do, while I prepared myself for the idea of seeing Damian again. But there are some things you can't prepare for.

Betrayal.

Love.

Damiano De Luca.

> **❝** There are two ways to be fooled. One is to believe what isn't true; the other is to refuse to accept what is true.

— SOREN KIERKEGAARD

Renata Vitali

One Month Later

"I wasn't sure I'd find you here."

I placed a bookmark between two pages and set the book down—*The Toynbee Convector*, to my dismay. "You weren't sure you'd find me at the place you know I stay at?"

I kept my face blank and the scoff I wanted to emit quiet. Damian didn't need to know how much he shook me. I almost couldn't believe that I'd once been so aloof. I didn't feel like the same person I had been when I had first stepped foot in Texas ten years ago. Nor did I feel like the person I'd been when I arrived for the funeral just over a month ago.

Irritation scuffed at my throat, its temperature rising with each step he took toward me.

Why are you so bitter he left you that morning? You wanted him to. It's not like you like him. You can't like him.

The voice in my head could suffer tax audits for the rest of its life, jump off a cliff, and be forced to watch *Barney and Friends* on repeat in Hell, for all I cared. Denial felt better than the alternative—admitting the feelings I had for Damian hadn't lessened over time.

"You're mad at me?" He laid next to me on the bed, his back propped against my pillow. "You changed your phone number. I just couldn't believe it."

I'd done that because I'd spent the first day back from New York glued to my phone, and waking up alone reminded me of how alone I'd felt over the past decade. Damian and I were heart-break. How could I want heartbreak?

He pressed on despite my silence. "I did what you wanted. If anything, *I* should be mad at *you* for making me leave—" His tone was light, but I swore I heard undercurrents of bitterness in him. He wouldn't admit it, but he wasn't over my departure.

And me? I wasn't prepared for an ambush this morning. The follow-up roundtable meetings were later today. I was supposed to have a few more hours. I'd just gotten into New York last night, and now we were fighting already?

I used anger to give me strength. "Nope." I sat upright and scrambled to face Damian. "Don't even finish that sentence." My head shook, along with my already shaky façade. Hell, I'd pretty much dropped the calm, cool and collected act last month, and it didn't look like it would make a return anytime soon. "Last month, you could have mentioned me leaving, but you said nothing. This isn't fair."

"There's no statute of limitations on how long I can bring up you leaving me."

"I left Texas. So what?!"

I was so sick of the guilt I felt over it. We'd been dating for a month. Tops. Why had I spent the past ten years agonizing over my mistake? I was a kid. Eighteen. Scared. Confused. I didn't deserve to suffer for it for the rest of my life. Maybe I needed to be told that everything was okay.

"You don't remember what you said?"

Yes, but I didn't think *he* had.

I ran a hand across my face. "I was young. I didn't mean it."

I'd also needed him not to chase me, though that didn't work out. He'd chased and chased and chased, and I'd used my family's resources to make sure I was never found. Even when everything in me wanted to come back to him, I reminded myself of how much it hurt to leave the first time.

Disbelief painted his features. "You honestly expect me to believe that?"

Our relationship was so starved of honesty that I couldn't expect him to believe anything that came out of my mouth. My reasons for coming to Texas? Apparently, a lie. My reasons for leaving? Definitely a lie. How many lies had we told in between? How about the last time we'd been in New York for Vince's funeral?

This was escalating far quicker than I could keep up. My hands formed fists at my sides. I shook my head. "I was never supposed to be in Texas in the first place! I was eighteen. A kid. We were both kids, and it's not like you loved me."

"I did though."

No. Way.

His eyes dipped to the stupid ring on my finger, one I'd been fiddling with all morning. "I fucking did!"

"You never said it."

"I did!"

"When we had sex—one time. And it was because of the sex." My hands shook. I tried to stop it, but I couldn't. "You never said it any other time."

"I didn't think I had to. I didn't think there was a rush. I didn't think you'd leave!" He shook his head. "And it wasn't because of the sex. I meant what I said."

"I... I—" I scrambled over him and off the bed, needing the space. I paced the length of the bed, choosing my words before giving up and heading to the door.

"Knight!" He stood and ate the two steps between us. "You don't get to walk away this time."

"Are you blaming me for this?!" I shook my head. "You're the one who lied to me. That was you, Damsel. Not me. You." I turned to face him. "I loved you, and you lied to me."

Damian shook his head. "I didn't lie to you."

I scoffed. "A lie of omission is still a lie."

Damian and I had seen each other for all of five minutes, and a full-blown argument had ensued. I wished I was better at saying no to Maman when she asked me to return. Then, I wouldn't be here, a knot the size of Texas in my throat as I tried to speak past it.

Damian's eyes were dark with frustration. "How can you stand there, so angry at me, when you have a goddamn ring on your finger?!" He took a step toward me, and I resisted the dueling urges to kiss him and extricate myself from this situation. "You're married, Ren; yet, you clearly still care about me."

Screw this ring.

I tore it from my finger and tossed it at his chest. "I'm not married, Damsel." Humiliation tingled across my spine. "My mom gave me the ring to wear on my ring finger before I left, so I'd have armor when I faced you. Happy?!"

This fight had been a long time coming. Honestly, it felt good to get this out, like it needed to happen before we could move forward. Each word I spoke eased my anger and healed a bit of pain. And now that I had this ring off my finger, a giant weight lifted off my shoulders.

The ring bounced off his chest and hit the floor. He stared at it before backing me into the bookshelf behind me. "You're not married?"

"No." I looked away.

"You try to be so strong"—he cupped my face and moved it until I stared into his eyes—"and you are. So, so strong, Renata. But you don't need to be strong all the time. You're perfect, even when you're fragile. You put up these walls you don't need to put up. You don't need the baggy clothes nor the tight pencil skirts and fancy evening gowns. You don't need the ring. You can wear whatever you want and be whoever you want, and you'd still be the best person I know."

It was too much.

His words.

Him.

I pushed him away. "You don't know me anymore."

"I know all I need to know."

I shook my head again, memories of running away sinking into me. "I didn't know you'd be so mad!"

"How could I not be?! The girl I loved left me!"

"It's not like we said I love yous."

"We've been over this. *I* did."

I froze, and memories of the night he had taken my virginity pushed to the front of my mind. I'd buried them, hoping to black out the pain of what came next—leaving him.

"And even if I hadn't said it, it shouldn't matter. You should have known. You had to have known." He dipped his head and closed his eyes. Tense lines traveled across his forehead. When he opened his eyes again, they landed on my tattoo—a scribbled line wrapped around my ring finger.

I forced myself not to fidget as he stared at it. "What? Why are you staring?"

His eyes met mine, dipped to my finger, then returned to my eyes. A strange look crossed his face, the one he would give me in our library when he'd thought I wasn't looking. Damian took a step closer to me.

Then, another.

And another.

His eyes dropped to my tattoo and returned to mine.

And then, like he couldn't hold himself back anymore, he kissed me.

28

> **It is not a shame to be deceived; but it is to stay in the deception.**
>
> — OLIVIA

Renata Vitali

Eighteen Years Old

Normal.

Two syllables. Adjective. Conforming to a standard. Synonyms: usual, typical, or expected. Antonym: my life.

Turning eighteen felt like it should have been a rite of passage. I didn't feel any more or less like an adult than I had at seventeen. I didn't celebrate my newfound adulthood with parties or friends. Heck, I'd forgotten it was my birthday until I woke up the next morning and Angelo De Luca told me eighteen was a little too old for his taste.

Maybe that was why I showed up to prom.

I wanted to feel normal, but in a town of mafiosos and their children, normalcy evaded me. Prom represented my last chance at normal high school memories. The crowded gym and paper decor screamed, "Normal!" The taffeta dresses and matching ties? Normal. Sitting at an empty table, watching other kids enjoy their senior prom? All too normal.

So, why wasn't I happy?

Maybe I didn't know what I wanted.

I certainly no longer wanted to be here.

I stood and headed for the hallway, grabbing a water bottle from the refreshment table on the way out. The library entrance nestled at the end of the hall welcomed me. I left the door open, so the hallway light could stream into the library, and took a seat on the floor.

I downed the water and spun the empty bottle, bored out of my mind but too stubborn to leave the only high school event I'd ever been to.

"You're the life of the party."

"No self-respecting woman should wish or work for the success of a party who ignores her sex. Susan B. Anthony."

"Not the kind of party I was referring to." He stepped closer until his feet were in my line of sight, next to the bottle.

I trailed my eyes up his body, taking in the three-piece suit he wore like he posed in a *GQ* feature. "No shit."

"So, you're in a grumpy mood, I see." He took a seat next to me and leaned against the bookshelf behind us. "What is it about libraries?"

"Nothing is less lonely than a room full of books." I breathed in. "And the smell. Definitely the smell."

He reached beside him and grabbed a random book, flipping through it quicker than he could possibly read. "Why are you here?"

"Why are *you* here?"

"Really?"

"Do you ever feel like the only real people in this world are the ones in these books?"

"Or maybe the world we're living in is a book, and we're just characters."

I rested my head against the bookcase and closed my eyes. "If that's the case, someone is reading me, becoming me, understanding me, and maybe I'm not so lonely after all."

He paused a beat, and the silence burrowed between us. "I'm sorry you feel lonely."

This was getting too real.

"Why are you here, Damsel?" I nodded in the direction of the gym. "You should be out there with your loyal subjects."

The lopsided grin he gave me shocked my system, and the calmness I'd always prided myself on fled. "Don't you mean *your* loyal subjects, Princess? You're the Vitali."

"I'm the Knight, and don't change the subject. Why are you here?" I leaned forward, and I didn't even consider why I held my breath as I waited for his answer.

"Let's dance."

"What?" I shook my head. "If we go out there together, we'll break their little minds." As far as I knew, no one knew about our friendship.

"So, we'll dance in here." I opened my mouth, but he cut me off. "Don't think too hard. If you want to dance with me, dance with me. As simple as that." He stood and turned to face me.

The second my palm pressed against his, I knew I'd made the right decision. A slow song drifted into the library, faint but enough for us to find a rhythm. My fingers gripped his shoulders as his hands slid around my waist.

I forced myself to keep breathing when he stepped forward, and my chest brushed against him. The first step we took was effortless. In sync without trying.

I rested my chin on his shoulder, and my nose brushed against his neck. I felt his Adam's apple bob against my cheek. "Thank you."

He didn't say anything for a moment, and the territory we drifted into felt dangerous. Risky. Like it could either be the best decision or the worst decision I'd ever made. I was almost thankful when he said, "Don't think too much of it," instead of something that would tip us past the breaking point.

Maybe he saw the million questions running through my head, because he dipped me and spoke into my ear. "Tell that brain of yours to shut up and let us dance."

"Why?"

He pulled me back up, and his grip on my waist tightened. "Because you'll find out."

That he cared about me.

"I already have."

His eyes darkened as they scanned my face. We'd stopped dancing after the dip, but he still held me, and I still clutched onto his shoulders.

My pulse was erratic.

Damn it, Heart.

My throat closed up.

Not you, too, Throat.

My knees buckled.

I give up, Body.

I kissed him.

Our lips pressed together, and instinct latched onto me as I explored his mouth. His tongue traced my lips. I parted them, and he slipped inside. His tongue stroked the roof of my mouth, and he took a step into me, backing me into the bookcase behind me.

The musty scent of books, and characters, and worlds mixed with his scent of bergamot and blackcurrant. I needed him closer, but I didn't know how to ask. My hands slid down his shoulders and pulled at the tucked edges of his dress shirt underneath his vest. I dipped my fingers under the shirt and explored the hard edges of his stomach muscles.

His mouth drifted from my lips to my jaw and down my neck. I cried out when his tongue traced my collarbone, then bit down. My right hand wrapped around his body and squeezed his butt cheek, but the phone in his pocket blocked my movement.

As if someone had dumped a bucket of water on my head, I lurched out of the lust fog. What had I done? We were... I didn't know what we were. Natural born enemies? Accidental friends? Neither felt right.

Maman hadn't contacted me yet, but I knew she would. I'd been eighteen for a week now. When she contacted me, I could leave. Damian only complicated things. He must have felt my waning enthusiasm because he backed up, giving me space.

My heart warred between feeling grateful and wounded.

It's not the first time he's hurt you, Heart. Remember when you first came here?

My heart wasn't having any of my logic.

He may have hurt me, but he heals so much better.

Damian's brows furrowed. "Knight?"

Panic lodged itself in my throat, and I forced some words out. Any words. "This means nothing."

Frustration flashed within his eyes. "Keep telling yourself that, Princess."

The lust fog may have eased, but I still felt heavy. Like layers of secrets and history weighed me down as I stood mere feet from the first boy I'd ever kissed. "I need air."

It took a moment, but he finally nodded. "I can take you home."

I agreed, grabbed the empty water bottle I'd chugged earlier, and forced myself to take steps toward the gym to get my coat from the coat check. A rivulet of sweat trailed down my cheek. I swiped at it with a hand that felt like lead.

My body swayed into Damian's as we entered the gym.

He caught me and steadied me just as he returned. "You okay?" When I nodded, his hand still on my elbow squeezed. "Stay here. I'll go get your coat."

I stumbled to the refreshments table a foot away, my dry mouth begging for a water bottle.

Laura met me at the table, a smirk pasted on her cherry-red lips. "Still thirsty?" She looked at the empty bottle in my hand, then the row of water bottles with one missing. Mine.

It took me a moment too long to piece it together. That fog in my head pressed down with each second. She'd put something in the water bottles, water bottles only I drank from. Everyone was in on it.

Was Damian?

I shook my head and swayed again.

Like earlier, Damian caught me. "Ren?" When I didn't answer, he turned to Laura, his arms still around me. "Laura? Care to explain?" The hardness in his tone eased my worries.

He didn't know.

I let myself check out as they talked.

Laura crossed her arms. "I-I…We were just having fun."

Damian's head brushed my cheek as he turned to look at the water bottles. "You drugged her? What if I'd drunk from a water bottle? Would you have drugged me?"

"One of us would have stopped you!"

"Are you insane? She's a Vitali, Laura. Her family could have us all wiped from existence!" The gym had quieted, and Damian's shouts rang across the gym as he addressed the entire student body. "Have you all gone fucking insane?! Why would any of you go through with this?!"

Silence.

"Someone better fucking answer me. Now!"

"Laura said it was your idea."

I didn't know who spoke up, but he sounded like a chipmunk. I'd never loved chipmunks, but I'd always loved animals. Why didn't I love chipmunks?

My knees buckled again, and Damian all but carried me now. "Your punishment will be given tomorrow, Laura." He raised his voice. "As for the rest of you, you're all fucking idiots."

I looked up at him. "I'm an idiot?"

He closed his eyes, sighed, and opened them again. "No. Now let's get you home." He bent down and carried me bridal style.

My head lolled back. "I feel like a princess."

"You are a princess."

"But I'm a Knight. I do the saving, not you."

"Consider me a fellow knight. We're in a battle together. I'm doing what any knight would do and helping a fellow knight."

"Damian?"

"Yes?"

"I don't know what we're talking about."

His lips turned upward before abruptly shifting downward. "Rest, Knight. We'll be home soon."

The driver opened the door. Damian slid us into the car, and I closed my eyes as I sat on his lap, my head resting on his shoulder. When I opened them again, I was on my bed, and the room began to spin. Damian stood at the foot of the bed, an oversized shirt of his in one hand.

He followed me as I ran across the hall and heaved into the bathroom toilet. I took the shirt he offered, and he turned away as I changed out of my dress and into the shirt, which fell down to my thighs. It smelled like him. His scent eased the dizziness and caused tingles to spread across my flushed skin.

I blinked a few times until his face became clearer. "What's happening?"

"Laura gave you GHB." He helped me back to my room and onto my bed.

"What does that mean?"

"It means you'll be drowsy, dizzy, nauseous, sweaty, and tired. But you'll be okay." He hesitated as he tucked me into bed and pressed a kiss to my forehead. "You probably won't remember a thing."

I remembered that we weren't friends. "Why are you helping me?"

His jaw ticked, and he swung his gaze to the side for a moment. "Earlier, you said the only real people in this world are the ones in books. But you're real, too, and when I'm around you, you make me real. You make me alive." He took my hand. "It's the only time I don't feel like I'm just going through the motions."

A lopsided smile grew on my face. "I think I like you."

"I think I more than like you. If things weren't so complicated, I could see myself with you forever."

"Like when a princess and prince marry and live happily ever after?" I yawned and closed my eyes.

"Yes. Just like that."

"I'd need a ring." I snuggled deeper into the covers. "The princess always has a ring when she lives happily ever after."

Some shuffling interrupted my near slumber, and when a hand touched mine, I opened my eyes. The edges of my vision blurred, but I could see Damian crystal clear.

With the Sharpie in his hand, he drew a ring around my wedding ring finger. "And we lived happily ever after." He popped the cap closed, blew cold air onto my finger, then kissed the top of it. "Sweet dreams, Princess."

When I woke up, a thin black line drawn across my finger caught my eyes. I didn't know how it got there, but it felt important.

29

> Deception is one of the quickest ways to gain little things and lose big things.
>
> — THOMAS SOWELL

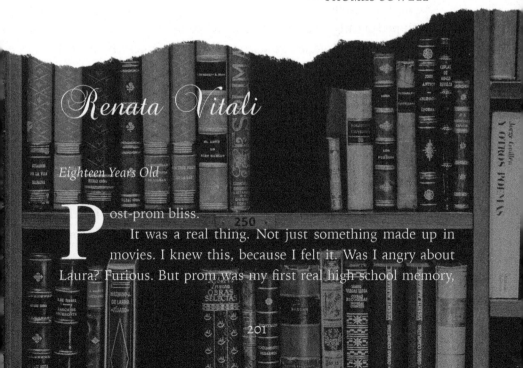

Renata Vitali

Eighteen Years Old

Post-prom bliss.

It was a real thing. Not just something made up in movies. I knew this, because I felt it. Was I angry about Laura? Furious. But prom was my first real high school memory, and I wanted to cherish the things I remembered about that night. Like dancing in the library with Damian and my first kiss.

We'd shifted that night. Our nightly library dates turned into heated make-out sessions until the sun started to rise. We'd spend lunch at school in the library, reading beside one another and stealing kisses, because not a damn teacher or librarian would dare say anything to me or Damian. And we drove his Range Rover instead of being chauffeured, so we could spend car rides to school alone together.

We didn't put labels on our relationship, but the school year had already ended; as an adult, I could leave without legal repercussions; and it occurred to me that, if Maman were to finally find a way to reach out to me, I didn't want to leave.

I grabbed my henna pen and touched up the line I had woken up with the day after prom. I'd been doing this regularly since, and I couldn't explain it. The henna didn't feel permanent enough, but the next step would be a tattoo.

How could I tattoo something I didn't remember to my body just because I felt an inexplicable connection to it?

Answer: I couldn't.

I slipped a ring over the henna to cover it up. Though it looked ridiculous, I added rings on all of my fingers because I didn't want to explain the henna.

Angelo cornered me when I left my bedroom to meet Damian in his room.

I eyed Damian's door, urging it to open, before flicking an unfazed glare at Angelo. "Yes?"

He rested a hip against the wall and leaned closer to me. "You and my son seem close lately."

"Hmm..." I examined my nails. "When I last dined with the Romano boss, he had more important things to deal with than who his son chose to spend time with." Snapping my gaze to him, I smiled. "When was the last time you were invited to dinner with the Romano boss?" I laughed. "... or any syndicate head?"

His beady eyes narrowed, and the way he towered over me could easily be construed as a threat. "Have you heard of my grandfather, Ludovico De Luca?"

Who hadn't?

Crazy ran in the De Luca family, and it started with a man who'd kill his own child. In a world where loyalty and honor knew no bounds, the De Luca family held no place. Damian's sanity was nothing short of a miracle.

I measured his unspoken threat. "I know infanticide gets you off, but if not for dignity, try to have some self-preservation in that witless skull of yours. When you run this family to the ground, the only person in this town capable of rebuilding it is in that room behind you."

"Don't test me, Vitali. Don't be stupid." He leaned into my face, and his rancid breath seeped into my nostrils. "You should fear me."

I laughed, harsh and in his face. "You're unworthy of my fear."

It was true. But when Angelo pushed past me, and my hand connected with Damian's doorknob, I froze as Angelo's crazed laughter sent chills through my body. The frequent threats. The back whipping. The unhinged behavior. I shook my head and cleared all the ugliness out of my mind.

Angelo wouldn't kill his own son if I stayed.

Would he?

> You can tell so much about a person by the way they leave you.

— REDVERSE BAILEY

Renata Vitali

Eighteen Years Old

"Knight?" He waited a beat. "Princess?" Another beat. "Ren?"

I lifted my head and lowered my hand. Damian had opened the door as I hovered outside his room. "Oh. Sorry. I spaced out."

"Are you okay?"

"Yeah." I moved around him and into his room.

"I heard my dad talking to you. What was that about?"

"Nothing." I forced a laugh out as I laid on his bed. "Has he always been a crazy rambler?"

Damian laid beside me and grabbed my hand. "For as long as I can remember."

I skimmed my eyes across the room for the first time in a while as he played with the rings on my right hand. We usually met in my room, and I hadn't seen his room since I'd stolen his phone on day one.

"What's that?" I tipped my chin to the left.

A facedown picture frame sat on the nightstand beside me. I took my hand from Damian's, leaned over, and stood it upright. Ludovico De Luca stared back at me.

Damian's shrug shifted the mattress. "My dad put it there a few weeks ago, after prom. Probably to fuck with my head. Who knows why he does what he does?" He laughed and leaned over me, dwarfing my body as he moved the picture frame facedown again. "I know we're related, but Ludo was one ugly moth-erfucker."

I rested my head on the pillow beneath me and bit my lip.

Damian still hovered above me, and he reached a thumb up to part my lips until my teeth no longer dug into them. "What's up?"

"Let's have sex!" I blurted.

Goodness. If I could die of humiliation...

Damian arched a brow. "I didn't know talking about Ludo was such an aphrodisiac."

I tugged at the bottom of his shirt, my brain working over-time to find the calmness I had once possessed. "Ludo? God, no. But your body is over mine, and you smell good, and you look like you do, and you talk like you do, and you act like you do, and I just want you."

Eloquent? No.

But my internal freak out took up 99.99% of my brain space as the picture taunted me. Ludo killed most of his family. I didn't know Angelo well, but everything I'd seen over the past eighteen or so months suggested he was capable of killing his son, too. I couldn't be responsible for that.

I needed to leave, but I was too weak to do so without stealing one last memory from Damian.

He buried his nose in my neck, and I felt his grin against my skin. "You know, I used to think you were like a robot. No emotions. Just articulate words delivered with no expression. Look what I've turned you into."

"Shush." I closed my eyes. I would miss his teasing. Back then, I hadn't thought he was even capable of something as light-hearted as teasing.

His mouth trailed up my neck to my jawline, where he placed soft kisses. I tilted my head and met his lips. We'd done this before. Him on top of me. Our lips meshed together. Our tongues meeting. It never got old.

My hands traveled all over his back. The ridges of his scars reminded me of Angelo's threat. I forced the fear down and focused on how much I needed Damian. His tongue stroked the roof of my mouth. I bucked my hips against him, searching for parts of him I needed.

My fingers raked his hair and tugged. He groaned into my mouth, and I reached between us and slid a hand underneath his Adidas joggers and Calvin Kleins. The smooth skin of his cock glided across my palm.

I wrapped my hands around him, and he thrust into them, his tongue mimicking the movement of his cock in my mouth. His hand reached between us, and his fingers pinched my nipples through my bra. Hard.

I cried out into his mouth, and he swallowed it. Tearing his shirt off, I used my legs to push his sweats and boxer briefs down. He leaned back, pulled my pants and underwear off in one quick movement, and leaned forward again to place an open-mouthed kiss between my legs.

I cried out when he slid two fingers inside me. I had touched myself before, but it had never compared to this. My throat closed up when I realized I'd never have this again. I'd leave, and we'd never meet again.

Damian curled his fingers until my wetness coated them. He pulled them out, tore my shirt in two, and snapped my bra in half, so my breasts were bare before him. I arched my back as his fingers entered me again.

He gathered my wetness, spread it around my nipple, and sucked it off. His tongue flicked the hardened bud before he bit down. My hips jerked forward and glided against his erection. I was so wet, it slipped past my lips and partially entered me.

His eyes closed, and he stilled. "Condom. Nightstand."

If this was our first and last time, I wanted to feel his skin against mine.

I shook my head. "Can we...?"

"Are you on the pill?"

"IUD. And I'm clean."

Truth was, I'd never had sex before. I'd broken my hymen falling off a horse in fifth grade. So, unless I told him I was a virgin, he'd never know. I kept my mouth shut. I didn't want to make leaving hurt more than it had to.

He slid into me, his movements slow and measured. I was so wet, he entered me with ease. Hooking my leg around him, I pushed him forward until he sank completely into me. I rested my arms beside my head as he moved in and out of me. He grabbed one of my hands, holding it as we made love.

I begged my brain to remember this moment forever. Begged it to remember the way his free hand explored my body. The way he pinched my nipples and rubbed slow circles around my clit. The way he dipped his thumb into my mouth after, so I could taste my own wetness. I had a feeling that when I was gone, these memories would be the only valuable things I took with me.

I came with my lips wrapped around his thumb. My moans nipped his skin. He pulled his thumb out of my mouth and kissed me as he flipped us, so I sat on top of him. Then he gripped my hips on both sides, and making love turned into fucking.

As he drove into me, faster than I'd thought possible, my walls clenched around him, and his climax followed. He came inside me, and I felt the pulses of his cock. His eyes closed for a moment, and he looked blissful.

I stared down at him and imprinted into my mind the way his face looked with all of his barriers down. Leaning forward, I pressed my forehead against his and closed my eyes, wondering where we would be if we had the world at the palm of our hands.

"Day, I lov—" I cut myself off.

I couldn't say it.

I couldn't do this.

Not when I knew I'd leave right after.

He cupped my face and waited until I opened my eyes and stared into his. "I'm in love with you."

"We're young."

"I know what I want."

"Me?"

A smile tipped his lips. "Yes, you."

I shook my head. "We can't."

"Why not?"

"I'm a Vitali."

He sat up, lifting me with him. "Pretty soon, my father will no longer have a throne, and there will be nothing in our way."

"Promise?"

"Always."

What are you doing? You have to leave him. Don't make him promise you a future and ditch him.

If Damian noticed my torment, he didn't let on. "I'm lucky you're here." He closed his eyes and relaxed, his guard so far down, I couldn't even see it. "I'm lucky they intervened."

"What?" I widened the gap between us. "Who intervened? I was sent here. By my father."

The look in his eyes said otherwise, while the look in mine threatened punishment if he wasn't honest. It took a minute, but he relented. "Your dad didn't send you here."

I shook my head. "Yes, he did. I was there when he told me I had to come here."

"Knight—"

"Tell me everything you know."

"I can't."

I had my opening. My out. I didn't want to take it, but I had to. Did it hurt that he kept this from me? Yes. Did it freak me out that someone else was pulling strings? A little. Was it a deal breaker? Not when I loved him.

I trusted him. He had to have reasons. But I could use this fight to leave him. To keep him safe from his dad, and maybe— just maybe—we'd find each other in the future. When Angelo no longer posed a threat.

My vision blurred, and my head spun as I succumbed to powerlessness. I swallowed my pain and frustration and forced out words I didn't want to say. "You're a liar."

"Princess, ple—"

"You're just like the rest of your family. Just like your dad."

His eyes flashed before he caressed my face. "You're mad. That's oka—"

I pushed him until he laid flat on his back with me on top. "And you betrayed me. Know this..." I raised my knee, so it pressed between his legs until he winced. My chest pushed down on his, and my lips brushed against his ear as I spoke.

I swallowed my uncertainty and forced the words out. Ones he couldn't misconstrue. Ones that wouldn't leave him with hope. "If ever I am gifted the opportunity to betray you, I'll take it. If life hands me the chance to destroy you, I will. Today. Tomorrow. Ten years from now. I will always want revenge. And you will never stop looking over your shoulder."

Then, I fled.

I left Devils Ridge.

I left my heart.

I left him.

And a part of me knew I was doing the wrong thing, but I did it anyway.

> An honest enemy is always better than a friend who lies. Pay less attention to what people say and more to what they do. Their actions show you the truth.

— UNKNOWN

Renata Vitali

The Present

Hope.
Noun.
Expectation and desire for something to happen.

It slammed into me the moment Damian's lips pressed

against mine. It shed the barriers I had built around me as I returned his kiss. It rekindled feelings I'd never fully repressed as we made our way to the bed. It convinced me that we had a future, if only we could get past the deception we were both responsible for.

I returned his kiss, my hands eager to explore him. I couldn't explain why he'd kissed me, but I was glad he'd taken the first step, because I couldn't bring myself to. It wasn't lost on me that he was always fighting for me.

Our movements were frantic. His hand tugged at my hair. Mine reached for his belt and yanked. When his fingers brushed against my slit, it struck me hard that we were really doing this. Excitement drove a path through my body.

How had I talked myself out of this the past month?

Why had I talked myself out of this the past month?

He felt so good on me, and I needed him in me. I reached into his pants and grabbed his thick erection. I stroked it twice, the smooth skin bliss against my palm.

He reached into my underwear, gathered my wetness, and pushed it back into me as he slid three fingers into me and curled them. "That tattoo on your finger means you're mine. It means you've always been mine."

I didn't understand what the tattoo had to do with anything, but fear over the last time my heart broke resisted his words. "It's just sex. We're fucking as much as we can this weekend to get each other out of our systems."

He laughed. "Keep telling yourself that." His teeth bit down on my neck, eliciting a groan from me. "Once I'm in you, you won't want me to leave."

His pants were halfway down his legs when my alarm rang out. I groaned against Damian's lips and apologized.

He watched me turn it off. "What's the alarm for?"

I cocked a brow. "The roundtable meeting in a couple

hours..." His features darkened, and my lips parted on a heavy breath. "Oh."

He hadn't been invited. I'd thought something had changed last month when he initiated the most peaceful roundtable discussion in the history of the syndicates. I guessed not.

"I have to go."

I nodded. "Of course." I considered what my dad would do if he found out he'd been excluded from an important meeting. "Don't spill too much blood."

Despite the gravity in his eyes, he allowed himself a small smile. "This isn't over."

"It's just sex," I reminded him, though the way my body arched toward him spoke volumes.

"It's more than that." I didn't answer, so he held out his hand. "Phone? Unless you're just going to switch phones and change your number again." He arched a brow and dared me to argue.

"I didn't switch phones. I just changed the number."

"So, you had my number this whole time?"

He left the rest of his question unspoken, because we both knew the answer. Not only had I changed my number, but I'd also had his and chosen not to call or text him. I'd spent so much time running from us that I'd become afraid of us. I couldn't tell him this, because it was bullshit emotions that could be picked apart with ease. It was mortifying how I could be fearless in every way but the heart.

I wanted to ease the hurt Damian felt, like he had when he'd distracted me with naughty texts at Vince's life celebration dinner. Instead, I pulled out my phone and unlocked it as he watched.

Renata: Roundtable discussion. Same location. Noon...
And now you have my number. You're welcome.

His phone buzzed, and he read his text. My eyes dared him to ask for more. Instead, he nodded his head and said, "This isn't over, Renata."

That was the problem.

I didn't want it to be.

Damiano De Luca

The De Luca family had been fractured for so long that, when I had taken over, I only trusted Cristian to become my *consiglieri*. Time passed, life happened, responsibilities became overwhelming, and I knew I needed to appoint an underboss if I wanted to get shit done.

I did the only thing I could think of. I turned to my advisor, and now he was both my *consiglieri* and my underboss. The only all-in-one *consiglieri*/underboss of his kind. That little fact gave him an ego the size of a Texas debutante's teased hair. Coupled with our lifelong friendship, his ego meant he never held back with me.

Like now.

"You went to see her." He popped an ice cube in his mouth, dipping his fingers into his Dalmore 62 like a fucking Neanderthal. "First thing you did in the city, too." He shook his head. "Not a good look, man."

I couldn't stomach thinking of Ren. She looked tired. Like she hadn't slept at all in the past month. Maybe that was my fault. Maybe we weren't good for one another. I cut the thought off before I could consider stopping my pursuits. When I was with Ren, everything felt better and more real than anything I'd ever touched. If I lost that again, that bereft feeling would return and sicken me.

I leveled Cris with a cut-that-shit-out stare as I took up more space on the hotel couch than I needed. "That's not why I called you to my suite."

He must have read the look on my face, because he replaced his carefree demeanor with a hard expression. "What happened?"

"They moved up the date for the roundtable discussion."

He shifted in the lounger next to me. "Okay... what's the—" He swore. "Oh. They didn't tell you, and you found out through your girl. Motherfuckers! What are you going to do?"

I raised a brow. "That's why you're here." I made a go-ahead gesture. "Advise me, *consiglieri.*"

"First things first." He leaned forward, rested his elbows on his knees, and rubbed his hands together. "Drop that peaceful, kumbaya bullshit. It's doing none of us any favors." I disagreed but let him continue. "We need more respect, to renegotiate our borders, and some cross-territory distribution benefits. This is our chance to gain at least one of these things. Giving up the chance for Vincent Romano, someone you barely even knew, is doing the syndicate no favors."

"I'll take your words under advisement."

"It's what everyone wants."

"Duly noted."

"You're not gonna do anything I asked, are you?"

I sighed and ran a hand across my face. Cris was right. When I'd passed on negotiations, I hadn't been thinking about the De Luca syndicate. I'd been thinking of Ren. But I had responsibilities here, and they were, first and foremost, the De Luca family.

I shot Cris a look. "I'll negotiate for a cross-territory distribution route, and if I can, a border renegotiation."

"Thank fuck."

I rolled my eyes. "I regret promoting you on a daily basis."

"Good thing I'm your only friend." He downed the rest of his drink like it was Two Buck Chuck and not from a six-figure bottle. "And as your friend, I feel compelled to tell you that this thing you have with the Vitali girl isn't good for anyone. If you end up together, you put us higher on the radar of the Vitali family, which isn't actually a good thing. If you separate, especially if it's an ugly separation, you put us higher on the radar of the Vitali family, in a really bad way. Either way, we're on the shit side of the Vitali family's radar. Not good for the syndicate, Damian. Think of all you've already sacrificed."

The worst part was how right he was.

"I didn't ask for your opinion."

He held both hands up. "Fine. Just think of the syndicate. It's literally your only job."

"I'll ignore the tone because you're right. You're my only friend." I cut off his laugh, the bastard. "I need to be the first for negotiations, and—"

"Your girl can do that for you," he finished.

I pulled out my phone and shot a text to her.

Damian: I need a favor.

Three dots popped on the screen and stayed there for a solid five minutes before my phone buzzed.

Renata: Sure.

Damian: I need to go first in the negotiations today.

Renata: Oh, is that all?

Damian: Is that sarcasm?

Renata: …

Damian: That's not all.

Renata: What else?

Damian: I need you to admit that we're happening. When the meeting's done, we're going to talk. We'll lay everything out. No more lies. No more miscommunication. No more fear.

Renata: I'm not scared.

Damian: That's what you got from that?

She didn't respond, and I could picture her muttering what I used to hear her say to herself when she thought she was alone, "Don't be weak. You're a Vitali. Vitalis don't feel fear." I'd never learned what she was so afraid of. Squeezing the truth out of Ren was like trying to squeeze the last of the shampoo out of the bottle. It was damned near impossible, and I'd be lucky to get a drop.

"What are you afraid of?"

My question must have taken Cris by surprise, because he was more flustered than I'd seen him in a while. I'd expected a half-assed answer, but instead, he stared me dead in the eye and said, "I'm afraid that something will happen to the De Luca family, and the whole entire town of Devils Ridge and all the other families and cities that depend on De Luca income will get hurt. I don't need to tell you that these are real lives at stake. Men, women, and children whose lives depend on the decisions we make each day."

His fears mirrored mine. I knew I'd asked for the De Luca syndicate, but the responsibilities could be crippling. The only reason I'd taken the job was because Angelo hadn't deserved it and no one else could do it. I wanted the De Luca name to thrive, so everyone who depended on it could thrive. Truly.

Cris held nothing back as he continued. "This meeting can do a lot for our syndicate. You're my best friend, which is the only reason I'm telling you this. I'm the only person who can say this without repercussions, and I don't take that lightly. When you go into the meeting in an hour, we need you to have your head on straight. No distractions. You know how many lives depend on you. You've never been like this with any other woman."

He was right.

Fuck, he was so right.

He shook his head. "I don't know what's so different about this girl that always gets you like this."

The difference was, I didn't love other women.

I loved Renata Vitali.

32

> Reality is easy. It's the deception that's the hard work.

> — LAURYN HILL

Renata Vitali

I didn't know how Damian had spent the last two hours, but he was here now, and no one but me seemed happy about it. Actually, I wasn't sure I was even happy about it. There was a word for people like me.

Commitment-phobe.

Every relationship I'd ever been around had ended in failure.

Papà always cheated on Maman. Maman still loved a dead man she'd never really had a real relationship with. Rumors floated around about suspicious circumstances after Damian's mom's death. (I still had no clue how he could even consider a relationship given the fact that so many thought his dad had killed his mom.) My relationship with Damian ended on my lie, and I'd blamed it on *his* lie.

Relationships didn't work, and I was comfortable admitting that. After ten years of trying to get over Damian, I knew getting back into a relationship with him wouldn't end well. Didn't mean I couldn't still care for him or enjoy what he could do for me physically.

I'd just gotten off the phone with Maman, who reminded me yet again to drop my walls, only this time, I found myself actually considering it despite my commitment phobia. The heavy glossed walnut of the long table rubbed at my elbows as I waited for people to get over Damian being here.

When things settled, I cleared my throat, opened the book, and began the proceedings. "We reconvene here today for a second round of peace negotiations in respect for Vincent Romano's death. If any syndicate opposes, you may do so now."

I started again after a long bit of silence. "The second round-table proceeding exists as an opportunity for renegotiations and a reminder to respect Vincent Romano in his passing. In a moment, I will open up the discussion, starting with the... De Luca family."

A moment of outrage spread across the table. I cleared my throat and cut a glare across to every leader in the room. My face said, "bite me," and theirs said, "I'd love to." Still, I stared them down, wondering how I couldn't wrangle up an ounce of fear when taking on some of the most powerful men in this country but felt so much anxiety at the idea of having a physical relationship with Damian, which I knew could lead to more.

The transcriber had stilled, along with the rest of the room. They were outraged by the favoritism, and they were right to be. But that didn't mean I'd take their shit.

I turned to Damian, and he held nothing back in his gaze. "What would the De Luca family like to request?"

He stared at me—really stared at me. A look of indecision and regret crossed his hardened face before it relaxed, and he said, "The De Luca family declines to put forth an agenda in respect for Vincent Romano's passing."

Everyone here would have to pass on negotiations or risk being outclassed by the De Luca syndicate. Marco Camerino's pissed off expression didn't lessen. Rafaello Rossi looked uneasy. The Romano family looked pleased, because historically, the bereaved syndicate always came out on the losing end, and at least they'd avoid that now. Ranieri Andretti seemed indifferent, but he held the bulk of the guilt for Vince's death in the first place. So, his feelings here were last on my list of priorities.

And Damian?

He'd given up his leverage again, even though we both knew his syndicate needed these negotiations.

He kept choosing me, and it was time I started choosing him.

The room cleared until only Damian and I remained. He closed the door when everyone left.

"What's that look you're giving me?"

I shook my head. "I don't know whether to be in awe of you or utterly appalled. Your syndicate needs you to represent them. You can't keep putting them second."

"I can't help it."

"I know."

And I did. He put me first. Always had.

"Do you, Ren?" He took a step closer to where I stood, my bottom resting partially on the table. "Because I keep making these gestures, and you keep pushing me away, but we both know you want me. Don't even deny it." I didn't dare. "What do I have to do to get through to you?"

I opened my mouth to speak, but the fear seized me. "I'm supposed to be strong, but whenever I think of being with you again, I freeze, and this irrational fear takes over. It makes no sense. You didn't break my heart. I broke my own heart by leaving you. I don't know why I'm like this. What the hell is wrong with me? Why can't I ever make this work?"

He had to understand me, had to understand the feelings I couldn't articulate. We were both made of the same components. Broken hearts. Broken childhoods. Broken parents who broke us, too. If anyone in this world could understand me, it would be him.

"You're scared. I get that. But if you can take a leap for anyone, let it be me."

Of course, he was right. I remembered how it felt a month ago to be in the ballroom, listening to people tell stories of Vincent, knowing how much I'd missed out on. I didn't want to miss out on Damian anymore.

I didn't answer for a bit. "Does it have to be a leap?"

He held back a smile, but I could see it in his eyes. "It can be a hop."

"I'm good at hopping."

> **❝** Skeptics are never deceived.

— PROVERB

Damiano De Luca

Dad called halfway through dinner. I sat at the table with the rest of the syndicate leaders. Ren was on the other side of Asher's restaurant, because she'd already showed favoritism in the meeting this morning and didn't want to overplay her hand at dinner.

When Dad called, I answered the phone and dipped into the hallway that led to the bathroom.

Dad didn't even wait for me to greet him before he spoke.

"You're representing the De Luca name, and you're fucking up. I told you that you're no good for this. You're a fucking embarrassment."

"What do you want, old man?" I didn't have time for this.

"Look, money's tight—"

I barked out a laugh. "I'm hanging up now."

"Wait! Hear me out."

I did, because what he'd been reduced to amused me. He'd given me scars on my back from his belt, and I'd taken away the empire that gave him the power to do that to me. It felt nice to rub it in his face a bit.

He heaved out words as quickly as he could, clearly afraid I'd hang up on him. "You wired me half of what I usually get this month."

"Your allowance has been reduced and redistributed to people who deserve it more. The Humane Society. ASPCA. The Human Rights Campaign, ACLU, Southern Poverty Law Center, and about a dozen women's health clinics."

To be clear, just about everyone on this planet deserved money more than my dad did, but I liked to give to causes he hated in particular. Probably the one joy I never denied myself.

"Bull fucking shit! That's my money! You've already got me in a retirement home with people whose greatest life accomplishments are their fucking grandchildren. I'm Angelo De Luca!"

He was such a damned headache. That was what he was. Every once in a while, he'd run his money dry, and I'd get a belligerent phone call, all of which ended the same—me hanging up on him.

"Is there an actual point to this phone call or is it merely to waste my time?"

"That girl of yours. Vitali." His words slurred every now and then, his fake dentures probably slipping out a bit in his drunken rambling. "You'll lose the syndicate if you choose her, and there goes my allowance. Don't screw up."

The fact that he knew Renata was here unnerved me. I knew he received intel from older soldiers, and I didn't go after them because they were related to people who served me well, but it still bugged me how informed he was.

My fingers tightened on my phone. "This is none of your business."

"It's my business when you run my money."

"I don't run your money. I run the De Luca syndicate's money, which is no longer yours."

"Drop the Vitali girl. She's dead weight."

"No."

"How does she have you so pussy whipped?"

"It's called love. You should try it sometime, Angelo. Maybe it'll make you less of an asshole."

His crazed laughter met my ear. I knew it had been a while since I'd heard it, because it actually chilled me.

"Love." He laughed again. "Love!" His Texas accent deepened as his laughter unhinged him. "Ain't no such thing as love! Love is me killing your Mamma before she could kill me." He snorted again. "Love. There ain't no such thing."

229

Renata Vitali

I sat through dinner that evening, relatively unscathed. The two Camerino soldiers across from me discussed the trip to Italy they'd taken, while the woman beside me—I think her name was Marquessa—scoffed.

She turned to me. "Well, I had dinner with the pope last time I visited the Mediterranean."

I nodded and smiled politely, keeping my irritation to myself. "That's nice."

"It was." She sighed and patted her updo. If I had to guess, I'd say she was in her forties, but talented plastic surgery had her looking thirty. "I had to cut the meeting short to meet with the Italian president. He's a busy man, you see, but he'll always make time for me."

I wondered if she knew that he was my godfather. I kept that to myself as I nodded. "How great of him."

One of the Camerino soldiers' wife smiled at me. "You're from Italy, right?"

"Yes, though it's been a while since I've been back to my home country."

"I don't even hear an accent!"

"I went to boarding school in the States and dropped it pretty quickly."

Marquessa huffed. "Boarding school in the States? I sent my children to England, where they could be properly educated. You can't trust teachers in America these days. None of them know how to do their jobs properly."

I clenched my fists beneath the table, wondering if Marquessa would have even bitten her tongue if she knew I was a public-school teacher. In the syndicate hierarchy, Marquessa wasn't anyone. She was just the highest-ranking member at this table—because I was technically out of the mafia—and on a power trip.

The Camerino wife frowned. "My high school teacher helped me with my college applications, sent in my letter of rec, and helped me fundraise to pay for the applications. I ended up at Degory and graduated summa cum laude."

Degory rivaled the East Coast Ivy League schools, and still, Marquessa scoffed. "I went to Oxford. My children did, too. On their own merit, mind you. There's no nepotistic legacy in England like there is in America."

Did this woman realize she was American?

I was two spoonfuls into my lobster when Marquessa leaned forward, patted my hand, and asked, "Why are you here again, dear?"

I looked around to see if anyone had heard her. A few heads turned our way, but they didn't say anything. I'd opted for a table further away from the main table, where all the syndicate leaders sat. I didn't recognize anyone here.

A few soldiers and that wife of a Camerino *caporegime*, maybe. Chances were, they knew I was a Vitali, but the gravity of the connection didn't register because I'd been out of this world for a decade. Judging from her earlier words, the *caporegime*'s wife knew for certain.

My eyes searched for Damian's, but he'd left the main table, where I should have been. We needed a public outing apart to assuage valid concerns of favoritism, and it would have dampened the De Luca name if it were Damian who sat on the outskirts. Better me than him.

Damian and I had done our push and pull. I gave him first pick at the roundtable. He gave up negotiations in Vince's name, knowing how much Vince meant to me. I gave him the seat at the main dining table. I had no doubt he'd do something for me soon.

I was there for him.

He was there for me.

Tale as old as time.

"How did you get into this party?" She studied me. "Vincent Romano's death has been the hottest ticket around town. Everyone who's anyone has been trying to join the proceedings. How are you here?"

I turned to her. Disbelief suffused me, but I didn't let it show. "Pardon me?"

She opened her mouth to retort, and I could predict a sophomoric, stick-up-her-ass response, but her eyes widened as she caught something to the side. "Oh, my."

Damian approached us, and he looked angry. I doubted the anger was directed at me, but it was there, and it roared. I'd never seen him like this. The woman beside me shifted in her seat. Though she'd bragged all night, she looked flustered in the presence of a syndicate boss. Despite her prejudices against the De Luca name, which she'd been trashing all night, she reacted to him in ways I hated but couldn't blame her for. After all, Damian looked in a league of his own.

He didn't stare at anyone but me when he reached my table. "Want to leave?"

Something had clearly happened, because this was the opposite of drawing attention away from our relationship. My eyes skimmed the room. People at neighboring tables stared at us. In the center of the room, Bastian looked in our direction, but I couldn't quite see from here to know for certain that his eyes were on us.

Something had happened, and Damian was looking at me to be there for him. I studied him. His hair stuck up a bit, like he'd run his hands through it a few times. His eyes were dark, his cheekbones and jaw all sharp and angry lines. In his hands, he clutched his phone in a tight grip. His knuckles became a little white at the tips.

I knew that, if I left with him like this, I wouldn't be "hopping." I'd be leaping.

But he needed me.

"What do you have in mind?"

"Depends. Are we hopping or leaping?"

I swallowed hard and took in his angry, shaking hands and the way my instincts wanted to do anything and everything to help him. "Leaping."

He was so focused on me—and perhaps erasing his pain—that I didn't think he even registered the people around us as he spoke, his words blunt and unapologetic. "We're going to the library, and I'm going to fuck you against a bookshelf until all the books have fallen to the floor and the only thing standing upright is us. I'm warning you now, before you choose to leave with me, that the sex will be angry, and I won't stop until I've fucked the ten years we spent apart out of our systems."

Marquessa gasped. Two Camerino soldiers shared insecure looks, ones that questioned their masculinity. To be fair, Damian didn't need dirty talk and crass words to be a filthy alpha male. He had it in his eyes. That undress-me stare, which always made me feel like he was inside me, even when we stood across the room from one another.

Except now, he was here, giving me an out in the filthiest way, and I didn't want to take it. I wanted to leap, fall, crash into him. I wanted to take his pain, bottle it up, and bury it somewhere it couldn't hurt him anymore. I wanted him to lose himself in me.

I stood, turned to my table mates, pasted a fake smile on my face, and focused on Marquessa in particular. "It was lovely dining with you all tonight, but my American public-school teacher, non-Oxford attending ass is about to get fucked a dozen different ways." I winked at Marquessa. "Next time you're in Italy, feel free to reach out to my family."

She tilted her chin up, but her eyes darted to the possessive way Damian wrapped a hand around my waist. "And who are they?"

"The Vitali."

I caught a hint of her widened eyes before I turned and left with Damian. A few minutes later, we sat in the back of his town car on our way to the library. The divider gave us privacy as his palm rested on my upper thigh.

He turned to me. "That's the first time I've heard you say your last name with pride."

"Don't get used to it."

His eyes dropped to the tattoo on my finger, and he nodded. "I didn't plan on it."

34

> Don't lie, because the same people who believe
> your lies are also the ones who believe in you.

— UNKNOWN

Renata Vitali

I sat at the edge of the night table in my little nook room. People read and studied elsewhere in the library, but it was quiet in here. Damian had promised me angry sex, and if he delivered, they'd hear. I couldn't bring myself to care.

Damian had brought up a bottle of whiskey with us, but he hadn't opened it. He sat on my bed, the bottle resting beside him. To the world, Damian De Luca was educated, filthy rich, and practically owned an entire town.

He controlled the largest continental state in the wealthiest country in the world. While much of that consisted of less-than-legal dealings, his generations old, above board ventures rivaled the biggest old money tycoons in this country. A large portion of De Luca territory included impressive oil lands, and I knew Damian had money and power.

While I saw that power in him, I also saw the parts of him he never let anyone else see. The fractured parts of his broken child-hood. Living with him, I'd heard his father beat him with belts, emotionally abuse him, and degrade him over and over again. He'd taken the abuse, his eyes calculated, waiting for a moment to strike. So, I wasn't surprised to hear that he dethroned his father after I left.

But I knew others had been taken by surprise. Papà had called me, demanding an explanation for the unexpected coup. He couldn't understand Damian, and I couldn't explain what others refused to see.

Damian's patience and strength earned him his throne, but they also pushed aside his equilibrium. Maybe this was the turning point. Maybe he finally let himself break, and I had the privilege of being here to pick up the pieces. Back then, I'd done nothing, but I wouldn't make that mistake again.

I waited for him to say something. He slid off his suit jacket, loosened his tie, and unbuttoned a few buttons of his shirt. His cufflinks came off next. He tossed them to the side and took his time rolling up his sleeves.

Every move he made felt deliberate, and I knew he didn't intend for them to turn me on, but they did. My nipples pebbled in anticipation. He was hurting, I was turned on, and our rela-tionship was too messed up for me to process.

"Do you believe in love?" The hoarseness of his voice ripped through the air.

"Damian—"

"I don't mean us. I mean in general." His eyes darkened as I hesitated, thinking of all the relationships I'd been privy to. "So, that's a no."

"No, I believe in love. I've just never seen it in real life."

Besides ours, which was a fucked-up kind of love if there ever was one.

He read between the lines. "Including ours."

My hands clutched the nightstand I sat on. "I didn't say that."

He gripped his shirt at the row of buttons and yanked, impatiently ripping his shirt apart and the buttons with it. "My mom loved my dad. Actual love. Not the kind you fake or think you have, but the kind you know with every fiber of your being exists." He strode toward me and stepped between my legs. "I never understood it, but she trusted him with her heart. Do you want to know what he did with it?" He didn't wait for me to answer. "He trampled on it, and then he killed her. My dad killed my mom."

I shook my head. I'd heard rumors, but they were just rumors. I remembered the phone he'd had clutched in his hands when he approached me at dinner earlier. "Were you on the phone with your dad earlier? Did he tell you this?"

"He said he killed her before she could kill him. Want to know why?"

I shook my head. I really didn't, but I'd listen because he needed me to. "Why?"

"Because there's no such thing as love."

"You don't mean that."

He'd always been the one of us who believed in love, giving me time to overcome my fear while he helped me. His words struck anxiety into me, and I felt the shift in my body as I realized that I didn't have as long as I needed to get my shit together. Things happened. Life changed. If I wanted Damian (and I did), I had to make a move.

His voice was rough and raw. "I told him I love you,"—my hands shook at his revelation—"and he told me there's no such thing as love."

"Your dad is a psychopath and a liar." I shook my head and took the biggest leap I'd ever taken. "I love you, Damian. Love exists, and I know this because I love you."

I wanted to bring him to me. To hold him. To be the one who renewed his faith in love. Instead, I waited for him to make a move. He didn't respond to my declaration, and while that cut deep, I persisted.

"Have you ever seen a wolf?" I placed a hand on his chest and leaned into him. "The wolf and the cougar are on the top of the food chain. Whereas the cougar is solitary, the wolf operates in a pack. He is faster, smarter, more ferocious."

His eyes were hooded, but they focused on me, urging me to continue.

I explored his body with my hands and hooked my legs around him. "The cougar will lose a battle against a wolf, and he will die alone. But the wolf finds his pack. Makes them better. And when he finds his mate, he mates for life, defending her viciously. Loyally. Forever. Until death do them part."

I used my legs to push him toward me, until his body pressed entirely against mine. "Angelo De Luca may be the cougar, but you are the wolf, Damian. Angelo will die alone, and you will thrive, surrounded by people who are loyal to you and someone who loves you."

His eyes shuttered before they opened and locked on mine. His hand cupped my face, but the touch was anything but gentle. "Last chance to leave, Princess."

"I'm staying." I turned my face, pressed a kiss to the center of his palm, and laughed gently onto his skin. "And I've told you already, Damian. I'm the knight."

"You're right. Tonight, I won't treat you like a princess, but I won't treat you like you're the knight either." His free hand traced a path from my outer thigh to my waist, and he felt dangerous in a way I craved. "I'm giving you a chance to leave." His expression—dark and anguished—should have been enough to make me run the opposite way.

But I needed to at least try to ease some of his pain.

"I don't want to leave." My voice firmed, and I tried again with more confidence. "I'm staying."

We'd finally begun to rip the veil away, and I felt everything falling apart in the best of ways. I was done with hiding things from him. I was done fearing the commitment. Angelo De Luca was a goddamned liar, and my dad was no better. Damian and I weren't our parents. We were better, and we'd make this work because we actually loved each other. It had taken ten years, but it was happening, and I couldn't be happier.

Damian's expression darkened, and his voice hardened. "Take off your dress."

I did.

I bared myself to him—body, heart, and all.

35

> You may be deceived if you trust too much, but you will live in torment if you don't trust enough.

— FRANK CANE

Renata Vitali

He took a step back and admired my naked body. My breasts moved as I breathed, and I wore no panties as I sat on the table before him. My nipples were so hard, it was almost painful. He stared at me, and I hoped being near me drove the bad away.

He didn't make a move, so I goaded him. "I want you to do whatever you want to me."

"Careful what you wish for."

I ignored his warning. "I want you to hold nothing back."

Still, he held himself back.

I lowered my voice until it sounded husky, and my eyes begged him to lose himself in me. "You promised me angry sex. You said you'll fuck me against the shelves until the books scatter to the floor, and the only thing left standing is us."

Like a flipped switched in him, he spoke with a hardened voice. "Spread your legs."

I parted them, feeling vulnerable and bare while his shirt hung open on his frame, and he still wore a pair of slacks.

"Every time I see you, I can't believe how stunning you are. You have no idea how hard it was to know you were out there, and I couldn't wake up next to you every morning."

I closed my eyes, too cowardly to face him. "I'm sorry."

"If we do this, you're mine forever. There's no going back." His eyes dipped to my hand. "Do you know what that tattoo means?"

I gave a nervous laugh. "Of course. I wouldn't tattoo something on my body that means nothing to me."

Truth was, it did mean something to me. I just wasn't sure why. I'd woken up one night with a ring drawn around my wedding finger in Sharpie; traced it regularly with a henna pen; and when that wasn't permanent enough, tattooed the exact line one drunken night in a shoddy tattoo parlor in the city.

His eyes dipped to my pussy, which laid bare before him. "Come here."

I slid off the table and approached him. He circled me until he stood behind me, reached around my body, and cupped one of my breasts in his palm. It spilled out of his hand, and we both looked down at where he touched me.

He pinched my nipple. "I've wanted to slide my cock between your tits for the past few weeks."

I leaned my head back on his shoulder. "I touched myself while picturing you coming on my face last night."

He leaned forward and bit down on my shoulder. "Dirty, dirty girl," he praised. His other hand pressed against my hip, and he slid it lower until he slipped past my lips and brushed against my clit. "This won't be what you're used to from me."

Damian's dad had just admitted that he'd killed Damian's mom. I'd be concerned if Damian acted normally. This was our push and pull. I hurt; he healed. He hurt; I healed. Breaking that cycle would be breaking us.

"I don't need normal." I reached behind me to touch him, but he swatted my hand away. I bit my lip and groaned. "Use me, Damian. Bite me. Tease me. Fuck me. Do whatever you need."

Just, please, be okay.

He tilted his head. "Are you on the pill?"

"IUD. I'm clean also."

His lips curved up, and his tone became mocking. "Are condoms too good for the princess?"

I ignored his taunts. "If we're both clean, and I'm on birth control—"

Damian's laughter cut me off. "Who knew you'd be so needy, begging me to take you bare?"

I rolled my eyes, though he couldn't see them. "Just fuck me already."

His breaths came out ragged and rough, and a thrill shot through me at being able to take his mind off his parents. But then his hand connected with my bare ass, and I shouted out. It hadn't hurt, but it had surprised me. Not being able to see Damian was driving me crazy.

I stilled as he lowered himself to his knees. Both of his palms gripped my ass cheeks, and he bit down on one of them. Hard. I screamed out, loud enough for people in nearby rooms to hear.

He spoke against my skin. "Both hands on the bookshelf."

I placed both hands on the nearest bookshelf. I could feel his breath on my pussy as it parted for him, my ass in the air as I leaned forward. He licked my slit from behind, his tongue going straight for my clit.

My heart beat out of control as he buried his face in my skin. I'd never been eaten out from behind before, and it was far more intimate than I was used to. His tongue stroked my outer lips. His teeth grazed the skin, and he sucked my right lip into his mouth until my moans drowned the room. He was so hungry for me, I could have mistaken him for a starved savage, prepared to eat me. I wasn't sure I wanted to come out of this alive.

"Damian," I groaned out his name. Barely.

"By the end of the night, you'll scream my name so loud, you'll lose your voice." His lips brushed my clit as he spoke filthy promises against my pussy.

He slid three fingers inside me, not even bothering to check if I was wet enough. But I was, and when his fingers parted my lips, my wetness dripped down my pussy. He licked it up as he thrust his fingers in and out. I moaned as he wrapped his lips around my clit and pressed opened mouthed kisses to it.

"Tell me how you want it." His demand scorched my skin.

"Faster." I panted at the feel of him. "Curl your fingers and press them against my g-spot."

"Beg for it."

I hesitated.

"Beg." His tone left no room for argument, and the last thing I wanted was for him to stop.

"Please, Damian."

"Beg harder."

"Please. Please. Please," I chanted. I rode his fingers, pushing my pussy against him until I was surprised he could even breathe. "Faster."

He maintained the same pace, lazy strokes along my slit. "What do you want?"

"Faster!" My frustration built as he refused to give me what I needed. Instead, he slowed, and I groaned. "What the fuck?" I tried to take matters into my own hands, pushing down until I rode his fingers as best as I could.

His dark, amused laughter sent chills along my body, and then he pulled his fingers out of me, stood, and slammed his erection into me. I screamed out in surprise as his hard thrusts pushed my body forward into the bookshelf. My voice echoed along the walls, and I hoped the library was nearly empty by now, because I was being loud with a capital L.

My grip on the shelf tightened as he picked up his already furious pace. His hands remained planted on each side of my hips to steady me, and he fucked me hard and fast. With each thrust, more books fell off the shelf and onto the floor. I couldn't bring myself to care. A knock on the door sounded, but we ignored it, my little pants filling the air.

A second later, a feminine voice traveled through the wooden door. "Excuse me? Are you alright in there?"

"Fine!" I managed to shout as Damian yelled out, "Fuck off," followed by a guttural growl.

I'd never seen him so unfettered. It only turned me on more. I did this. I had him unhinged. I drove away the pain and suffering his dad had caused. I'd always seen the side of Damian that others hadn't had the privilege of viewing, but even I hadn't seen how deep his demons went.

They hid behind a reserved façade, and an educated vocabulary, and bespoke suits, and patience. And now that the lid had been pulled off, Damian didn't hold back as he chased them away with each thrust.

I assumed the person outside the door had left, because we weren't interrupted again.

Damian's pace didn't relent, but he suddenly spoke out loud, "I'm not him."

I wasn't even sure if his words were meant for me, but I

replied, "No, you're not. You're better." He picked up his speed, and I groaned. "Oh, God. Damian!"

He grabbed one of my legs and led it to the bottom shelf. I lifted it onto the shelf, following his instructions without a word. With my leg raised, he slid deeper inside me, pressing harder against my G-spot. I was so close to coming, and I barely held on as it was. I didn't want this to end.

He bit my shoulder, leaving teeth marks. "We won't be them."

I shook my head as much as I could with his relentless pace. "We won't."

Damian had always internalized his pain, and I'd always figured he'd find his breaking point. I just didn't know he'd be balls deep inside me when it happened. But I was happy to help him, every part of me excited that he had chosen me to chase his demons away.

"Damian!" I needed him to slow down. If he kept this up, he'd make me come, and it'd be over. "Too fast. Too much. I can't take it."

"Yes, you can." He reached around me and rubbed my clit with his fingers, bringing me over the edge. "And fuck, you look so fucking beautiful taking my cock." He pressed dozens of little kisses along my neck, the only soft part about the way he pounded in and out of me.

I came on him hard, and he didn't stop his relentless fucking, his fingers merciless in teasing my clit. He leaned against my back and whispered filthy words in my ear as my walls spasmed around his erection.

I've never slid into a pussy so tight.

I can feel your walls clamping around me, like you don't want my cock to leave.

Come all over my cock, baby.

Your pussy is such a needy little cunt, Princess.

And then, he hit me with the words, his voice haunted, "Tell me you love me again."

My eyes glazed over, the pleasure too much. "I do." I tried to turn to look him in the eyes as I told him, but his fast pace had me clenching my eyelids shut and holding the shelf as tightly as I could. So, I settled for chanting the words, feeling freer with each iteration. "I love you, Damian. I love you, I love you, I love you."

I was spent when he slid out of me, barely able to hold myself up without the help of the bookshelf I clutched and his arm around my waist. I dropped to the floor, turned, and leaned against the bookshelf with my legs tucked under me.

I stared at his erection with hooded eyes. "You haven't come." He didn't answer, but I persisted. "Let me help you come."

His eyes flicked over me, taking time to stare at my heaving breasts. "I'm a mess right now. I shouldn't have fucked you that hard."

"I liked it." My voice came out spent and husky. "You should have fucked me harder." My eyes traced his long erection, cataloging each vein and the perfect ridge of its head. I licked my lips. "Let me make you come."

Indecision warred across his face until he walked forward, and I kneeled in anticipation. "I'm not ready to be gentle," he warned.

I nodded. "I like rough."

And I did. This rough, nothing-held-back, do-as-we-pleased sex felt liberating. He didn't judge me for loving it, and I didn't judge him for needing it. If anything, I loved that he knew I could take it.

"Open." He reached out, and his thumb pushed my chin down until my lips parted. "Wider."

I opened wider as he leaned forward, stuck his fingers inside me, gathered my wetness, then spread it across his erection. He stroked his erection a few times before guiding it into my mouth.

I leaned forward and rubbed my nipples on his thighs as my tongue slid across his cock, tasting myself. I tasted a little sweet, almost like nothing.

"Can you taste your cum? Can you taste how much I turn you on?"

"Yes," I tried to say around his erection, but it came out muffled, so I nodded my head instead.

"Good. Don't fucking forget that, because I hate when you make me chase what's already mine, Renata. And make no mistake, you're mine." He stepped back, releasing himself from my mouth. "On the bed. On your back."

I scurried to the bed and laid down. He grabbed my legs and slid me lower until my face was near the middle of the bed. My heart charged as he climbed up my body, his hard length in my face and his fists holding his body up above me.

"Open your mouth."

Holy crap.

I did as he asked, my tongue dying for another taste of him. He thrust into my face, his movements unapologetic and merciless. I moaned against his cock, causing him to groan as the vibrations traveled along his erection.

He fucked my face, not letting up for a second. I gasped for air, and when that didn't work, remembered to breathe through my nose. A rush of his body soap and musk entered my nose until I was drunk on every part of him—his taste, his touch, his scent, and the chiseled eight-pack that flexed each time he pushed deeper into my mouth.

I reached a hand out and ran it across his abdominal muscles, my movements jerky. His thighs rubbed against my pebbled nipples with each thrust, and I groaned around his cock. His cum surprised me, pulsing into my mouth as he pulled out of me.

I watched as he stroked himself with his right hand and shot jets of cum all over my face and breasts.

He leaned back and looked at the mess he'd made on me. "Push your tits together."

I swallowed the cum he'd left in my mouth and squeezed my breasts together. He swiped the cum off my face with his fingers, rubbed them in circles around my nipples, and dipped them between the valley of my breasts with the rest of his cum until my entire chest was coated.

Then, he stroked himself again, his cock still mostly hard, and slid his length between my breasts. After a few more pumps, he leaned back and looked down at me. "Now, I've fucked every part of you but one." His lips turned up in a smile, and while his eyes still looked haunted, he also looked satiated. "I'll get to that later."

Oh, dear Lord.

He let me take control later that night, riding him the way I wanted to ride him. Teasing him the way I wanted to tease him. And letting him come when I wanted him to come. We were sticky and sweaty and a little messed up, but we were happy.

Between rounds, I traced the scars his dad had left on his back. Stubborn, raised edges, which had healed as much as they could. I had listened from my room that night as Angelo De Luca whipped Damian, the lashes unrelenting. But I wasn't that scared teen anymore. I wouldn't be run out of a city again.

And when I fell asleep with Damian's arms wrapped around me, I knew we'd be okay. We weren't our parents. We were better. Because Damiano De Luca loved me in ways no one I'd ever met and would ever meet knew how to love—patiently, through time, with no limits, with no expectations.

And I loved him.

The unapproachable parts he showed the world.

The uninhibited parts he showed me.

And especially the bruised, savage parts he could never hide from me.

36

> Sometimes, it's not the people who change. It's the
> mask that falls off.

— UNKNOWN

Damiano De Luca

I woke up with Renata on my chest. The room still smelled of sex, and I bet if she were awake, the cum I'd left all over her chest would cause her all sorts of discomfort.

Shit.

Yesterday.

That dull ache I'd lived with most of my life intensified. I'd always suspected my dad had done something to my mom, but

I'd never known for sure. As much as it fucked me up to find out the truth, it also relieved me. It was one less lie in my life, and I felt more free than I had in a long time.

And Renata... Once again, she'd seen me in pain, and she tried to fix me. Only this time, it had been the straw that broke the camel's back, pushing us together in filthy, naughty, desperate ways. I couldn't say I was unhappy about that, and I sure as hell appreciated her.

I slid Ren's arm and head off of me as gently as I could. The bed creaked as my weight lifted off of it, and I walked to the little bathroom connected to her room. I was already naked as the day I'd been born, so I strode into the shower and let the water hit me. Ice cold shards hit me before the temperature shifted to extreme heat.

The door opened, and Ren entered.

"Morning, Princess." I studied her beneath the showerhead, watching for signs that I'd pushed her too far. The water droplets fogged the clear glass door, but I could still make out her face.

She wore my shirt, her bare body still on display, thanks to the way I'd ripped the buttons when taking it off last night. A lazy smile drifted onto her face as she watched me watch her. It was sleepy and lacking her usual walls, and I knew we would be okay. At least, I hoped we would be. I'd bared every fucked up feeling I had since childhood to her last night. I wouldn't blame her if she wanted to run the other way.

She yawned and leaned against the sink, content to watch me shower. "Are you going to explain yesterday?"

She didn't sound mad. I didn't know if it was her mafia upbringing or that spine of steel, but the way she took yesterday in stride didn't surprise me as much as it should have. Well, I hoped I was reading her right.

I rubbed at my face, splashing water onto the glass divider. "I'm sorry about that."

"No need to apologize." The corner of her lips quirked up,

and I realized I'd been anxiously waiting for more signs that she was okay with how rough I'd been last night. "I liked it."

"I didn't know what you'd like." I shrugged and tried to play it off.

"I think how wet I was and the fact that I was chanting your name like it was the only thing running through my head—which it was—should have showed you that I liked it."

Holy fuck.

My cock, which had been dormant, nearly shot up at her words. I thought of stinky socks, molded walls, and expired processed cheese until I got myself under control.

She had a teasing smile, like she knew what I'd been thinking of, when I spoke again. "I wasn't sure if you liked rough sex. I was gentler when we did it in Devils Ridge."

"And I appreciate that"—again with the smirk—"since it was my first time."

Good God.

Stinky socks, stinky socks, stinky socks.

I was a grown ass mafia leader, chanting about stinky socks to keep my erection at bay. Perfect. Ego, meet blow.

I eyed the amusement on her face. "I took your virginity?"

"Yup." She popped the P. "But about yesterday..."

"I'm sorry."

"You've already apologized. Unnecessarily, might I add."

I'd given up washing myself by now, so I just leaned against the tile and let the hot water rain down on me, courtesy of New York City taxpayer dollars. "My dad told me what happened to my mom, and I kind of just lost it. I mean, I already suspected that he had something to do with her death, but thinking it and knowing it are more different than I'd thought they'd be."

"Will you be okay?"

"Yes. Maybe not immediately, but I'll be okay eventually. I've lived the past sixteen years without my mom. It's nothing new on that end. And I already hate my dad enough without this added to it. Though admittedly, it does make me hate him more. I didn't even think it was possible."

"What are you going to do?"

"I'll cut him off from the De Luca coffers. I've already taken away his empire. I considered sending him to jail, but I have a feeling he's suffering more around senior citizens who have families that visit them than he would in jail, where he'd find camaraderie amongst the incarcerated."

"You seem okay."

Not like last night, I read her unspoken words.

Shit.

"I really am sorry."

"Hey, Damsel?" she teased.

"Yes, Knight?"

"Stop apologizing for something I enjoyed. It's getting annoying."

"Okay. Fine." I studied her. "Where does this leave us?" Naked in her shower was probably an awful time to ask this question, but our relationship had never boasted good timing.

"It's so tempting to dive right in, full speed, isn't it?"

I nodded. That was exactly what I wanted—to make up for lost time.

"Let's take it one day at a time. Technically, we only dated for a week."

"It was a good week."

She sighed. "It was."

Until it wasn't.

"But?"

"But we live thousands of miles apart, in separate worlds, and have a history that isn't the greatest. Don't get me wrong. I'm ready for this. I'm letting you in. I think it's unfair and unrealistic for either of us to leave the other waiting, and frankly, I want you more than I've ever wanted anything else. I just don't want to ruin this before it starts again."

"Okay. I can live with that." Sudden laughter spilled past my lips. "Maybe we should even go on our first date."

She leaned her head back and groaned. "See? We haven't even gone on a first date!"

"I was kidding."

"I'm not." She paused. "Actually, that's a perfect start. Go on a date with me."

"Are you asking or telling?" I'd say yes either way.

"Telling." She straightened up from the sink. "And Damian? There's a bookshelf with half its books still on it. You didn't fuck me hard enough."

Well, damn.

Game on.

37

> **"** Trust takes years to build, seconds to break, and forever to repair.

— UNKNOWN

Renata Vitali

The knight is the only chess piece able to move freely, jumping over other pieces to reach the square it wants. That ability to jump means the knight is at its most powerful in closed positions, when forces close in and it seems trapped but isn't.

I saw myself in the knight. Trapped by my father, by the lies in my life, by my last name. I wanted the power to break free. I wanted to be the knight, able to jump over my problems. But no one tells you that the best chess pieces are the ones off the board. The ones that don't even exist on a chessboard.

All my life, I'd always wanted to be the knight. But maybe it was okay that I was the princess. Off the chessboard. No mind games. Just living. Breathing. Happy. When Damian called me princess, I didn't even feel the urge to correct him.

He handed me my towel as I got out of the shower. He'd dressed in fancy sweats and a plain white t-shirt. "My driver dropped off my clothes and some breakfast."

I dried off, threw on panties and an oversized shirt, and took the breakfast sandwich he offered me. "Thanks."

There was nowhere else to sit, so we ate on the bed.

I picked at the bagel, took a deep breath, and let my walls fall. "When I left, I told myself it was because I had to. That I was doing the right thing, but I knew I wasn't." I had his rapt attention as he dropped his half-eaten sandwich back into the bag. I gave him mine, too.

He took it, set them aside, and focused on me. "Why did you leave?"

"Your dad cornered me in the hallway. He brought up Ludovico and implied he'd do the same to you. That he'd kill his own son." I stared at the wall I faced. Offering information I didn't need to went against my instincts, but he deserved answers, I finally felt ready to give them, and I needed to get this out.

For the first time in a while, hope had surfaced. Maybe we had a future. Maybe the lies and deception could stay behind us, and I could be happy again without fear of getting hurt. The walls I had built around me were dropping, but to totally destroy them, I needed to take a big step. I needed to own my truths.

I glanced up at Damian. "And then, I came into your room and saw the picture of Ludovico your dad had left on the side of your bed. You laughed it off, but it shook me. I was so damn worried about you, and it was weird for me because I'd never worried about someone other than my mother. It was nice to have someone to care for. But there was so much responsibility to it."

Damian moved, so we sat with our sides pressed against each other.

I closed my eyes and leaned into him as he stroked my hair. "I knew I had to leave. You gave me an out when you said someone else had sent me to Devils Ridge. I took it. I called you horrible things. I threatened you. And I left."

When I opened my eyes and met his, there was no judgment in them. It made what I had to admit next harder. "But there was another part of me that knew I was making the wrong decision. That it was the wrong thing to do. My ego over being lied to, and feeling fear for someone else for the first time ever, and the house of lies we'd built around us... they wouldn't let me find you again. I could have gone back, but I chose not to because I was scared. I didn't know how to handle the fear other than to bury it."

"Dad threatened you?"

I nodded. "Sort of. He threatened *you*, knowing I loved you. But it doesn't excuse leaving."

"You were eighteen, and the head of a mafia syndicate threatened you."

"Don't make excuses for me." I shook my head. "I'm a Vitali. I had more power than him."

"You were eighteen."

I sighed, backed away from him, and laid flat on the bed. "Leaving was still wrong."

"You know how I was mean to you when you first came to Devils Ridge?"

"Ha!" I accepted the subject change and rolled my eyes. "How could I forget?"

"It was because I caught you in my room. At the time, I was

making power plays to overthrow my dad. I was so goddamned paranoid." He hesitated. For some reason, when he looked at the ring tattooed around my finger, his features smoothed, and he continued. "There was someone behind the scenes helping me. A benefactor. I would get anonymous packages, instructions, and tips. Things like that."

My brows furrowed. "I've never heard of a benefactor."

If Papà caught wind of this, he'd blister.

"For the longest time, The Benefactor pulled my strings. Helped me when I needed it—before I even knew I needed help. I still don't know why. But there you were, this stranger from a powerful family, searching my room." He arched a brow. "And don't even deny that you were snooping."

I laughed. "I was definitely snooping. I needed a phone."

"And you stole mine." He let out a groan. "That just made it worse. I had messages in there from The Benefactor, and I'd spent months wondering what you knew. You never let up."

"Because I knew nothing."

"Well, I know that now."

"And you have no idea who The Benefactor is?"

"I've been trying to track him down, but I haven't had any luck. That night, I was talking about The Benefactor when I said your dad wasn't the one who sent you to Devils Ridge."

"For the record, I wasn't mad at you for that. Was I shocked? Yes, but something about being sent to Devils Ridge felt wrong. Like it was too drastic a punishment for catching my dad cheating. Since my dad's always been off the rails, I never questioned it. I just used the revelation as an excuse to leave you in a way you wouldn't question."

Damian sighed and leaned back. "Maybe you were right to leave me. I'd like to think I could take on my dad, but fuck, he killed my mom. You gave me an opportunity to battle him on my own terms rather than him taking me by surprise. But I wish that hadn't required a fight that took ten years away from us."

A lump jammed my throat. That fight still hurt. Bringing up Angelo's threat was one thing. Talking about the actual fight in detail was another. One day, I would be able to talk about it more. Today was not that day.

I sat up and stared down at Damian. "You know, you promised me a date, and I'm a little miffed that we've never been out on a date before."

"We had library dates."

"But we've never been *out* on a date. Those were in your house."

"Speaking of the house, I never sold it. I live in a townhouse close to Devils Ridge High, but I never sold the mansion. I couldn't tell you how many times I've wanted to knock it down with a wrecking ball, but I could never bring myself to sell or destroy it."

I remembered how much he hated the De Luca house. "Why not?"

"The library."

Our library.

I bit my lip to keep from smiling. "There are other libraries."

"Not the same."

"We made memories in this library last night." My hand slid down his chest and dipped below the band of his sweatpants.

He grabbed my hand and led it to his erection. We stroked it together. His hand gripped the base of his cock. I wrapped my palm around the top, my thumb brushing against his head. He twisted up, and I followed his lead, working his length with him.

He leaned up and nipped my neck.

I let out a soft sigh, and my hand stilled. "The library's crowded out there. We already had someone interrupt us last night. It's an old library. There's no soundproofing."

"Let them hear."

He flipped me, so he hovered over me. Moving down my body, he slid my sleeping shorts and underwear down. I slung my legs over his shoulders and interlocked my ankles. He gave my pussy an open-mouthed kiss before he carried me to the bookshelf, his lips still pressed against my core.

"Oh, God." I reached behind me and gripped one of the shelves.

Books fell to the floor. I couldn't even bother to keep my voice down. Damian's hands squeezed my ass, pushing me closer to his face. His nose brushed against my clit, and I groaned loud enough that footsteps paused outside the door.

Damian slid his tongue inside me, fucking me with it. Over and over again as I rode his face. I came with a scream, and my core clenched around his tongue. This time, every book on the shelf had fallen to the floor.

When he set me back on the bed, lowered his sweats, and moved to enter me, I stopped him with a quirked brow. "We're still going on a date."

He looked too satisfied. "Whatever you want."

"Now."

"Now?" He had his erection out and paused mid-stroke.

"Yup. Date first."

He clenched his eyes shut but tucked himself back inside his sweats. "Date it is."

I smiled at him. It was toothy and one-hundred percent genuine.

The atmosphere felt lighthearted. Playful. Not weighed down by the eternal forces we'd always been plagued by.

It felt right.

> **❝** Honesty is the first chapter in the book of wisdom.
>
> — THOMAS JEFFERSON

Renata Vitali

We stood outside the bustling subway entrance. A dirty white tile laid beside the stairwell underground. Etched shooting stars surrounded messy text.

I turned to Damian. "We're here."

"Chinatown? Are we getting soup dumplings?"

"No, here." I pointed to the tile. "Read it."

He cut me an odd stare before relenting. "One day, I'll see you every day, and we'll be forever, like dreams." He cocked a brow. "What is this?"

"A Toynbee tile."

"A tile named after the story?"

"Could be. Or they could be named after the historian— Arnold J. Toynbee. There are some more theories. No one really knows for sure." I grabbed his hand and led him across the street. "Toynbee tiles are messages embedded in tiles in streets all over major US cities. Four South American cities, too."

"Who makes them?" He was indulging me—I knew that—but it just made me like him more.

A few more steps, and we'd get to the next tile. "No one knows who creates them—past and present. But it started in the 80s. Honestly, I'd bet there are hundreds of creators. People who just want to cement their place in history." I stopped in front of the next, a few blocks from the last one. "Here's another."

A crack split this one in two, but it only added to its appeal. It was history, stomped on, worn out, but forever here. In a fucked-up way, it reminded me of my relationship with Damian. A little too much.

Damian looked down and read aloud. "Will it always hurt this much? Or is this Forever making me work for it?"

The grin on my face was one-hundred percent stupid.

He took in my face. "What?"

"Nothing."

"This is cheesy and dramatic."

"The tile?" I bit my lip to keep from laughing.

"Yes."

The laughter slipped past my lips. "I won't argue with that."

His eyes narrowed at my laughter, but he let it slide. "Are we doing a tile tour? That's... either very original or so New York City hipster."

"Yes, this is a tile tour. Bear with me, Texas."

"I don't mind the history, but I wouldn't say no to some incentive."

I looked both ways before pushing Damian into the brick wall between two stores. I placed each of his hands on my hips to give me coverage from the crowded street.

He gave me a look. "What are you doing?"

I felt carefree and devious as I dipped my hands into my skirt from the waistband. "Giving you incentive." Tearing the fabric on each side, I pulled my panties off of me and tucked my shirt back in.

"Are those your panties?"

"Yes." I slid them into the pocket of his suit pants, my fingers brushing against his length as I pulled my hand out. "For every tile we see, I'll give you a piece of me."

He thought I meant my clothes. I meant everything. He had made the first move when we were kids. It was my turn to take a leap.

The heat in his eyes traveled straight to my core. "Next tile. Now."

I laughed, and we walked a few blocks away, into Little Italy. I turned to him. "Most people think spaghetti and meatballs were invented in Italy, but they were actually first made here."

"How do you know so much about New York? I thought you went to boarding school in Connecticut."

"My mom lived near my school. She'd take me to the city at least once a month. We'd do a ton of cool things here. I fell in love with the city." Even though sharing things went against my nature, this felt so right. "You'd like my mom. She stays under the radar." I noted his frown and elaborated. "Yeah, she and Papà aren't really good at the whole married thing."

A derisive scorn filled his handsome face. "I'd know something about that."

I sighed and took in the scent of Little Italy. "Here's the next one."

Situated in between two pizzerias, just before the alleyway entrance, a tile read:

> I treaded the water when
> I wanted to dive in head first.
> Now, I've finally reached
> the deep end, but it's empty.
> Next time, I won't take too long.

Damian wrapped an arm around my waist. "Are they all like this?"

"Like what?"

"Sad."

"Just these ones." I wondered if showing these to him hurt more than they helped, but he needed to see them. I needed to show them to him.

So, instead of stopping, I angled my body so he blocked the view of me from everyone outside the alleyway. I wore a bralette, which I snapped at the straps and slid off me. My nipples formed tight little buds that pressed against my shirt, but other than that, I was okay enough for public consumption.

I placed the bralette into his other pocket and scraped my nails slowly against his thigh through the fabric. He let out a groan, and I pushed past him before he could say anything. The next tile laid where Stuyvesant Town, Gramercy, and Murray Hill met.

Under a canopy of green leaves, Damian read the tile. "If I had a second chance, I wouldn't need another one." He turned to me. "Do you think these are all written by the same person?"

"The ones I've shown you? Yes. But there are so many more around the city, and I doubt they're all written by even a handful of people." I grabbed his hand, though my thighs and calves ached from the walking. "Two more."

"My incentive," he reminded me.

I turned to him, wrapped a hand around his neck, and kissed him. It was the kind of kiss people usually only achieved after years of dating. Part passion and steam. Part familiarity and comfort. Under the canopy of the trees and leaves that surrounded us on every side, it felt picturesque and more intimate than any other naughty gift I could give him.

His tongue slid into my mouth and stroked my tongue, and I sighed into him before pulling back. "The last syndicate meeting is in an hour and a half, and we have two more tiles."

I led the way to the next tile, at the border of Midtown East and the Upper East Side, near Central Park. It read:

> Reality feels so permanent.
> I wish for a reset button.
> That time machines exist,
> like in the Toynbee Convector.

"I'd give you another incentive, but it took us forty-five minutes to walk here, and it's an hour walk to the next one." I couldn't believe we'd already spent hours walking around the city to see a few tiles, of which we had no clue the significance of.

"Fine, but I get a question first."

"We can walk and talk."

He took my hand, and we began our walk down the length of Central Park. "What's with the tiles?"

"Every time I'd miss my mom at boarding school, I'd send her a letter with a wish. I never got any letters back, but when I saw Maman, she'd take me into the city for an adventure. They always ended at a Toynbee tile."

"So, they make you feel close to your mom?"

"Yes."

"Are you gonna give me any more than that?"

"No. It'd ruin the big reveal."

About a minute from the next tile, I finally spoke again. "The tiles my mom would take me to were mine. The letters Maman got never had responses because she'd respond to them with the tiles."

"Those were her words back there?"

"No." I took a deep breath, my heart running marathons in my chest. "They're mine. From the letters. Maman stamped my wishes forever into the ground, into history, to show me that dreams are forever. That anything I wished for could be forever. This one... this is the one from a letter I gave my mom. The first one I sent to her right after I left Devils Ridge."

We both looked down and read.

I want my Damsel.

The edges of the tiles had aged, and there my declaration stood, cemented in history for everyone to see. His eyes studied the tile, his expression thunderstruck.

My hand gripped his shirt and turned him until he looked at me. "I've always wanted you, Damian. Even when I ran from you, my heart stayed with you, and you were always mine. I want a world where you'll always be mine. I'm not stopping. I'm not hopping. I'm not even leaping. I already dove, and I don't want you to catch me. I want you to fall with me."

We missed the meeting after that. His driver picked us up and took us back to the library, where we stayed for the rest of the weekend. For the first time in a long time, I felt happy and free.

39

> Deceit is the false road to happiness; and all the joys we travel through... vanish when we touch them.

> — AARON HILL

Renata Vitali

We spent the rest of the summer together. Summer vacation was one of the greatest teaching perks. I had the luxury of having a big enough trust fund that I didn't need a summer job, and I spent the time I had off with Damian.

The De Luca syndicate spanned Arizona, New Mexico, Texas,

and Oklahoma. Damian had stuff to take care of in Oklahoma. So, we spent the rest of August and most of September in a lake house there.

It wasn't exactly taking things slowly, but it felt right. The days blended together in near-domestic bliss. Sometimes, Damian had to drive to Oklahoma City to speak with business associates, but most times, his business was close to Broken Bow, where we stayed in one of the De Luca vacation homes.

He'd be gone for an hour or two a day, which I spent reading on a hammock in the backyard. Damian spent most of his time on Broken Bow Lake with me. By the end of our first week here, my pasty, New England skin was tanner than it had ever been since I'd fled Texas.

I'd gotten used to seeing Damian in suits, but he dropped the suit in Broken Bow, unless he had a business matter to deal with. It was nice seeing him relaxed, shirtless in sweats or swim trunks, depending on our plans for the day.

We spent every night together and woke up every morning beside one another. When he had to leave for the city, he would find his way back by nightfall, even if he hadn't finished his business and had to wake up extra early to leave for the city again the next morning.

One night, after meeting the Oklahoma *caporegime*, he returned home at the edge of dawn. I stayed up waiting for him, curled up with a worn paperback of *Nightmare Abbey*. He entered the room and watched me from the doorframe.

I had just finished the part where Marionetta torments Scythrop. I'd been rereading the scene, thinking of the time I'd last read it. He had entered the library and let me borrow his phone, and we both pretended we hadn't already been in love.

Damian approached the bed, his eyes sleepy as he took the paperback from me. "Nightmare Abbey. I didn't take you as an anti-romance type of girl."

It thrilled me that he remembered our conversation all these years later. I pressed a kiss to his lips as he hovered above me and recounted my words. "Was it my lack of faith in humanity that persuaded you otherwise?"

Renovating the library became my new pet project. Damian came home to me choosing paint swatches, and when I woke up the next morning, he had the room painted the color I'd chosen. We built new shelves by hand and fitted them to the walls. He ordered classics I loved, and we had a shelf dedicated to the books we'd read together in Devils Ridge as teens. He convinced me to frame the words on my Toynbee tiles all over the library.

Every day, he found ways to erase the pain of our pasts. He'd surprise me with limited edition paperbacks, which we'd read in the library all day long. Sometimes, we'd swim naked in the lake, and I'd convince him to read steamy passages to me from romance novels. He'd agree on the condition that I let him reenact them.

We'd fuck when he returned from working and defaced the lake with our inability to keep our hands off each other. He had me on every surface of the library, and many times, we had to reorder the shelves after all the books had fallen to the floor. Sometimes, we made love. He'd kiss away the bad memories, and I'd kiss the scars his father had left on his back with a belt.

Every now and then, Maman would call. I ignored her phone calls, even though I knew she'd approve of my relationship. After all, she'd been the one to try and convince me lately to let my guard down. But I didn't want to break the spell, and I loathed the passing of time. Summer would end, and I'd have to return to reality—Maman, Papà, school, and the thousands of miles, which separated us.

Between the picturesque scenery and the lazy days spent in love at a lake house, I'd let my guard down and convinced myself that life was perfect. Not that everything was actually perfect. I hadn't heard from my dad in nearly a year. I was ignoring my mom's calls. I'd see Damian press the ignore button on his phone nearly every time his *consiglieri*-slash-under boss called. But this was the closest to perfect I'd ever experienced.

A day before I had to leave for Connecticut, we spent the day naked in bed, exploring each other. We hadn't talked about what we'd do after I left, which made me a little anxious. I knew he wanted to—he kept dropping hints—but I wasn't ready to burst our little bubble of happy.

He sighed, and it was a rare moment of seriousness over our break. "My dad called this morning. Apparently, Cristian called my dad, who called me."

"Is that why you've been acting weird all morning?"

"I got another package from The Benefactor. I thought I was done with these packages a while ago. I don't even know how he found us."

"What was in the package?"

"The Benefactor wants me to drop Cris and promote someone of their.choosing."

"So, The Benefactor helps you take over the De Luca syndicate, then years later tries to plant someone in your ranks." I bit my lip. "It sounds like a takeover. Or at least some sort of power play."

"That's what I'm afraid of. I have this bad feeling that The Benefactor jeopardizes everything I've worked to build with the De Luca syndicate. We spent years undoing all the damage my father had done." He ran a hand across his face. "I can't really talk it over with Cris. I don't know how he'd react, and I haven't been too forthcoming with him about The Benefactor."

"You can talk to me about it."

I could tell he didn't want to, which hurt me, but I understood. I didn't want to talk about my mom despite his many, many hints. An hour later, Maman called again, and I hit ignore.

Damian eyed my phone. "She's persistent."

"I actually like that about her," I admitted, though I didn't elaborate on why I was dodging Maman's calls.

"I need to meet this mom of yours." Another hint of his.

"We can head to the Hamptons." He stilled, but I continued, not thinking much of it, "As soon as we're done representing our families in the city, we can make an overnight trip."

"Where is she?"

"The Hamptons."

"Your mom lives in The Hamptons? As in New York?"

"Yup."

"Do you know any other mafiosos in the Hamptons?"

"No. Just my mom." I laughed a little. "She made sure of that."

"The mom you're close to?"

My brows pressed together. "Yes. You're acting weird." I rolled onto my back and stared at the ceiling. Regret laced my words. "She's my best friend. We tell each other everything."

Well, except for the fact that I was dating Damian De Luca.

"Is this why you've been ignoring your mom's phone calls? Why you won't talk about her except surface level bullshit?" He shook his head and backed away from me. "I tracked the packages! You didn't think I'd find out? You know how much I've sacrificed for this syndicate, Renata!"

"Excuse me?" I scrambled after him as he left the bedroom, my mind spinning with no signs of stopping. "What are you talking about? I'm so confused."

"Nice try, Ren." His scoff held more disdain than a Westboro picketer. "I get that you're a Vitali, and the Vitali have secrets, but why wouldn't you say anything about The Benefactor? We're supposed to trust each other."

"Wha—"

We reached the kitchen, and he turned to face me, his eyes so damned hurt. "I told you how much The Benefactor bothers me. You said it yourself. There's a power play going on. I just didn't know you were involved."

"Da—"

"Just so you know, your mom wasn't as sly as she thought she was. I traced every package back to New York and, later, the Hamptons. I just didn't know any mafia members lived there." He raised his brow like I'd kept that info away from him on purpose.

My mind still reeled over his accusations. Namely, Maman being The Benefactor, which was impossible. But also, the way he was so quick to lash out at me for holding back on him, which I hadn't been. I get that our past was layered with lies, but I thought we'd moved on. Why couldn't we move on?

I shook my head. "I haven't lied to you. You have to trust me."

"I told you to drop your walls. I told you to trust me. But it's you who couldn't be trusted." His words slapped me, and even though my head didn't whip to the side, my gut did.

I raised my hands, wild gestures as frantic as my thoughts. "This world we're in? It's built on lies. There will always be another revelation. One after the next, after the next. We will never find love if we can't take the leap."

He turned and entered the pantry. "Look what trust brought my mom."

"Your dad is sick! A psychopath!"

Gosh, the comparison wasn't even close.

"Look what trust brought *your* dad. Does he know his wife schemes behind his back?"

Damian was crazy. Absolutely crazy. There was no way... My mom couldn't be The Benefactor... But she hadn't contacted me the entire time Papà exiled me to Devils Ridge. When I tried to talk about it later, tears always brimmed her eyes, and I could never bring myself to press harder.

And Maman was so connected for a Vitali first lady, wasn't she? Friends with every wife and their powerful husbands. In a secret relationship with Vincent Romano. Married to the head of the freakin' Vitali. I knew she was smart and held power, but she seemed fragile and unassuming.

What was it she'd told me all those years ago?

… *Silent threats do not warn you*, ma petite guerrière. *They attack, lethal and unapologetic.*

What if she *was* The Benefactor?

I shook my head. Why was I even considering Damian's conspiracy theories? Maman lived sequestered in the Hamptons. She rarely left her home. How in the world could she be The Benefactor? She would never deceive me like that. She wasn't that type of person. I refused to believe it. Hell, I'd recently just learned a benefactor even existed!

Damian dug around in a box. Silence slithered between us with the occasional ruffling from within the box.

I broke the silence first. "My mom is not The Benefactor. No way. Just no fucking way that would be possible." Silence. "You believe me, right?"

I needed Damian to see reason, because Maman… she just couldn't be The Benefactor. It made no sense. And me and Damian? This was our chance to make it. We couldn't let our relationship slip by like last time.

Damian's face told me he didn't believe me, so I changed my line of reasoning. "My mom and dad never loved each other. It was all a farce. Us? We're real." Still, he kept digging, ignoring my words. I was shouting now, grasping at straws, at anything that would erase the past ten minutes. "I sacrificed my happiness for you, Damian! I sacrificed a happy future with you when I left Devils Ridge because I wanted you safe from your asshole father. It was the hardest thing I've ever done."

I took a step closer, begging him to even look at me, which he didn't bother to do. "So, you may have daddy issues, Damian, and that's okay, but don't you dare project that onto my mother, me, or our relationship."

Swallowing back the anger that unhinged me, I lowered my

voice. "Don't you get what a big sacrifice leaving you was for me? I loved you, gave you my virginity, and left after your father threatened me." Angelo was the enemy. Not Maman. I took another step toward Damian. My heart fractured with each second he ignored me. "Doesn't that mean anything to you? Are you really that ungrateful?"

He ignored my words, pulled something out of the box, and showed it to me. A leather-bound book from the Vitali archives. The one my mom controlled. The one no one had access to without her help. Hell, Damian probably didn't even know what he held.

Recognition lit up my face, followed by a truckload of Denial with a capital "D".

He must have seen it, because his eyes narrowed, and disgust curled his lips. "What do you know? My dad was right about one thing."

"What?" I asked out of reflex. I didn't want to hear his answer. I didn't want to hear any of this.

I trusted Maman.

She wasn't The Benefactor.

Papà was the bad parent.

Damian stared me down, his voice as hollow as his eyes. "Love doesn't exist."

"He's wrong. Your dad is wrong." I shook my head. "And if you truly believe that love doesn't exist, you're wrong, too." My mind raced, fracturing as I pictured my future without Damian. "Love exists. It's real. We have it. You'll never find what we have with anyone else. If you want to create a family without me for your De Luca throne, and I know you'll need a family, a farce is what you will settle for. Because you love *me*, Damian. Anyone else is just a lie."

I waited for him to wake up.

To see the truth in my words.

He didn't.

Renata Vitali

It was silent as Damian drove me to the airport. I hadn't
brought much with me, just enough things to fit in my
backpack. It made leaving all the more painful, like I had
nothing to take with me except what I'd come with.

A part of me wanted to cling to Damian like ivy. The other
part of me considered that I'd be pushing my luck. If he was

remorseful, he didn't show it. Silent as shadows, we spent the hour drive to his private airstrip bathing in tension.

It wasn't lost on me that, just as I'd dropped my walls, Damian had built his quicker than a lightning's flash. I couldn't blame him. The circumstances didn't look good. I knew how it felt to have trust issues.

That didn't mean this didn't hurt. It also didn't mean that the hurt and anger didn't push itself to the forefront of my mind. It did. I brimmed with anger. My fingers shook, and we both were so damned angry, I doubted either of us could form sentences.

At the airstrip, the male flight attendant opened my door for me and led me to the plane's stairwell. I turned back to see Damian, but he'd already driven away. I knew he needed time, but once you've already waited ten years for someone you love, you can't bring yourself to do it again.

I forced myself to sleep as I settled on the plane. The back of the private plane had been fitted with a small bedroom, and I wondered how often Damian slept in this same bed. The sheets and pillowcases smelled of laundry detergent, but when I peeled the case back, I caught Damian's scent.

I slept on the bare pillow and woke up two hours later to Damian's scent. Nostalgia crept into my heart, and despite how angry I was at Damian, I decided I needed to find answers for the both of us. Because what if Maman *was* The Benefactor? I didn't believe it, but there were facts I couldn't ignore.

The stewardess arrived soon after I pressed the call button on the nightstand. She was as perky as I was mad. "How may I help you, ma'am?"

"Ask the pilot to reroute the flight to the Hamptons." I remembered my manners a beat later. "Please."

"Of course. Which airstrip?"

"Nob Bay."

I would go to the Hamptons.

I'd confront Maman.

And when I was done, I'd wipe my hands of heartache. My heart hurt enough for a lifetime.

I reminded myself that Gaspard, Maman's majordomo, had done nothing wrong as he reached out for a hug. After returning it half-heartedly, I pulled back. "Is my mother here?"

We stood in the doorway under a massive arch. A set of luggage stood idly near the entrance, and a few staff members brushed past us.

Gaspard nodded and led me to the library, where Maman and I usually spent our time together. "I'll let her know you've come. She's been missing you, my dear." His stern look brushed off me. "She's been sad that you haven't returned her calls."

I ignored his words despite the pang they caused. "Where is Mère?" It felt oddly comforting to say 'Mère' to someone who understood the difference Mère and Maman. Not comforting enough to erase the discomfort I felt from Damian's accusations.

"She's with a guest." Normally, his French accent drew comfort.

Instead, I just felt sad. "Who?"

He arched a brow but didn't comment on my barrage of questions and their less-than-polite delivery. "A law enforcement officer."

"Is she in trouble?"

"No."

Which meant he either worked for the Vitali or worked for her. "Does this law enforcement officer have a name?"

"Yes."

"Does he have a law enforcement agency?"

"Yes."

"But you won't tell me?"

He didn't need to. When I told Maman that Ariana De Luca was in the FBI, she hadn't been surprised. Which meant she'd already known, and the law enforcement officer must have been connected to the FBI. Goodness, how many jars did Maman have her fingers in?

I tried to rack my brain for when my briefing mentioned Ariana. She showed up in Romano territory after the bounty on Niccolaio Andretti's head was raised. Bodies had dropped. That had to be the catalyst.

"It's best you bombard your mother with your questions and not me, little one." Gaspard dipped his head in a small bow. "I'll let your mom know that you're here."

"Gaspard?"

He turned back to face me. "Yes, Renata?"

"Please, leave the door open."

He nodded, and when he left, I took a seat in front of Maman's chess set. The porcelain set represented carved memories of my childhood. Weekends at Maman's, spent begging her to play chess with me.

"Not this set," she'd tell me before pulling out a different set.

We'd play, and she'd teach me the Vienna game. I'd almost been convinced that her porcelain set was merely decoration, except I'd seen her move the pieces one at a time. Sometimes, a month apart. Sometimes, a year apart.

But today, the dark king stood at a checkmate.

Oh, God.

How could I not have seen this? I loved Maman, but I was her pawn. Literally. Memories flashed into me as I saw them with new eyes, recounting the events that coincided with the chess moves I remembered Maman making.

Maman sent me to Italy as a surprise for Papà's birthday. *Pawn to E4.*

I caught Dad cheating on Maman and was sent to Devil's Ridge. *Knight to C3.*

Maman helped Damian take over the De Luca syndicate as The Benefactor. *Bishop to C4.*

Damian and I fell in love, entwining the Vitali with the De Luca. *Knight to E5.*

A five-million-dollar bounty was placed on Niccolaio Andretti's head. *Queen to H5.*

Bodies dropped all over New York as Niccolaio evaded his bounty. *Queen to E5.*

Ariana appeared in Romano territory. *Knight to D6.*

Vincent Romano was killed. *Knight to B5.*

Maman sent me to Romano territory to represent the Vitali at Vince's funeral. *Knight to F7.*

Damian and I reconnected as Maman encouraged me to drop my walls. *Queen to C7.*

What was Knight to D6? And worse, what was the Checkmate?

When I'd seen Maman after running away from De Luca territory, we'd read together. I glanced at the chessboard, but it didn't strike me that she moved five chess pieces in the year I'd been gone. I hadn't thought anything of it.

"Renata, darling, it's lovely to see you!"

My eyes shot up to Maman as she entered the room. She

looked as demure as a Catholic nun. I never would have expected this from her.

"Maman." I forced myself to relax, hoping my face didn't give anything away.

"Have a seat." She gestured to the chair in front of her chess set. Fitting. "Not that I'm not happy to see you, but why are you here? You've been avoiding my phone calls."

I nodded at the chess set. "What is this?"

"A game. The Vienna opening is quite effective."

Chills traveled the length of my arms. "You're a liar, Maman."

Her smile slipped. "I can assure you the Vienna opening is effective. Far more effective than your father's preferred King's Gambit." She reached out, knocked over the dark king, and sent me a serene smile. "Game over."

"This isn't just a game, Maman."

"No, it's not."

"All those years ago, you sent me to Italy on purpose. You knew Papà was having an affair, and you knew I'd find out."

She leaned back in her seat. "Ah, so you've figured it out..."

"How are you so calm about this?"

"I didn't raise an idiot." Actual pride beamed in her eyes. "I knew you'd figure it out eventually."

"I don't know how you did it, but you convinced Papà to send me to De Luca territory."

How could I have missed this?!

Maman pressed the call button for a butler. "I may have suggested it to his consiglieri."

Papà's consiglieri married Maman's childhood friend. Thanks to that friendship, he'd always had a soft spot for Maman.

"And you've been helping the De Luca syndicate. Damian... to what end? Are you trying to take over Damian's syndicate?" I shook my head. That would never happen. Not even over the dead bodies of every other syndicate. I met Maman's eyes again.

"You're tethering yourself to the De Luca family by helping them. And through me."

"Yes."

"And you've just met with someone from the FBI, which has to be connected to Ariana De Luca. But she likely came to L'Oscurità as a result of the bodies dropping after Niccolaio Andretti's hit raised to five million dollars. How did you pull that off?"

"I had nothing to do with the hit. It was merely a fortuitous event, which moved a few pieces on the board in my favor."

"But that hit resulted in Vince's death. How could you do that to him?"

She looked away. "He had cancer. He knew what he was doing?"

"Was he involved?"

She didn't answer.

My eyes narrowed, and my voice hardened. "Maman, was Vincent Romano involved in all this?"

"Yes." Her fingers reached out and toyed with the slain dark king. "Vincent was a good man. We both knew this. Ask yourself why he would involve himself in something nefarious."

Answer: he wouldn't.

Which meant there had to be some good end game here, but I couldn't see it. I couldn't see past the damned betrayal.

Pull yourself together, Ren.

"You sent me to New York for Vince's funeral, reconnecting me with Damian. You kept telling me to let my guard down, which means you want me with Damian. To what end?"

Her eyes dipped to the chessboard, tracing the length of the fallen dark king. "Checkmate."

"Please, tell me the dark king is not Papà."

"I could tell you no, but I'd be lying, my little warrior. And what would be the point in lying at this point?"

The butler entered the library, and Maman ordered a peach

water like my perception of her hadn't just done a total one-eighty in the span of a day. I wanted to leave, but I was frozen, incapable of looking away from her.

She waited for me to speak, the picture of patience. Her butler asked me if I wanted anything, but I couldn't even open my mouth to decline. Maman waved him away with a flick of the hand only she could make graceful.

I'd been so blind. So goddamned blind. In the mafia fold. Out of the mafia fold. It didn't matter. I was a puppet either way. I swallowed, but my mouth was too dry.

Maman's lips quirked upward. "Did I break you, *ma petite guer-rière*? Did I blow your mind?" Maman laughed a little, stood, and pushed in her chair. "It's been lovely seeing you, my darling daughter. However, I hadn't expected company, and I have plans for tonight." She patted my shoulder and left the room.

Her butler came into the room and looked around for Maman. "Miss Vitali? Miss Vitali?" He touched my shoulder and gave it a gentle shake. "Miss Vitali?"

I turned to him. "Where's my mother?"

He held up the peach water. "She said you'd be needing this."

Cunning, manipulative woman.

My anger flared. I grabbed the water, because yes, I did need it. After draining the glass, handing it to the butler, and thanking him, I headed to the doorway, where I heard Maman speaking to Gaspard.

"We were talking." I eyed her and crossed my arms. "Where are you going?" I had my suspicions, but as the lies buried me in their treachery, the need to hear more truths heightened. I needed to hear her say it.

She gifted me a serene smile. "I have pressing matters to attend to."

"More important than your daughter?"

"Oh, honey. Don't misconstrue this." She gestured around at

the gaudy marble monstrosity she called a home. "This is all for you. When I pass away, this legacy will be yours."

"I'm not interested in your legacy of lies."

She reached out and cupped my cheek. "I have to leave now." Her hand dropped, and my face burned where her hand had been.

My eyes scraped their way down the length of her. She wore a pair of Lululemon yoga pants, a loose Vince henley, and Givenchy sneakers. Travel clothes. I'd spotted a small overnight luggage set earlier, too.

Maman was headed for Italy. To dethrone Papà.

Checkmate.

Game over.

And the dark king fell.

41

> Our capacity for self-deception has no known limits.

— MICHAEL NOVAK

Damiano De Luca

One Week Later

Fun fact: A wolf who has been driven from the pack or has left of its own accord is called a lone wolf. Lone wolves avoid contact with packs and rarely howl.

I knew this because I'd looked up wolves after Ren had called me one. I felt a little like a lone wolf this week. Fielding Cristian's calls came easier than it should have. His competency made me grateful, because I knew he could run the De Luca family while I stayed in Oklahoma and figured my shit out. I didn't think I'd talked to a human since Ren left. Most of our business consisted of oil lands contracted out, anyway.

Another fun fact: Wolves mate for life.

Ren hadn't lied when she'd said that. She did, however, lie when she implied she was that lifetime mate for me.

My phone rang again. Cristian. I hit ignore, slid it back into my back pocket, and picked up my axe. A block of wood split in two as I swung at it. The flannel wrapped around my waist doubled as a towel for my sweat. I dragged the fabric across my forehead and shirtless torso as a black, unmarked SUV pulled up to the property.

I tossed the flannel to the side, gripped the axe tighter, and raised my hand above my head to block the sun from my eyes. Bastian stepped out of the car, his three-piece suit at odds with my shirtless torso, jeans, and work boots.

He took me in as he approached. "Are you posing for a bodice ripper?"

"Your lexicon is as outdated as your haircut."

"Hey, I mean it in the best of ways. The book could be called, *Her Lumberjack's Moist Depths*. I'm sure there are women into that sort of thing." He looked around. "Though there doesn't seem to be one here." He arched a brow. "Trouble in paradise?"

"Worried your girl will be in jeopardy if I'm no longer cozy with the Vitali family?" I swung the axe into the halved tree trunk, picked up my shirt, and headed into the lake house without inviting Bastian. My phone rang, but I hit ignore and slid it back into my pocket.

He followed anyway. "No. She left the FBI. Turned in her badge. Everything's been taken care of." He loosened his tie and took in the house. "I'm here for a meeting with an alcohol supplier. Your consiglieri cleared it. You'd know this if you'd pick up your phone."

I chugged a bottle from the fridge, tossed it into the recycle bin, and turned to face Bastian. "Cut the idle chit-chat. Why are you here, Bastian? In my house?"

"Ariana told me something interesting."

Obviously, it had to do with me, because he was here. If he thought I'd let him hold it over my head or use it as leverage, he was more daft than I gave him credit for.

I beat him to it. "She's my sister. I know."

He seemed unfazed by my brute honesty—something new I'd been trying, though I didn't exactly have an audience to lie to lately. "So, why the fuck haven't you talked to her about it?"

I wanted to. I did. But spending time with Ren seemed more important, and now that she'd left, I'd been too preoccupied trying to figure out why the lies even mattered so much when I loved her more than I hated the lies. Lies I was starting to consider she hadn't even had a part in. Stranger things have happened.

"If you haven't noticed, I run an entire syndicate. I don't have time to shit rainbows and make small talk over pumpkin spice lattes."

"Trust me. Ariana is worth making time."

I studied him. "I assume she wants to meet with me."

"I told her you're not your dad."

"I'm not." I ran a hand over my head and really took him in. There was something about him that had changed. He looked... peaceful. Maybe I was a miserable asshole, but that tempted me to fuck with him. "You know, if you guys marry, you'd be my brother."

"Stop. I still have to digest my dinner."

"Look around. The De Lucas aren't that bad."

His eyes took in the surroundings. A box of shit Ren had left laid at his feet. He eyed it from his spot at the edge of the island. "Look, here's some unsolicited advice—"

"The worst kind. No, thanks."

He ignored me. "—You're not your dad. You don't have to act like him. Maybe you should unlearn everything he's taught you and embrace the best parts of being in a syndicate. And there are good parts. It's taken me a while to figure this out, but these good things exist. Take time to discover them.

"You have a rising syndicate, earning potential in your business ventures and oil lands, and enough money that you could live like a Saudi prince for the next ten thousand years and not have to work a second.

"Your dad jeopardized these things when he ran the De Luca syndicate. Now that you're in charge, you can do things differently. You can build, expand, and thrive. Blocking people out... Well, that's your dad's M.O. Don't turn into your dad. No one liked him. No one even respected him.

"When you take the time to discover the best of this world, you'll learn that it's the relationships. The loyalty, trust, and honor. You may not be used to these things thanks to your upbringing—and I don't mean this disrespectfully—but it doesn't mean you can't start embodying them today.

"If you think about it, there was no real reason to keep the fact that you knew Ariana is your sister from her. A lie of omission is still a lie. You lied for no good reason. Think about that. Own up to your lies. Only then can you own your truths, De Luca."

"Why are you telling me this?"

"Because you don't look happy, and my girl's the type of girl that would want her brother happy." He checked his watch and straightened up. "I have to go. I'll show myself out."

He left, but his words stayed with me.

Own your truths, De Luca.

Ren and I were both guilty of lying. To others. To each other.

To ourselves. She was as guilty as I was, and I needed to own that. I needed to admit that we'd both been wrong, apologize for my part of the bad stuff, and get my girl back.

I had everything I'd thought I wanted—money, autonomy, control of the syndicate. Why wasn't I happy?

Because I didn't have Ren.

And I didn't deserve her until I shed all the lies.

Own my truths, indeed.

42

> 66 Though deception is seen as an attack upon the other, deception is a tool of emotional suicide.
>
> — UNKNOWN

Renata Vitali

The children screamed as they ran out of the classroom. My migraine bit at my sanity, and I forced myself to yell out, "Walk, please! Walk! Dylan, stop pushing Andy or I'll send you to the principal's office!" I groaned and pressed my forehead against the whiteboard. "Why must children have vocal chords?"

"Ren? Are you okay? You're normally so calm and unfazed." Silence. "Ren?!"

"What?!" I faltered as I took in Sally's stunned eyes. "Oh, my God. I'm sorry. I didn't mean to snap at you... I'm a mess."

"You're a second-grade teacher. I think you get a hall pass."

"Thanks. It's just been a crazy week." Try a crazy life. "Did you need something?"

"One of the parents brought pizza." She gestured behind her even though the lounge was to the right. "It's in the teacher's lounge."

"Thanks, Sal." My weak smile fooled neither of us. "I'll be right there."

"I'll save you a few slices." She took in my no doubt haggard appearance. "Good thing it's Friday, right?"

Yup. Definitely haggard.

I was thankful when she left. I barely held on as it was. Sanity seemed like such a stranger these days, and I craved an ugly cry session like a reality star craved attention. I eyed the clock. I had thirty minutes of lunch left. Not enough time.

I pushed the tears back, but they wouldn't recede. One slipped past my lashes and down my cheek. Then, another. Oh, God. My heart was breaking, as slow as the Earth's rotation. I never stopped to let myself feel it, but I knew it was happening as much as I tried to prevent it.

My body sank to the floor. I drew my knees to my chest, rested my cheek on them, and for the first time since I fell in love with Damian more than ten years ago, let it happen. I let myself break. The tears didn't make me feel weak. They cleansed me, pushing away the bad memories until I could only focus on the good. The parts of Damian I fell in love with.

I never feared for my life in Texas. Not because of my name— Angelo was prone to reckless lashing out that could turn dangerous in a split second, and my name wouldn't provide enough logic to prevent violence. No, Damian had been my protector, even when he didn't want to admit it to either of us.

Our library dates saved my soul, and that loneliness I'd felt my entire life receded around him. He protected me when Laura and the rest of the student body drugged me. We fell in love in little moments—battles of wit, tiny shows of affection, resolute faith in one another.

So much for that faith.

My phone rang, and I forced myself to sober. I answered it without looking at the caller ID and pressed it to my ear as I gathered my things.

"Renata, honey—"

What the...

My brows pressed together. "Papà?"

The urgency in his voice had my pulse racing. "I need you to go to your mom's and grab something for me, Renata."

I'd opted to stay out of their mess when I left Maman's. I wanted nothing to do with the mafia. It would take nothing more than a miracle to drag me back—kicking and screaming, mind you.

I shook my head, even though he couldn't see me. "Can't you ask her to?"

"It's a tape, baby girl." He'd never called me that before. "She's using it to blackmail me. What's on it could send me to jail. You don't want your papà in jail, right?"

"Papà, this is between you and my mom. I'd appreciate it if you left me out of it."

"Do as I say, Renata." He'd cut the begging and returned to his demanding self. Oddly, the familiarity relieved me.

Still, I wasn't taking his shit. "I'm not a kid anymore. You can't send me off to Texas as punishment."

The curious part of me wondered what Maman had done on her trip to Italy. Papà sounded like a man hanging together by a thread. It wasn't what I'd gotten used to hearing from him. I also hadn't heard anything about the Vitali since then, though I wasn't exactly in the loop.

Papà's harsh tone scathed me. "There are other ways to punish you. I know you're fighting with your mom, but you still care about her. So, either you go to the Hamptons and grab the tape in the safe or I send a strike team to do it for me, and it won't be pretty."

He must have sensed my hesitation because he pressed on. "Damiano De Luca."

I froze at his name. I wasn't delusional enough not to realize that I still cared. Damian was my first—and only—love. Your first love is the man you'll always compare every other man to. He's the person you never get over, even when you've managed to convince yourself that you've moved on.

I'd dated over a dozen men since Damiano De Luca. I compared each and every one to him, and it had fractured those relationships before they even started. I could keep living, going through the motions, maybe one day even find happiness without him. But I would never get over him. And that included loving him every second of every day.

Papà had me by the neck. He had all the leverage he needed just by mentioning Damian's name. His laughter rung loud and dry. "You didn't think I didn't hear about how you two fell in love when I sent you to Texas?" He scoffed. "*I* did that. *I* gave you love." He lowered his voice. "I could take it just as easily."

Déjà vu swayed me, warping me back to the hallway in Devils Ridge, where Angelo made a similar threat to me.

"Fine," I bit out.

"There's a videotape in the safe. The code is six digits. Three couplets. Your birthdate, plus fourteen on each couplet."

Of course, the safe code derived from my birthdate. My parents had a fucked-up way of showing their love for me. Papà hung up as soon as I grunted my agreement. By the time school ended and I drove from Connecticut to New York, night had fallen.

The army that met me at Maman's driveway startled me. I recognized some faces as boys from my high school in Devils Ridge. They'd grown into men and, for reasons which evaded me, gathered on Maman's stone-paved driveway. A liaison from the Romano family leaned against the front door beside Bastian Romano and Ariana De Luca.

I stilled when I saw who stood next to Maman. He commanded attention beside her in a uniform of all black clothing, black tactical gloves, and a bulletproof vest. He had several weapons attached to his body, including an assault rifle swung across his chest.

When my car was parked, and the engine cut off, his eyes landed on mine.

"Damsel," I whispered.

And even though I knew he couldn't actually hear me, I also knew he'd still heard me.

43

> " Sometimes, deception can be therapeutic.

— NOLAN ROSS

Renata Vitali

I came to the conclusion that there was no way I'd get into the safe with this many people around pretty quickly. It took all of point-two seconds for the urge to leave to settle in. Damian took a step toward me, but I didn't think the movement was conscious. After all, his eyes didn't seem as inviting as his body.

I wanted to hate him, but staring at him, I couldn't bring

myself to feel the hatred. Just resignation at the fact that my heart would always belong to him.

Maman approached the car door, her eyes delighted. "Did your father send you here?"

My eyes slid to Damian before returning to Maman. "Yes."

Lying would be pointless. I wanted nothing to do with this mess, and judging by this army and the blackmail tape Maman had on Papà, Papà seemed to be on the losing side. Damian was safe. I could go now and sleep knowing my father couldn't hurt him, but my fingers wouldn't turn on the car and my foot wouldn't hit the pedal.

Maman's laughter twinkled in the otherwise silent night. "He's a bit desperate, isn't he?"

I nodded, my head stiff. "Sounded like it."

"He wanted you to steal the tape?" Her words seemed less like a question and more like a statement.

"Yes. He said either this or he'd send in a TAC team." The temptation to stare at Damian gutted me.

"And I assume he threatened his"—she nodded in Damian's direction—"life."

My hands fisted, hidden at my sides and blocked by the car door. "Yup."

"Good thing I have my army."

How could someone so devious smile so pretty?

"Yup." I nodded, my movements halfhearted. "Good thing."

It struck me again how calculated Maman was. She'd gathered a veritable army in the strongest mafia territory in the world. In helping Damian ascend to the De Luca throne, she'd garnered the favor of a strengthening syndicate. For good measure, she tried to intertwine our families by pushing me and Damian together.

Maman had Vince's heart and support, which meant she had the Romano family's backing. This explained why the Romano allowed her to live in their territory all these years. Plus, the

Romano family had to play along with this tactical gathering because doing otherwise meant admitting they had unknowingly let a sleeper into their territory.

The Andretti family was finally at peace with the Romano family, something I suspected Maman and Vince had played a hand in. Going against the Romano family would restart a war that had only just ended.

The Rossi family connected with the Romano family in heritage. Bastian Romano's mother was a Rossi, who shared an arranged marriage with Bastian's dad. So, if the Romano family was okay with Maman gathering here, the Rossi family would be, too.

And finally, the Camerino family couldn't go against four families, and they were already too spent on their territorial war with the Rossi family to take on Maman. So many little pieces created this puzzle, a feat no other man or woman had achieved. If I weren't so disgusted, I would have been impressed.

Maman had taken over the Vitali, and there was nothing anyone could do about it.

"I'll let you and your boyfriend talk before you leave." She arched a brow and stared me down. "Unless you've decided to appreciate all that I've done to procure this empire for you and would like to be an adult and talk with me."

I shook my head. "No, thanks."

"Hmm." Her lips flattened. "You may not realize it now, but this is a good thing, little warrior. Look around. This is unity. For the first time in history, the five syndicates are unified. We're stronger together." She reached out to touch me, thought better of it, turned, and walked away.

My eyes met Damian's again.

Maman spoke of unity, but I'd never felt so divided.

44

> ❝ Patience is the weapon that forces deception to reveal itself. It is insurance against being deceived or making wrong decisions.
>
> — MICHELLE MCKINNEY HAMMOND

Renata Vitali

In a weird, messed up way, Maman's words spoke of peace. Cooperation. Solidarity. The irony made me snort.

"Laughing to yourself?" Damian rested a forearm on the top of my SUV door and leaned forward, peeking in my window at me. It was so casual, I would have thought we were okay, had it not been for my conflicting emotions and the tense lines on his face.

I'd wasted my window of opportunity to leave on wallowing at the state of my life. I'd had two major relationships in my life —the mother-daughter bond I shared with Maman and what Damian and I shared. Now, I had nothing.

I stared up at Damian, wondering how this conversation would go. So much had been left unsaid between us, and my anger hadn't abated. Neither had my heartache. Damian looked just as tired as me, which satisfied the part of me that needed to know he still cared.

He heaved a sigh. "How have you been holding up, Princess?"

So, we were going the civil route. I could live with that.

There were so many ways to answer his question. Instead, I swallowed the urge to yell at him and settled for my go to phrase. "I'm not the princess." The familiarity only heightened my nostalgia, which rose to my throat and formed knots until I couldn't breathe.

"Knight."

"I'm not the knight either. I'm the pawn, Damian." Bitter laughter bubbled in my throat like a bath bomb churning in hot water. "A fucking pawn."

"You're a pawn like I'm a fairy princess."

"My mom used me as a pawn, and then you accused me of being complicit in that. I lost my mother and the love of my life in the same day. There's no trust between us. I shouldn't be surprised. The first thing I did when I met you was lie about snooping in your room, and then I stole your phone. What a way to start a relationship."

He heaved a sigh. "Your mom told me what she did. I suspect not everything, but enough to explain that you weren't involved in"—he waved his finger in a circular gesture—"all this. I was wrong, and I'm sorry. There's no excuse for how I reacted, but I'd like to explain."

"Okay."

"Everyone in my life has lied to me, and it was easier to run from you than accept that our relationship isn't as perfect as I wanted it to be. But the thing is, I conflated my relationship with you back then to my relationship to you now. That's not fair to either of us. We deserve a second chance, not a continuation of a first chance that was destined to fail."

"I can't give you another chance, Damsel. I can't handle it. I like to pretend I'm strong, but I'm human, and nothing drills that into me more than when I'm around you."

We were silent for a moment. Too much needed to be said, but none of it would be easy.

He broke the silence first. "For what it's worth, I thought it was hot when you stole my phone. No one else in the town had the guts to go against me. Except maybe my dad."

"Fuck Angelo De Luca." I bit back a smile when he barked out a surprised laugh. This got too friendly for my liking. I needed to remind him that we weren't friends. "You and my mom seem cozy for someone who accused me of being her coconspirator."

"You're here, aren't you?"

I wasn't even going to dignify that with an answer.

He paused for a response, but when I didn't reply, he continued, "I talked to Bastian. He came to visit me in Oklahoma."

"Did he find out about Ariana being your sister?"

"Yes. He wanted me to talk to her."

"Have you?"

"She's here, but we haven't had a moment alone. I think I'd like to get to know her sometime. Not today when I'm being leveraged into defending a mad woman,"—I snorted—"but later. When I'm ready to talk to her."

"I'm happy for you."

And I was. I didn't question why he told me this. I chalked it up to instinct. While I'd only ever had Maman and Damian,

305

Damian had only ever had me. I wanted to be here for him like I wanted NBC to stop canceling my favorite shows, but we were too fractured to be together... maybe, at the very least, we could be friends?

Friendship.

It was a good goal.

His silence encouraged me to ask, "Why don't you seem mad at me?" Not that I did anything worth his anger in the first place, but last I checked, he still thought I had a part in Maman's scheming and lied to him about it.

I watched as he rounded the car and got into the passenger seat.

He shut the door as he settled into the leather seat. "Bastian also said something that's kind of stuck with me. I've got to own my lies before I can own my truths."

"Lies?"

"I've told a lot of them to a lot of people. Some on purpose. Some unintentionally. Those are the worst. They take the longest to realize."

I leaned my head back against the headrest. I understood what he meant. I'd been telling myself I didn't love Damian since the moment I started falling for him. I'd also been lied to over and over again. It didn't feel good to be on either side of the deception.

I glanced at him and took in the severity of his expression. "So, you're owning your lies right now?"

"Yes."

"Confess away."

"I first liked you when you stood up to my dad on your seventeenth birthday. I heard what you said to him when anyone else would have cowered in that bath. I wanted you when you turned a debate of Freud's "Dostoevsky and Parricide" into a flirting opportunity—and don't deny you were flirting, because I was, too. I fell in love with you when my dad punched me in the face,

306

and you told me to get back up because you knew I was stronger than self-pity. Every moment after that, from our library dates to the dance to that night in my bedroom, I fell in love with you more."

Holy hell. How did he expect me to survive this conversation with my ovaries intact if he kept going on like this?

Friendship, Renata. Pull yourself together, woman.

He continued, unaware of my inner turmoil. "When you left, Cristian would ask me, 'How do you know you even like her? How do you know what love is?'"

I remembered why I'd never liked Cristian.

"What did you say?"

"I told him that I don't know." He gutted me with his words. "I told him that no one knows what love is, but there's something about you I'll never be able to let go. That's the closest to knowing any of us get."

He leaned back against the seat and eyed the ceiling of the car. "But I was wrong. There's a way to know. I can't define the feeling, but that doesn't change the fact that I know I love you. I realized this when I saw you in New York. That piece of you I'd never been able to let go of didn't loosen. It saw you, tightened, and tugged me closer."

His words thrust me over a cliff, clinging onto the ridge for dear life.

"Oh."

A stupid response, but I didn't trust myself to say more. We needed to stay friends. We'd tried having a relationship twice. At least as his friend, I still had him in my life.

"You're my first love, Knight. I gave my heart to you."

Maybe that was the problem. He couldn't let go of me because his first love was the only person who would ever get all of him. No matter how much time passed, I would always hold a piece of him no one else would.

It was the piece of him that discovered love. That learned love in late night library dates, when friendship transformed to love, when one soul lifted the burdens of the other, and in that first kiss we could never go back from.

How much of what he said was that missing piece he'd given me talking? How much of it was real? Truth was... I didn't just want to be his first love. I wanted to be his last love. But here we sat. Civil, for reasons which blew my mind. We had an opportunity now to be friends, to always be in one another's lives without risking losing each other.

"We have a choice right now to become friends and stay in each other's lives without risking another ten years apart. I think we should take it."

He let loose a humorless chuckle. "We have a lot of choices in life, but I know for a fact that this is not one of them. You can say whatever you want about outside forces involved in our relationship. But to me, meeting you will always be fate. I made the choice to befriend you. But falling in love with each other? That's beyond our control. We can try to stop it all you'd like, but we will always be in love with each other, and anyone else would just be settling."

"I can't risk this."

"It's a bigger risk to spend our lives knowing we're best together and not taking the leap. That ring you have tattooed on your wedding finger is permanent proof you're in love me. That you will always love me. I'm imprinted in your skin, Ren. Forever. There's no hiding from that. Do you remember when I drew that on you?"

"You drew this on me?"

I held my left hand to my chest and clutched it with my other hand. As if hiding my tattoo would change its origin, or the fact that I didn't know where the original Sharpied line came from but my own intuition told me I needed it etched into my skin permanently.

He eyed my hand and nodded. "That night Laura drugged

you, I took you back to your room. You asked me why I helped you. I told you that the only time I don't feel like I'm just going through the motions is when I'm with you. That's still true, by the way. You told me you thought you liked me, and I told you that, if things weren't so complicated, I could see myself with you forever. And then, I drew that ring around your wedding ring finger."

He reached for my hand, and I let him grab it—couldn't help myself. "I didn't realize it until recently, but things don't have to be so complicated. We can simplify it." He leaned forward, brought my hand to his lips, and pressed a kiss to my tattoo. "Choose me, and I'll choose you. We'll put each other first. Everything else is just background noise."

I wanted to. I did. But I couldn't make the choice right now. What would help me to take the leap? I wasn't the type for grand gestures. I wasn't even the type for little ones. So, knowing what I wanted escaped me.

"I don't have an answer for you."

"That's okay." He studied my face. "But I'm going to keep trying."

"Okay."

"Don't change your phone number again."

My smile slipped past. "Okay." I finally let loose a laugh, and it felt free. "Was changing my phone number dramatic? Maybe. But in my defense, it—"

A screech of tires pierced the air. Damian flung his body across mine, covering me in an instant. I didn't need his protection, but he did it anyway. Across Maman's courtyard and driveway, soldiers drew their handguns and assault rifles to a ready position.

Four unmarked Escalades stopped in the driveway, over two dozen men armed with rifles evenly distributed between them. Papà's tactical team. They took one look at our group, which outnumbered theirs four to one, and paused their movements.

Maman stood on the steps to her home. She leaned against a column, one foot hooked around the other, the picture of nonchalance. And why would she care? She was well-connected in the mafia world. She spent her time gaining allies, whereas Papà spent his time making enemies.

Maman and the intruders stood at a standoff. Still, she looked unconcerned. Confident, even. She had an army. Papà had a small tactical team. They'd retreat, and the Vitali family would be hers.

The opposition team's cars retreated, backing out of the driveway. Damian pulled back a little, and our eyes met with hardly a hand's width separating us. His eyes dipped to my lips. I leaned into him before remembering that I wasn't ready to risk losing him by entering a relationship with him.

I leaned back into my seat, and he backed away from me. "You didn't have to do that."

"Instinct." He paused. "And even if it wasn't instinct, I would have done it anyway."

I couldn't be mad at that. "Thank you."

And despite everything, despite the years of deception from all sides, I realized that he always made me feel safe.

45

> **“** There is nothing more deceptive than an obvious fact.

> — ARTHUR CONAN DOYLE

One Week Later

Damian: Still no answer?

Renata: Ask me again tomorrow.

Damian: It's tomorrow.

Renata: Observant.

Damian: Cute.

Renata: Tomorrow.

Damian: I'm starting to think you just want me to text you every day.

Renata: ...

Damian: Let me guess... Tomorrow?

Renata: ...

Damiano De Luca

I nodded a greeting at Bastian, who sat on the customer side of the empty bar. At midday, the bar was closed as it prepped for dinner service.

Ariana glanced from me to Bastian. "I'll give you guys some space."

"Actually, I came to see you."

Bastian looked between us. "Fucking finally."

Ariana shooed him away, then returned her attention to me. "I was wondering how long it would take for you to show up."

"Hey, you could have come to me."

She rubbed a rag across the counter in large circles. "We're still short staffed." A smug smirk crossed her lips. "My former bosses may have filtered out all the qualified job applicants, so I'd get the job."

It still blew my mind that I, one, had a sister; two, she was a fed; and three, Bastian Romano fell in love with a goddamned fed.

"And those former bosses are just okay with you working here?"

"I don't work for them anymore. There's not much they can do." She didn't elaborate, and I didn't ask. "You're not like your dad, are you?"

"Fuck no." I paused. "Technically, he's your dad, too."

"Is he that bad?"

"Worse."

She sighed. "I guess my mom was right to run."

"She was probably better off outside Devils Ridge," I agreed.

"She died giving birth to me."

Shit. "I'm sorry."

And I was. Not just because she was my sister—and holy shit, I had a sister—but because I liked her as a person. The night shift came and went, and by the time all the employees left, Ariana and I still sat in a booth, talking.

Ariana shrugged. "There are a lot of issues when it comes to my mom, but I didn't really know her. I miss something I've never had but know I should love."

"Are you always such an open book?"

We'd dived straight into the deep stuff, not bothering with the pleasantries. In one night, I learned more about her than I knew about some of the kids I'd gone to school with my whole life.

"No. Never, actually." She took a sip from her coffee mug and looked up at me. "We have decades of lost time to make up for." I already knew firsthand how that felt with Ren. "I figured if it took you this long to come see me, you had to talk yourself up to it, and the least I can do is be open and honest with you since I couldn't bring myself to see you either." She looked around the bar and sighed. "I'm also averse to lying. I used to work undercover. It gets so damn tiring."

"That may be my favorite thing about you so far."

"That I worked undercover?"

"No, that you're committed to honesty."

"I hear you're having some trouble with that."

"Your boyfriend has a big mouth."

"He said you didn't look happy when he saw you in Oklahoma, and you couldn't get over the lies Renata's mom embedded your life in. We both know better than anyone else that our parents' actions hold no bearings on our own."

"I know that now. Hell, maybe I knew that then, too."

"Then, what happened?"

Something about her drew me in—maybe the way she looked at me like she genuinely cared, her face so similar to Nana's. It made me want to confess everything. I figured she must have developed that ability working undercover, but I liked it. I liked the idea of having a sister, someone tied to me by De Luca blood who hadn't been tainted by the De Luca madness.

"I couldn't stop the accusations from spewing out of my mouth. Our relationship never moved on from Devils Ridge ten —almost eleven—years ago. So, all that frustration I felt in Oklahoma..." I shook my head. "It was really what I felt from Devils Ridge after our relationship ended the first time."

"And now?"

"I'm trying to release every lie I've accumulated in my life, so I can move forward and be someone Ren deserves."

"Is that what this is?"

"A little. Yes, I've lied to you and want to apologize for it, but I also want to see you. I'm sorry I didn't tell you when I found out that you're my sister. I'm also sorry it took me this long to come see you."

She reached out and squeezed my hand over the tabletop. "I'm sorry I didn't tell you I'm your sister. I knew since birth, and I could have approached you when I turned eighteen. The truth is, I was afraid. I'd heard a lot about your dad, and when rumors reached the bureau that you took over, I could have reached out. My job didn't matter enough to me to prevent me from doing so. It was the fear that you'd be the monster my aunt always told me your dad is."

I shook my head. "I don't blame you. He's a real piece of work, but I promise you, I'm not like that. At all. I want to get to know you."

"I'd like that. How does the truth feel?"

"Like I should have done this in the first place."

"Hindsight's a bitch like that. What are you going to do now?"

"Go get my girl."

46

> The essence of bravery is being without self-deception.
>
> — PEMA CHÖDRÖN

Renata Vitali

I checked my phone again. My desk chair dug uncomfortably into my thighs as I tapped my feet.

"Miss Vitali?"

"Yes?"

I looked up at Charles, one of my students whose mother always picked him up late. Nearly an hour had passed since the bell rung. The same amount of time had passed between Damian's last text to me, and my patience ran thin. Which, I knew, was a sign that I still cared. Fuck caring. And fuck not having Damian, too.

Last week, after snapping at Sally again, I figured I owed her an explanation for my short fuse. I gave her the gist of it. I had an ex, who recently came back into my life for a short-lived summer romance. He wanted me back, and despite the fact that I loved him, I couldn't bring myself to take the leap because our past kept coming back to haunt us.

Sally claimed that I wanted Damian to fight for me. It didn't have to be that drastic, but taking the leap of faith scared me, and I needed some reassurance that we wouldn't relapse. Second chances could either be an opportunity to prove you've learned from your mistakes or another opportunity for someone to hurt you. The latter made me cautious.

"Miss Vitali?"

"Huh?" I blinked a few times in rapid succession and focused on Charles. "Sorry, Charles. What did you need?"

"I was gonna say that your foot tapping is annoying, but now my mom is here." He waved the iPhone no eight-year-old had any business possessing. "Bye, Miss Vitali. I liked the finger painting in class today. You'd be cooler if you let us do that every day."

I cocked a brow. "I'm not cool?"

He shook his head, his chubby face solemn. "No. Mr. Rice is way cooler. I had him last year."

Oh, boy. Someone save this boy from the wrath of an underpaid, overworked teacher.

I pasted a fake smile on my face. "Mr. Rice is pretty darn cool. Have a nice night, Charles."

We both stood, and I opened the door for Charles. The two of us jumped back when we saw someone on the other side.

Damian.

I glanced at Charles before my eyes darted to Damian. "This

is highly inappropriate."

"I thought school was over."

It was. Charles' mom needed a watch like I need a gin and tonic right now.

Charles turned to me. "Is this your boyfriend?"

His mom rushed into the hallway, her hair a haggard mess. "I'm so sorry. I had to—" Her voice trailed off as she caught sight of Damian. "Um, wow." She fixed her hair and smiled. "I'm Stella."

Damian didn't bother looking at her. Instead, I had his full attention as he nodded to the classroom. Because I needed her gone without a barrage of who-is-that-hot-guy questions, I gave Charles' mom a polite smile and waved when I would usually give her some passive aggressive attitude after she came barreling in an hour late, her face still pink from her facial or her wrists bright red from the shopping bags she carried.

I shut the door and locked it after I entered the classroom. Damian gave me time to stare at the door while I gathered myself before I turned around and faced him. My classroom was a chaotic, Harry Potter themed mess you couldn't help but stare at, yet I owned his attention as I took a seat behind my desk.

He followed me there, leaned against the edge of the desk, and stared at me.

"You're here," I whispered.

"It's tomorrow."

"I guess it is."

"I didn't want to wait ten more years." He used his foot to turn my chair, so my body faced him directly. "I don't want to waste ten years, knowing the only woman I want is you, and everyone else I meet would amount to nothing, because all I'd be doing is comparing them to you every second of every day."

"What do you want from me?"

"I want you to realize how much I love you."

"I do."

How the hell could I not when I loved him so much, I knew that words would never adequately explain how I felt. I refused to believe he didn't feel the same way. He was the right guy with the wrong timing, and I knew deep down that he deserved a second chance, and a third, and a fourth, and more, until we worked. But I, fearless Renata Vitali, was too chicken to take the leap.

"I don't think you do, Princess." He grabbed my hand and pulled me up until we stood face to face, my body between his legs, and his arm wrapped around my back. "I love you. Every good memory I have is with you. Every breath I take is for you. Every dream I have is featuring you. It's. All. You. From the second I caught you on my bed and you stole my fucking phone, I was yours. I can't let ten more years go by, Renata. The last ten years nearly destroyed me. I searched for you. Spent millions searching. Took time off to question anyone and everyone I could. Nearly started territorial wars trying to find you. And every night, I'd go to bed wondering if I was searching hard enough. My favorite part of the day was when I went to bed and dreamed of you. I'd lay on my empty sheets, wondering how ten years have changed you. Were you taller? Did you still dye your hair god awful jaundiced corpse yellow? Did you still live in sweats twenty-four seven? Did you still stay up late reading classics you've already read a million times before? My dreams always filled in the missing pieces, but they were never enough. When I woke up, you were never there, and I had to wait till nighttime to see you in my dreams again. I know you're it for me because every time I do something that should make me happy, I'm not fucking happy, because there's no greater happiness than being with you."

The first tear slipped past as he put into words everything I'd felt over the past ten years. Everything I tried to bury inside me. He didn't give me time to fully process his words before he handed me something.

A photograph.

I took it from him and stared, unsure what I was looking at. A close up to a pile of ruins. Chunks of dark wood. Some cracked marble. Was this a junkyard?

I glanced back up at him. "What is this?" My eyes returned to the photograph as I stared, oddly transfixed by the destruction.

"My dad's house."

My head shot back up, and I swallowed. "What?"

Our library.

He'd destroyed our library.

No, no, no, no, no, no, no.

"I moved into the lake house in Oklahoma."

"That's great." I cleared my throat, my heart withering at the thought of all those memories destroyed.

You still fucking care, Renata.

I tried again, hoping I was at least half convincing in my false happiness. "I'm happy for you." I tried to be. I really tried.

"I moved it."

"What?"

"I moved the library into the lake house."

I shook my head. "What? How?"

"I had the entire thing cut out and shipped to Oklahoma, where I built it into the house as an add on, right next to the library you renovated. The old with the new. I'm ready to move on, Princess. I destroyed Dad's place, and the only things I've taken with me are the good memories. Our library is sitting there, in my house, waiting for you to make more memories. Make more memories with me, Ren. Let me be the Day to your Knight again. Let me prove to you that we're fate."

Holy hell, this was him fighting for me.

I just had to leap.

I opened my mouth to speak. Fear gripped my muscles. My eyes met his, took in his expression, and I knew I was making the right decision.

EPILOGUE

> Deception isn't black and white. Sometimes, there's more to the story. Sometimes, it's the only step to overcome before your happily ever after.

— PARKER S. HUNTINGTON

Renata Vitali

One Year Later

I remind myself that I pretty much live with a ninja as I tiptoe down the stairs and into the library. Flicking on the light, I scour the shelves for the paperback I want and head for the divan from Devils Ridge.

Damian didn't lie when he said he had attached the old library to the new one. It's literally attached by some extra wall frames and an extended foundation. The dark Victorian decor clashes with the light farmhouse-style beach house, but I love it.

When I step into the old library, all the good memories from the first time I fell in love with Damian greet me. Everything is pretty much the same, except he flew to New York and took pictures of every Toynbee tile of ours. Those pictures are now framed in bookends on some of the shelves.

I grab a Sharpie from the desk and return to the divan. My fingers open the paperback. *The Toynbee Convector*. Skimming through the book until I land on "The Toynbee Convector," I slide a photograph onto the page and close the book.

We're reading it tomorrow. I can't wait until he opens it and finds the ultrasound I had taken yesterday. I can't wait for a lot of things lately. Every second of life with Damian excites me, and I can't believe I went ten years without him.

The door creaks open. I set the book beside me on the divan, hoping it doesn't draw Damian's attention.

His eyes are a little sleepy, but I know he's alert because we always are. It's not the type of training we can turn off. "You're up late."

"I couldn't sleep."

He sends me a sly grin and crosses the room to me. "I can help you with that."

"Oh? How so?"

"I hear orgasms help you sleep better."

"That's mostly for men." I place my hand on the front of his thigh, my head eye level with his growing erection. "I have a better idea."

"A better idea than orgasms?"

"I think you'll like it."

I stay seated, though he stands in front of me, his head tilted down to meet my gaze. I can tell he thinks I'm about to pull out his erection, but instead, I lean around him and grab the Sharpie. His smile slips, and it takes everything in me not to laugh.

Grabbing his left hand, I press my lips to it and sigh onto his skin. "I love you, Damian. I have spent a decade missing you, and whenever I think of it, I can't believe how stubborn we were. How stubborn *I* was. The truth is, I've always known that you're it for me. I knew it when we were kids, and I know it now." I uncap the pen. "I don't want to spend another second without you. I don't want to spend another second as anything other than your wife. You've already put a ring on my finger. Will you let me put one on yours?"

"You're asking me to marry you?"

"Yes, but technically,"—I raise my left hand—"you put a ring on me first. I just want that to be clear."

"Crystal clear." He gives me his hand, and a stupid grin lights up my face as I draw a line around his ring finger.

I meet his eyes. "Do you know what this means?"

"What?"

"I basically just emasculated you by being the one to ask you to marry me." I don't actually believe that, but I know his reaction will amuse me. I smirk at his narrowed eyes. "I think you need to reclaim your manhood."

I squeal and drop the Sharpie as he lifts me and grinds his erection into my core. My legs knock against the paperback, and it falls to the ground. The ultrasound slides out.

"What's this?" Damian sets me down, bends over, and picks it up. The widest smile I've ever seen on him crosses his face, even wider than when I drew that ring on his finger. "You're pregnant?"

"Yup. Sixteen weeks. I didn't even realize it because my cycle has been irregular since I removed my IUD."

"You're not even showing."

"I am, but I think you've been distracted by my new curves."

"Did you propose because you're pregnant?"

I shook my head. "No, I found out I was pregnant when I took a test two days ago. I've been planning this for about a month."

He eyes *The Toynbee Convector*. "You've been waiting for us to get to this book."

I nodded to the ultrasound picture. "The baby was just a happy coincidence."

The baby.

Our baby.

It strikes me that I have everything I want in this library. Damian. Our baby girl. Rings on our fingers. I used to think Damian was a twisted prince who couldn't love. I used to think he'd become the king and destroy me.

But our demons have been put to rest. Our past no longer plagues us. And Damian may not be the Damsel anymore, but I feel like a fucking princess.

Damiano De Luca

"So, let me get this straight. She didn't insist on a giant diamond ring?" Niccolaio eyes the tattoo on my finger like it's a Rubix cube he can't crack.

"No." I arch a brow. "Did Minka?"

"No."

"Okay."

"Okay."

Ranie shakes his head, his eyes glued on his wife, who stands at the edge of the lake in a candy red bikini half the size of her baby bump. "You guys are stupid."

Bastian tosses the last of his cheeseburger to my dog and ignores the glare I cast his way. "At least their wives have something on their fingers."

I pat Pages, my tiny Shih Tzu—a living, panting blow to my masculinity, but my wife wanted him, and I wanted her happy. "If that gives Pages the shits, you're cleaning it, Romano."

"You're a six-two guy with a five-pound Shih Tzu named Pages. If you think I'm cleaning your dog's shit, I can schedule a CT scan for your damaged brain. I'm sure Liv would do it."

Marco shakes his head. "My girl's not touching any of you assholes."

Ranie twists the platinum band on his finger. "Gallo's eight months pregnant. If my wife's wedding ring still fits on her finger after eight months with a bun in her oven, my sperm's not as super as I thought. And I can assure you that's not the case. My son's gonna be huge. You should have seen the size of his package on the ultrasound."

We all had, in our group chat from hell.

Didn't miss the second or third pictures he sent either.

Asher's eyes remain closed, like he can't believe he's spending a Saturday with us, but he can suck it up because my girl wanted everyone here, so everyone had better damn well be here. "I'd be more concerned with your son, who's pissing into the fire pit."

None of us ask how Asher saw that with his eyes closed. We all look to the side, and sure enough, Luke is swinging his package around like it's a lightsaber, splashing piss all over my custom-built fire pit.

Marco laughs and downs his spiked Arnold Palmer. "Father of the year, Ranie."

His daughter runs up to us, her Converse soaking wet from running at the edge of the lake. "Why does Luke's bagina look different from mine? He says it's 'cause he's cooler than me."

Marco covers Charlotte's ears and yells out, "I'm gonna fucking kill you, Ranie!"

Ranie flips Marco the bird as he walks over to Luke, makes his son zip himself back up, and tells him not to get caught next time. *Andrettis don't get caught, Luke.* Gallo waddles over to them and overrules Ranie, saying there will not, under any circumstances, be a next time.

Marco uncovers Charlotte's ears and kneels, so they're closer to eye level. "Remember what I told you about Brett Keith?"

"The guy who mom used to like?"

He narrows his eyes. "Mom never liked him. But yes. Him."

"You said, 'Never trust anyone with two first names.'"

Bastian snorts and pats Charlotte's head. "Your dad's really mature, Charlie Girl."

Marco pushes Bastian's hand away. "I also said never to trust boys."

"Because Brett is a liar." She scrunches her brows together and tilts her head. "Aren't you a boy?"

His eyes dart to mine, but I'm content to watch him fumble through fatherhood. I salute him with my beer bottle and take a sip.

His eyes return to Charlotte, who bites her lip and stares at Marco with wide blue eyes. "I think your mom just called you."

"But I didn't hear anything."

"Me neither." A smirk curves my lips. "Have you ever heard of the term 'pathological liar,' Charlie?"

Marco guides Charlotte in Greyson's direction. "Okay, go play with your brother."

"But—"

"Go, Charlotte."

She runs away, just as Raf, who was on the phone with his father-in-law, ambles over to us. He takes in the kids running around; Liv, Lucy, and Minka, lounging near the lake; Ranie, Carina, and Luke by the fire pit; and me, Marco, Bastian, and Asher, chillin' with beers in our hands—a casual Saturday barbecue.

He shakes his head. "You guys can't tell me that this isn't surreal."

I take in the view with him. "Definitely."

Seven years ago, a gathering like this never would have been possible. The Andretti-Romano war seemed endless. The Camerino-Rossi war drew more blood than a Red Cross donation van. The De Luca family garnered little respect.

I can't stand Ren's mom—hell, Ren still refuses to talk to either of her parents—but Margot Vitali did what she promised. I'll give her that. She united the five syndicates. Now we have a new generation, who will grow up never having experienced any of our wars. It took me a while to understand how a man like Vincent Romano could be complicit with dethroning Ren's dad, but watching my daughter play with kids from every syndicate, I get it.

Asher finally peeks his eyes open. "We all wish Sof could be here, man."

"I miss her." Raf runs a hand across his face, but he has a half-smile on it as he watches the kids play. That's how I know he's okay.

I catch Sadie as she tries to run past me and into the house. "Where do you think you're going?"

Her arms are crossed, and she looks pissed with a capital P. "To grab my voodoo doll, Daddy!"

"Your what?" I shake my head. "Why?"

"I hate Scarlett!" Her little feet stomp, and it'd be amusing if it was her mom dealing with the temper tantrum, not me. "I hate Scarlett so much!"

Scarlett is Raf's daughter. She's the opposite of her mom, which means she's Raf's twin. Dark hair, devious smile, and those I-know-something-you-don't eyes.

"You don't mean that."

But Sadie's eyes form little slits, and shit, maybe she does mean it. For a blonde-haired, blue-eyed angel, she has a streak of fire. One I'll need to worry about until she's old and graying. "Scarlett keeps talking to Rowan. Rowan is mine! She's stealing him from me, Daddy! Scarlett's a thief."

Oh, dear God, I hope Scarlett succeeds. Rowan is almost as much trouble as Marco's son Greyson.

Raf rolls his eyes and mutters, "Asher, I swear, your son better stay away from my daughter."

Asher takes a sip of his beer, unfazed. "Because he reminds you too much of yourself?"

Before Sofia wrangled Raf, he slept his way around the Rossi territory and New England, where he went to boarding school with Bastian and Marco.

I shake my head and focus on my daughter. "Where did you get a voodoo doll?"

"Everyone has one now!" Sadie crosses her arms and tilts her chin up, looking way older than her five years. "They're a therapeutic way to channel rage."

I swear, kids grow up on TV doctors these days. The urge to toss out all the flat screens, tablets, and smartphones in the house grips me again. Last week, Sadie overheard me and Ren fucking in the bedroom. I'm not sure what she made of all the grunting, but she asked if I found a revolutionary anger management regimen.

The kid has a Mensa-certified brain people only dream of, coupled with the maturity of a kindergartener. A headache, but my cute little headache.

"Gosh, Daddy. Get with the program." She runs off before I can ask her any more questions.

I set my beer down, nod to the guys, and head into the kitchen, where I just saw Ren enter. At the entrance to the kitchen, I lean against the wall and watch her work. Her clothes have been getting tighter and tighter around areas I'd like to grab and bite down on.

"I know you're watching me, Damian." She still hasn't turned to face me.

I don't mind. My view's unparalleled. I could watch Ren dance around the kitchen all day.

"You going to explain why we're throwing this?"

"I can't invite my friends over for a nice Saturday barbecue?"

It's been known to happen, and it's not like none of us have private jets we can hop onto at a moment's notice. But Ren's been avoiding alcohol, and lately, all it takes is a brush of my tongue against her nipple, and she's coming harder than a hail storm.

My girl's pregnant, and I know she wants our friends here when she spills. I reach into the fridge and pull out a giant catering to-go box. It has the logo from our local sports bar on it, so I know Ren hasn't touched it. I hand it to her.

"What's this?"

"Can you plate it, so I can bring it out to the guys?"

"Sure." She lifts the lid and nearly drops it when she sees the cake inside. It's in-your-face blue, and the lettering reads: IT'S A BOY! Ren looks up at me. "How did you know I'm pregnant?"

"Last night, you rubbed yourself on my leg in your sleep. I

had to clean it off in the restroom after you came." I laughed. "You didn't even wake up. Other pregnant women are into fried pickles and Snickers, but not my wife. My wife likes to fuck."

"Damian!" Her eyes dart around the kitchen, probably checking to make sure Sadie isn't lurking around. "How do you even know it's a boy? It's too early to tell."

"I just know."

She arches a brow. "You just know?"

"Yup."

And I do.

Just like I know I'm blessed.

Just like I know I'm in love.

Just like I know we're forever.

Just like I know I'm her Day, and she's my Knight.

The End.

ACKNOWLEDGMENTS

Chloe, you beautiful, pure-hearted soul; you pretty girl, with the clear blue eyes and the goofy grin; you energetic fun-seeker; you love of my life, my biggest heartbreak and biggest smile; I love you. I loved you yesterday. I love you today. And I'll love you tomorrow. I wish you were here.

Rose and Bauer—my two wonder pups! Thank you for distracting me as I write and keeping me company when the last thing I want to do is write. Thank you for making it take ten times longer than usual to publish a book. Thank you for making my life a million times better than it would be without you two in it.

L, thank you for being my partner in crime.

Ava, get better WiFi.

Oh, and thank you.

Juli, your teasers give me life. Thank you for loving the Five Syndicates as much as I do and for sharing that love with the world. <3 I love your IG page and Facebook posts, your sweet messages, and your passion for reading. I love your bubbly personally. And I am honored to have you as a reader—to have been your first read.

Leigh, thank you for being my momager, for helping me process this crazy, hectic career.

Harloe, my little Harlot. I love your face and your soul and how happy you make me. I've found a forever friend in you.
Thank you.

Rafa and Fran, the cover gods brought you both to me. Damian wouldn't be Damian without you both.

Desireé and Zach, you both are Damian and Renata. I cannot imagine anyone else being Damian and Renata but you two. Thank you for bringing my characters to life, for all you've both done for me (including all the frantic messages I should totally be ashamed of lol).

Jayvin, thanks for letting me harass you during football season, you MVP you.

Heather, you are the shiniest diamond, the largest cut, the best clarity, the rarest find. I love who you are; I love everything about you. Thank you for making me laugh, for helping me smile, for being a true friend.

Heidi, you are my person. You just get it. You get me. Do you know how rare that is? Rare enough for me to vow to steal you from your hubs. Back off, Brian.

Krista, you feel like a sister—a bubbly, bright, sister of my very soul. Thank you for being in my life.

Brittany, you weirdo. How can you not love aliens?! I'm sorry, we can't be friends until you bow down to Jeffrey the Facebook alien.

Elan, you're so needy. Gosh.

Amanda. You are so vivacious and full of life. I love everything about you—but most of all, our friendship.

Amara!!!!!!!!!!!!!!!!!! I hope you read that as me shouting your name in my American accent. I could get voice messages from you all day. You make me want to move to Australia, if not for your Aussie accent, then to be your BFF.

Gem and Janice, your keen eyes help keep my manuscripts pretty and clean. You two are so bad ass. I swear, y'all deserve monuments.

Bloggers, thank you for helping me get the word out on my books. I know I sometimes can't comment on every post and I sometimes don't see everything, but holy cow, I appreciate it all.

I know, without a doubt, that my career would be a sliver of what it is without you all.

Readers—loves of my life, apples of my eye, bookish babes.
Thank you for taking the time to read this. I (literally) cannot do this without you.

XOXO,

ABOUT PARKER

Parker S. Huntington is from Orange County, California, USA. She has a Bachelor's of Arts in Creative Writing from the University of California, Riverside and is currently pursuing a Master's in Liberal Arts in Creative Writing and Literature from Harvard University.

She was the proud mom of Chloe and has two puppies, Bauer and Rose. She also lives with her boyfriend of six years--a real life alpha male, book-boyfriend-worthy hunk of a man.